CONTENTS

PART ONE
A PLOT IN THE MAKING

CHAPTER ONE

The Eavesdropper

On a pleasant, sunny afternoon near the end of May, when the late spring was just merging into early summer, Mr Thomas Pedley (Tom Pedley to his friends, or more usually plain Tom) was seated on a substantial sketching stool before a light bamboo easel on which was fixed an upright canvas measuring eighteen inches by twelve. To an expert eye, his appearance, his simple, workmanlike outfit, the leisurely ease with which he handled his brush, and the picture which was growing into shape on the canvas, would all have suggested a competent and experienced landscape painter.

And such, in fact, was Tom Pedley. From his early boyhood, some forty-odd years ago, drawing and painting had been his one absorbing passion, coupled with that love of the countryside that marks the born landscape artist. To him that countryside, largely unspoiled in his early days, was an inexhaustible source of delight and a subject of endless study and meditation. In his daily rambles through meadow or woodland, by farmyards or quiet hamlets, every journey was a voyage of exploration yielding fresh discoveries; new truths of characteristic form and subtle, unexpected colour to be added to his growing store of knowledge of those less obvious aspects of nature which it is the landscape painter's mission to reveal. And as the years passed and the countryside faded away under the withering touch of mechanical transport, that knowledge grew more and more precious. Now, the dwindling remnants had to be sought and found with considered judgment and their scanty material eked out with detail brought forth from the stores of the remembered past.

The picture which was shaping itself on the canvas was an example of this application of knowledge gained by experience. On the wall of a gallery it would have suggested to the spectator an open glade in some vast woodland. In fact, the place was no more than a scrubby little copse, the last surviving oasis in the squalid desert of a "developing" neighbourhood. From his "pitch", ensconced in a clump of bushes, Tom could hear, faint and far away, the strident hoots of motor cars, the rumble of omnibuses, and the clatter of lorries; and but a hundred yards distant was the path by which he had come, a rutted track that led from a half-built street at one end to a dismantled farmyard at the other.

Nevertheless, apart from the traffic noises, the place was strangely peaceful and quiet, its silence accentuated by the natural sounds that pervaded it. Somewhere in the foliage hard by, a thrush sang joyously, and on a branch just overhead a chaffinch repeated again and again his pleasant little monotonous song. And the solitude was as perfect as the quiet. The rough path seemed to be untrodden by the foot of man, for, during the two hours that Tom had been at work, not a soul had passed along it.

At length, as he paused to fill his pipe and take a thoughtful survey of his picture, the sound of voices was followed by the appearance of two men walking slowly along the path, conversing earnestly though in low tones. Tom could not hear what they were saying, though the impression conveyed to him was that their manner was rather the reverse of amicable. But in fact he gave them little attention beyond noting the effect of the dark, sharply defined shapes against the indefinite background; and even this interested him but little as his subject required no figures, and certainly not one in a bowler hat. So he continued filling his pipe and appraising his afternoon's work as they walked by without noticing him – actually, he was almost invisible from the path – and as they passed out of sight he produced his matchbox and was about to strike a light when a third figure, that of a woman, made its appearance, moving in the same direction as the others.

This time Tom's attention was definitely aroused, and he sat motionless with the unlighted match in his hand, peering out through the chinks in the bushes which concealed him. The woman's behaviour was very peculiar. She was advancing rather more quickly than the two men, but with a silent, stealthy tread; and from her movements she seemed to be listening and trying to keep the men in sight while keeping out of sight, herself.

Tom watched her disapprovingly. He disliked "snoopers" of all sorts, but especially those who were eavesdroppers as well. However, this was none of his business, and, when she had passed out of his field of vision, he lit his pipe, took up his brush, and straightway forgot all about her.

But he had not finished with her after all. He had been painting but a few minutes when she reappeared; and now her behaviour was still more odd. She was returning at a quicker pace.but with the same stealthy movements, listening and looking back over her shoulder with something like an air of alarm. Suddenly, when she was nearly opposite Tom's pitch, she slipped into an opening in the bushes and disappeared from his sight.

This was really rather queer. Once more he transferred his brush to the palette hand, and, as he listened intently, felt in his pocket for the matchbox; for, of course, his pipe had gone out, as a painter's pipe continually does. Very soon his ear caught the sound of footsteps; light, quick footsteps approaching from the direction of the farmyard. Then a man came into view, walking quickly but with a soft and almost stealthy tread and looking about him watchfully as he went.

Tom, sitting stock-still in his leafy ambush, followed the retreating figure with an inquisitive eye, recognizing him as the shorter of the two men who had passed down the path and wondering what had become of the other. Then the man disappeared in the direction of the street; and still Tom sat like a graven image, waiting to see if there were any further developments.

He had not long to wait. Hardly had the sound of the man's footsteps died away when the woman stole forth from her hiding place and stood for a few seconds listening intently and peering up the path in the direction in which the man had gone. Then she began slowly and warily to follow; and presently she, too, passed out of sight among the trees.

Tom thoughtfully lit his pipe and reflected. It was a queer affair. What was it all about? The woman was obviously spying on the men; apparently listening to their talk, and mighty anxious to keep out of sight. That was all there was to it so far as he was concerned; and as he was not really concerned in it at all, he decided that it was a "dam' rum go" and dismissed it from his mind.

But the dismissal was not quite effective. The incident had broken the continuity of his ideas and he found it difficult to start afresh. For a few minutes he struggled to pick up the threads, adding a touch here and there; then, once more, he leaned back and surveyed his work, finally getting up from his stool and stepping back a pace or two to see it better as a whole. Now, one of the most important things that experience teaches a painter is when to leave off; and Tom, having considered his picture critically, decided that the time had come. He had painted steadily for a full two hours, and he was a rapid worker in spite of his leisurely manner; rapid because he knew what he wanted to do, made few mistakes, and painted very directly with a rigid economy of work.

Having decided that his picture was finished, excepting perhaps for a little work in the studio to "pull it together", he proceeded forthwith to pack up, closing the folding palette and stowing it in the light wooden colour box, strapping the painting in the canvas carrier; and rolling the used brushes in the painting rag. When he had put these things tidily in his satchel, he folded up the easel and stool, fixed them in the carrying-strap, slung the satchel on his shoulder, and, having taken a last look at his subject, pushed his way through the undergrowth towards the path.

Arriving at the rutted track, he stood for a few seconds looking up and down it as he refilled his pipe. He was not an inquisitive man, but he felt a mild curiosity as to what had become of the man who had passed and had not returned. His previous explorations had given him the impression that the path, or cart track, came to a dead end where the wood petered out and the new devastations began. Apparently, he had been wrong; there must be some continuation of the track, perhaps holding out possibilities for the landscape painter.

Having lit his pipe, he strolled along the path for some three hundred yards until he emerged from the shade of the wood into open daylight. And then both his questions were disposed of. The track, or at least the cart ruts, was visible, passing through the remains of a gateway and meandering through the devastated farmyard towards an area in which stacks of bricks and dumps of various building material foreshadowed a new eruption of houses similar to those that were to be seen beyond. Hard by, on his right hand, was an old, rat-eaten hayrick, and, a few yards farther away, a ruinous cart shed of which the thatched roof had rotted away, exposing the decayed rafters. At these melancholy relics of the vanished farm Tom glanced regretfully; then he turned back and retraced his steps along the path.

He had trudged some two hundred yards when there was borne to his ear the sound of horse's hoofs and the rumble of wheels, evidently approaching from the direction of the street; and as he came nearly opposite his "pitch", a two-wheeled cart appeared round a curve. He stopped to watch it and to note the interesting effect of the rustic-looking vehicle on the winding track, standing out sharply in dark silhouette against its background of sun-lighted foliage. As it drew near, he backed into the wood to make way for it and exchanged greetings with the man who was leading the horse; and when it had passed, he turned to look at it and make a mental note of its changed appearance in the altered conditions of light, until it disappeared round a bend of the track; whereupon he resumed his advance towards the town, stepping out briskly and becoming aware of an increasing interest in the meal which was awaiting him at the end of his journey. At the top of the path where it opened on the half-built street, he paused for a few moments to look disparagingly on the unlovely scene, which but a year ago had still been country; then, having exchanged a few words with an elderly bricklayer who appeared to be standing guard over a stack of bricks, he strode away towards the main road to take up his position at the bus stop.

Here he had a considerable time to wait, and he spent it pacing up and down, looking expectantly at each turn in the direction whence the omnibus would come. From a young policeman who presently strolled past, he obtained a rather vague statement as to the time when it was due, with the discouraging addition that the last one had passed about five minutes ago. So Thomas resumed his sentry-go and meanwhile turned over in his mind once again that very queer episode in the wood; and he was still cogitating on it when the omnibus appeared and put a welcome end to his vigil.

It was not a long journey, in terms of modern transport, and the rather squalid domain of the speculative builder soon gave place to the established town. Tom's natural stopping place would have been the Hampstead Road, but he elected to alight at Marylebone Church and approach his destination by way of Osnaburgh Street and Cumberland Market; whereby he presently emerged into a quiet, shabby street of tall, shabby, but commodious old houses, and so to a green-painted wooden gate bearing the number 38A and flanked by a small brass plate on the jamb inscribed "Pedley" and surmounted by a big brass bell pull.

As Thomas inserted his latchkey and opened the gate, he disclosed a feature common to many of the adjacent houses; a narrow passage opening into a paved yard. For Jacob Street was largely a street of studios. Once it had been a fashionable street, the abode of famous painters and sculptors. Now, the famous artists had gone, but the studios remained; some tenanted by artists of humbler status, but most of them converted into workshops. In either case, Jacob Street was a highly eligible place for persons of small means who wanted roomy premises; for, as studios are in little demand nowadays and are useless for residential purposes, the rents were surprisingly low, though the accommodation was, of its special kind, admirable.

The studio into which Tom admitted himself after crossing the yard was better adapted for residence than some of the others, being more moderate in height, and he had further adapted it by erecting a light wooden partition in one corner, enclosing a large cubicle which served him as a bedroom. With this and a tall folding screen to enclose the fireplace in winter, or to conceal the sink and the gas cooking stove when he had visitors, Tom had converted the great bare studio into a convenient and fairly comfortable flat.

Having cleaned his palette, washed his brushes, and washed himself in a big bowl in the sink, he opened a haybox (disguised by an upholstered top to look like, and serve as, an ottoman) and took out a couple of casseroles which he set on the neatly laid dinner table, opened a bottle of beer and decanted the contents into a fine white stoneware jug, drew up a chair, sat down with a sigh of contentment, and lifted off the lids of the casseroles; one of which proved to contain potatoes (cooked in their jackets) and the other a nondescript kind of stew based on a dismembered fowl.

The table and its appointments offered a summary of Tom Pedley's character and personality. His simple philosophy of life was fairly expressed in his own statement that "a man's wealth can be estimated in terms of what he can do without". Now, the things that Tom could do without were the luxuries and extras that consume money. For entertainments other than museums and public galleries he had no use. He had hardly ever ridden in a taxi, he never smoked cigars, and his single bottle of whisky had lain unopened for a couple of years. He lived plainly, spent little, wasted nothing, and took care of what he had.

By thus thriftily ordering his life, he was able to indulge himself in the things that mattered to him. The beer jug was a museum piece, as was also the fine ale glass with its charming engraved design of hops and barley. The little French cheese reposed in a covered dish of Moorcroft ware, the pile of apples in a handsome bowl of beaten bronze, and a finely carved wooden trencher supported the brown loaf. Every object on the table, even including the casseroles, was pleasant and comely to look at, though not necessarily costly, and had been the subject of carefully considered choice. For Tom was an artist to his fingertips. To him art was no Sunday religion. He loved to have beautiful things around him, not merely to look at but to live with; and he could afford to indulge his fancy, since he did his own domestic work and knew that his treasures were safe from the devastating duster of servant maid or charwoman.

So Tom sat in the fine "Chippendale Windsor" chair at the picturesque gateleg table and consumed his dinner with placid enjoyment, keeping himself entertained, as is the way of solitary men, with a train of reflections. Principally, his thoughts tended to concern themselves with the curious episode in the wood, which seemed to haunt him to a quite unreasonable extent. For it had been but a trivial affair, and he was not deeply interested in it. Nevertheless, his memory persisted in recalling the incident and filling in details of which he had been unaware at the time, until he was able to visualize a curiously complete picture of the scene and the action. Then his lively imagination took charge and wove a little story around those three figures; and this interested him so much that it presently occurred to him that here was the making of quite a good subject picture of a simple kind, and he decided to try an experimental sketch and see what he could make of it.

When he had finished his dinner, he proceeded to wash up, still turning the project over in his mind. The washing up was not a protracted business, for he had learned to economize in the use of plates and dishes. There was, in fact, only one plate and a knife and fork, and, when these had been dealt with and tidily stowed away, together with the casseroles, in a great French armoire, he was ready to begin. Taking his fresh painting from the canvas carrier, he set it on an easel, and, selecting a smaller spare canvas, put that on another easel alongside, set his palette and fell to work, first roughing in some of the background from his painting and then proceeding to the disposition of the figures.

The subject of the projected picture was to be "The Eavesdropper", and this seemed to require that the woman should be the principal figure, placed as near as possible in the foreground and painted in some detail on a sufficient scale. Accordingly, he began with her, first blocking in a flat grey silhouette to get the form and the pose and then proceeding to colour and detail. And as he worked he was surprised to find how much he remembered and how little he had to invent. The gleam of sunlight which had fallen on the woman as she retired, lighting up her hair like burnished gold and picking out bright spots on her clothing, came back to him vividly, and when he had put in a few lively touches of positive colour to render the effect, there seemed little more to do. Roughly as the figure was indicated, it recalled the appearance of the woman exactly as he had seen her.

The same was true of the male figures, though as they were more distant they could be painted more simply. In their definitely urban dress they were not very pictorial, but, as this was only a preliminary sketch, Tom decided to keep to the actual facts. And here again he was surprised to note how much he had seen in those casual glances without conscious observation. In fact, when he had put in the two figures from memory not only had he rendered admirably the argumentative pose and action but he had put in more distinctive detail than the distance of the figures required.

For over an hour he worked away with great enjoyment until the little sketch was completed so far as it need be. Then he "knocked off", cleaned his palette, washed his brushes, and, after a glance at the old "hood" clock on the wall, proceeded to smarten himself up with a view to an informal call on his bachelor friend, Dr Oldfield, who lived hard by in Osnaburgh Street; with whom it was his custom to spend an occasional evening in pleasant, companionable gossip and perhaps a game of chess. But they were not often reduced to that resource, for the doctor was something of an artist, and they had plenty of material for interesting and sympathetic conversation.

When he had refilled his tobacco pouch from a tin and brushed his hat, Tom stood awhile before the easel considering critically the newly finished sketch. It had been interesting enough in the doing but, now that it was done, he found it a little disappointing. As a subject picture, it was somewhat indefinite and lacking in matter; in short, it was hardly a subject picture at all, but rather a landscape with figures.

However, it could be reconsidered and perhaps elaborated if that should seem worth while; and, having reached this conclusion, Tom took his gloves and stick and set forth en route for Osnaburgh Street.

CHAPTER TWO
Mr Blandy

One afternoon about a week after his expedition to the wood, Tom Pedley was engaged in his studio in tidying up the painting that he had done on that occasion. At the moment he was working with a sharp scraper, cutting off objectionable lumps of paint and generally levelling down the surface preparatory to some further touches to "pull the painting together". He had just stepped back to take a look at the picture as a whole when the jangling of the studio bell in the yard outside announced a visitor; whereupon he went out, and, traversing the yard and the passage, threw open the large outer gate, disclosing a small person carrying a leather bag.

"Why, it's Mr Polton," he exclaimed in a tone of relief.

"Yes, sir," said the small gentleman, greeting him with a pleasant and curiously crinkly smile. "I thought I might take the liberty of calling – "

"Now, don't talk nonsense," Tom interrupted. "You know quite well that I am always delighted to see you. Come along in."

"It is very good of you, sir, to say that," said Polton, as Tom shut the gate and led the way down the passage, "but I hope I am not disturbing you. I see," he added with a glance at the scraper, "that you are at work."

"Only doing a scrape down," said Tom, "and you wouldn't disturb me if I wanted to go on. But it's close on teatime. I should have been knocking off in any case."

13

As he spoke, he glanced up at the old clock, and Polton, following his glance, drew out a large watch and remarked that the clock was about ten seconds fast; "Which," he added, "is not bad going for a timepiece that is nearly three hundred years old."

As Tom proceeded to fill the kettle and put a match to the gas ring, Polton placed his bag on the table, and, opening it, brought forth a green baize bundle tied up with tape. Unfastening this, he produced a brilliantly burnished tankard which, after a gentle rub with his handkerchief, he held out for Tom's inspection.

"This, sir," said he, "is what brought me here. You said some time ago that you were on the lookout for a pewter tankard, and you made a drawing, if you remember, sir, to show me the shape that you wanted. Now I happened to see this one on a junk stall in Shoreditch, so I ventured to get it for you."

"But how good of you to think of me!" exclaimed Tom. "And what a perfectly magnificent specimen! And a junk stall, too, of all unlikely places. By the way, what am I in your debt for it?"

"I got it for a shilling," Polton replied.

Tom looked at him in amazement. "A shilling!" he repeated incredulously. "You don't really mean a shilling. Why, it's quite a valuable piece."

"Well, you see, sir," Polton explained in an apologetic tone, "it had had some bad usage. It was very dirty and it had been all battered out of shape, so it really was not worth more than a shilling. I didn't take advantage of the man. But pewter is a kindly material if you know how to deal with it. I just took out the bruises, put it back into shape, and cleaned up the surface. That was all. I am glad you like it, sir."

"I am perfectly delighted with it," said Tom. He paused, and for one instant – but only one – he thought of offering a consideration for the time and labour that had wrought the transformation. Then he continued, "Here is the shilling, Polton. But it isn't payment. I take the tankard as a gift. You have turned a bit of worthless junk into a museum piece which will be an abiding joy to me, and I am more grateful than I can tell you."

Polton crinkled shyly, and, by way of closing the subject, wandered round to the easel to inspect the painting. For some seconds he stood, regarding the picture with a sort of pleased surprise. At length he remarked:

"A wonderful art, sir, is that of the painter. To me it looks almost like a kind of magic. Here is a beautiful woodland glade that you have made to appear so real that I seem to feel as if I could walk into it. You must have gone a long way from the bricks and mortar to find a scene like that."

Tom laughed. "A very natural delusion, Polton, but, as a matter of fact, I was almost in sight of the bricks and mortar when I was painting. That bit of woodland is just the last remnant of the country in the midst of a new housing estate. It is within a bus ride of this place, and not a long ride at that."

"Indeed, sir," exclaimed Polton. "Now whereabouts would that be?"

"It is out Hendon way. A place called Linton Green; and the wood is still known by its old name, Gravel-pit Wood."

As Tom spoke the name, Polton started and gazed at the picture with a most singular expression.

"Gravel-pit Wood, Linton Green," he repeated in a strange hushed voice; "the very wood in which that poor gentleman was murdered!"

"Oh!" said Tom in a tone of mild interest. "I never heard of that. How long ago was it?"

"The murder was commited last Tuesday."

"Last Tuesday!" Tom repeated incredulously. "Why, that is the day on which I painted the picture. Do you know what time it happened?"

"It would have been somewhere about four o'clock in the afternoon."

"Then," Tom exclaimed, "I must have actually been in the wood at the very time when the murder was being committed!"

"Yes, sir," Polton agreed. "I rather thought you must when you mentioned the wood, because the police have issued a description of a man who was seen there about that time; and it seems to be a description of you."

The two men looked at each other in silence for some moments; then Tom commented with a grim smile:

"Well, this is a pretty kettle of fish. Do you happen to remember any of the details? I hardly ever see a newspaper, so this is the first that I have heard of the affair."

"I remember all about it," replied Polton, "but I needn't trust to my memory, as I have cut out all the reports of the case and I have got the cuttings in my pocket. You see, sir," he added deprecatingly, "I am rather interested in murders. Perhaps it is because I have the honour of serving a very eminent criminal lawyer. At any rate, I always cut out the reports and paste them into a book for reference."

With this explanation, he produced from his pocket a large wallet from which he extracted a sheaf of newspaper cuttings. Sorting them out rapidly, he selected one, which he handed to Tom.

"That, sir," said he, "is the one which will serve your purpose best. It is from a weekly paper and it gives a summary of the case with all that is known at present. Perhaps you would like to glance through it while I get the tea ready. I know where you keep all the things."

Tom thanked him and sat down to study the cutting while Polton, having examined the kettle, opened the big armoire and began noiselessly to set out the tea things on the table. The report was headed "Mysterious Crime in a Wood", and ran as follows:

"In the new and rising suburb of Linton Green, near Hendon, there still exists a small patch of woodland now little more than a dozen acres in extent known as Gravel-pit Wood. Here, about five o'clock in the afternoon of last Tuesday, a most shocking discovery was made by a labourer who was engaged on the new buildings. This man, Albert Whiffin by name, was sent by the foreman with a message to the clerk of the works whose temporary office was in the half-built street on the other side of the wood. He approached along the cart track which crosses the wood and had nearly reached the entrance when his attention was attracted by a white object among the grass at the corner of a disused cart shed, and he went off the path to see what it was. Drawing near, he saw that it was the ivory handle of an umbrella and naturally advanced to pick it up; but as he reached the corner of the shed and was just stooping to pick up the umbrella, he was horrified to perceive the body of a man lying among the nettles and rubbish in one of the stalls of the shed. A single glance convinced him that the man was dead, and he made no further examination, but hurried away with the umbrella in his hand, ran across the wood, and reported his discovery to the clerk of the works. The latter sent off a messenger on a bicycle to the police station, and within a few minutes a sergeant and an inspector arrived and were conducted by Whiffin to the shed where the body was lying. It was seen to be that of a well-dressed man about sixty years of age, and the identity was at once established by visiting cards in the pocket, confirmed by the initials engraved on the silver band of the umbrella. These showed the deceased to be Mr Charles Montagu, of The Birches, Hall Road, Linton Green.

"But how had he met with his death? The circumstances plainly pointed to murder; and this was confirmed by evident signs of a struggle in the nettles and the long grass. But, strangely enough, there were no wounds or other injuries. The clothing was somewhat disordered, the collar was crumpled, and there appeared to be slight bruises on the neck; but nothing that would serve to account for death. When, however, the divisional surgeon arrived and made his examination, he decided, provisionally, that death was due to poisoning either by prussic acid or some cyanide. Thereupon a search was made for some container, which resulted in the discovery among the nettles of a small bottle bearing traces of a liquid which had the smell of bitter almonds.

"As to the time at which death occurred, as the surgeon made his examination at 5.35 p.m. and he decided that deceased had been dead not more than two hours, it would seem that it must have taken place about four o'clock. The time is important in connection with the only clue to the mystery. About half past four, a carter taking a load of bricks along the track through the wood met a man coming from the direction of the cart shed. This man was seen also by a bricklayer's labourer, emerging from the wood into the half-built street; and he was seen again by a young constable, who noticed him particularly and has given a description of him which agrees exactly with that of the other two witnesses and which has been circulated by the police, with a request to the man to communicate with them.

"The description is as follows: Height about five feet ten, strongly built, age from forty-five to fifty, grey eyes, brown hair and short brown moustache dressed in a buff tweed knickerbocker suit with buff stockings and brown shoes, buff soft felt hat with rather broad brim; brown canvas satchel over left shoulder, folding stool and some kind of stand or easel strapped together and carried by a handle in the left hand and a couple of wooden frames, apparently picture canvases, in a holder carried in the right hand.

"The constable, who encountered the man at the bus stop in the Linton Green Road, waiting for the east-bound omnibus, reports that he seemed to be rather anxious to get on, as he inquired when the next omnibus was due and was apparently annoyed to learn that the last one had only just passed. He spoke in a deep, strong voice with the accent of an educated man. The conductor of the omnibus also noticed the man and remembered that he alighted at Marylebone Church but did not see which way he went after alighting.

"At the inquest, which was held on Friday, little further light was thrown on the mystery. The medical evidence proved that deceased died from poisoning by a strong solution of potassium cyanide, either taken by himself or forcibly administered by some other person. There were slight bruises on the neck but nothing to indicate extreme violence, and, in a medical sense, there was nothing to show that the poison was not taken by deceased himself. The police evidence, however, was more definite. The poison bottle bore a number of fingerprints, but although these were very imperfect, the experts were able to say, positively, that they were not those of deceased or of any person known to the police. This fact, as the coroner pointed out in his summing-up, taken with the signs of a struggle, made it nearly certain that the poison was forcibly administered to deceased by some other person. The coroner also commented on the significance of deceased's profession. Mr Montagu was a financier; in effect, a moneylender; and a moneylender is apt to have enemies with strong reasons for compassing his death. In the present case, no such person was at present known. As to the mysterious artist, his identity had not yet been ascertained as he had not been traced and had not come forward, and nothing was known of his connection, if any, with the tragedy.

"At the conclusion of the summing-up, the jury promptly returned a verdict of Wilful Murder by some person or persons unknown; and that is how the matter stands. Perhaps, when the police are able to get in touch with the elusive artist, some fresh facts may come to light."

As Tom finished his reading, he handed the cutting back to Polton, who returned it carefully to his wallet and, having put the teapot on the table, silently awaited comments.

"Well," said Tom, "as I remarked before, it's a pretty kettle of fish. I am the mysterious and elusive artist and a possible candidate for the title of murderer. However, the elusiveness can be mended. I had better pop along to the police station tomorrow morning and let them know who I am."

"Yes, sir," Polton agreed earnestly. "That is very necessary. But why wait till tomorrow? Why not go round this evening? The police may succeed at any moment in tracing you, and it would be so much better if you were to go to them of your own accord than to leave them to find you. Don't forget that they have reasonable grounds for suspicion. This murder has been the talk of the town for nearly a week. The papers have been full of it, including the excellent description of you. Probably you are the only person in London who has not heard of it."

Tom laughed, grimly. "By Jove, Polton," said he, "you are talking like a prosecuting counsel. But you are quite right. I am a suspected person, and it won't do for me to look as if I were in hiding. I will amble round to the police station this very evening."

But Tom's wise decision came too late. Less than half an hour later, when they had finished tea, and Polton, having insisted on washing up, was in the act of stowing the tea things in the great armoire, the jingling of the studio bell was heard from without and Tom went forth to answer the summons. When he opened the gate he discovered on the threshold a tall clerical-looking man, who saluted him with a deferential bow and a suave smile.

"Have I the pleasure," the stranger inquired, "of addressing Mr Thomas Pedley?"

"You have," Tom replied with a faint grin. "At any rate, I am Thomas Pedley."

"So I had supposed," the other rejoined, glancing at the brass plate, "and I am delighted to make your acquaintance, as I believe that you may be able to help me in certain investigations in which I am engaged. Perhaps I should explain that I am a police officer, and if you would like to see my authority – "

"No, thanks," replied Tom. "I think I know what your business is, and, in fact, I was going to call at the police station this very evening. However, this will be better. Come along in."

He preceded the officer across the yard and ushered him into the studio, where Polton was discovered standing on a stool setting the clock to time by his watch.

"Well, I'm sure!" the officer exclaimed. "Here is a delightful surprise. My old and esteemed friend, Mr Polton! And what a singular coincidence. Have you known Mr Pedley long?"

"A good time," replied Polton. "We first met in an antique shop in Soho; Parrott's. You remember Parrott – his name was really Pettigrew, and he was the villain who murdered Mr Penrose."

"I remember the case," said the officer, "though I was not concerned in it. But there is another coincidence; for, by a strange chance, it is a murder case that is the occasion of my visit here."

Tom did not quite perceive the coincidence but he made no remark, waiting for the officer to open the proceedings. Meanwhile Polton tentatively approached his hat, with the suggestion that "perhaps they would rather discuss their business alone".

"You needn't go on my account," said the officer. "There are no secrets"; and as Tom expressed himself to the same effect, Polton gladly relinquished the hat and sat down with undisguised satisfaction to listen.

"Now, Mr Pedley," the officer began, "I am going to ask you a few questions, and it is my duty to explain that you are not bound to answer any if the answer would tend – in the silly official phrase – to incriminate you."

"I'll bear that in mind," said Tom, with a broad grin.

"Yes," said the officer, with a responsive smile. "Ridiculous expression, but we must observe the formalities. Well, as a start; can you remember where you were and what you were doing on Tuesday, the eighteenth of May?"

"Last Tuesday. Yes. In the afternoon I was in Gravel-pit Wood, Linton Green. I got there about two o'clock and I came away about half past four, or perhaps a little earlier. In the interval I was painting a picture of the wood, which I will show you if you care to see it."

"Thank you," said the officer. "I should like very much to see it, presently. But meanwhile another question arises. It appears from what you tell me that you must actually have been in the wood while the murder was being committed, and yet, although there was an urgent broadcast appeal for information and similar appeals in the Press, you never came forward or made any sign whatever; not even though those appeals were coupled with a description of yourself, and so, in effect, addressed to you personally. Now, why did you not communicate with the police?"

21

"The explanation is perfectly simple," replied Tom. "Until a couple of hours ago, when Mr Polton told me about it, I had no knowledge that any murder had been committed."

The officer received this statement with a bland and benevolent smile.

"A perfectly simple explanation," he agreed; "and yet, if I were disposed to cavil – which I am not – I might think of the broadcast and the daily papers with their staring headlines and wonder – but, as I say, I am not."

"I dare say," said Tom, "that it sounds odd. But I have no wireless and I hardly ever see a paper. At any rate, it is the fact that I had never heard of the crime until Mr Polton mentioned it and showed me an account of it which he had cut out of a newspaper."

Here Polton interposed with a deferential crinkle. "If it would not seem like a liberty, sir, I should like to say that Mr Pedley showed me the picture and told me where and when he had painted it; and he seemed very much shocked and surprised when I informed him about the murder."

The officer regarded the speaker with a smile of concentrated benevolence.

"Thank you, Mr Polton," said he. "Your very helpful statement disposes of the difficulty completely. Now, perhaps, I may have the privilege of seeing the picture."

Tom rose, and, fetching a rough studio frame from a stack by the wall, slipped the canvas into it and replaced it on the easel.

"There it is," said he; "not quite finished but perhaps all the better for that as a representation."

"Yes," the officer agreed, "as my interest in it is merely topographical, though I can see that it is a very lovely work of art." He stood before the easel beaming on the picture as if pronouncing a benediction on it, but nevertheless scrutinizing it minutely. Presently he produced from a roomy inner pocket a small portfolio from which he took a section of the six-inch Ordnance map pasted on thin card. "Here, Mr Pedley," said he, "is a large-scale map of the wood. Do you think you could show me the position of the spot which this picture represents?"

Tom took the map from him and studied it for a few moments while he felt in his pocket for a pencil.

"I think," said he, indicating a spot with the pencil point, "that this will be the place. I am judging by the curve of the footpath, as the individual trees are not shown. Shall I make a mark?"

"If you please," the officer replied; and when Tom had marked a minute cross and handed the card back to its owner, the latter produced a boxwood scale and a pair of pocket dividers, with which he took off the distance from the cross to the nearest point on the path and measured it on the scale.

"A hundred and seven yards, I make it," said he. "What do you say to that?"

"Yes," Tom answered, "that seems about right."

"Very well. You were about a hundred yards from the path. From where you were, could you see any person that might pass along that path?"

"I could, and I did. Not very clearly, because I was sitting on a low stool and I could only see out through the chinks in the foliage. But while I was working there I saw three persons pass down the path, and two of them came back."

"And do you suppose that those persons saw you?"

"I am pretty certain that they didn't. They couldn't, you know. Sitting low among the bushes, as I was, I must have been quite invisible from the path."

"Yes," the officer agreed; "but you could see them. Now, what can you tell me about them?"

"All I can tell you is that they behaved in a rather queer way. At least, one of them did;" and here Tom proceeded to give a minute and circumstantial account of what he had seen.

"But, my dear Mr Pedley," the officer exclaimed, beaming delightedly on the narrator, "this is most important and illuminating. The woman is a new feature of the case. By the way, did anyone else pass?"

"No. These were the only people that I saw until just as I was coming away, when I met a man bringing a cart full of bricks through the wood."

"Then there can be no doubt as to who those people were. One was Mr Montagu, the other was the murderer, and the woman must have been connected with one or both of the men. What time was it when they passed down?"

"About four o'clock or perhaps a few minutes earlier. It would be about ten minutes or a quarter of an hour later when the man came back."

"Yes," said the officer, "that seems to agree with the evidence. And now we come to the most important point of all; can you give us any description of them, and do you think you would recognize them if you saw them again?"

"As to recognizing them, I am very doubtful. Certainly I couldn't swear to any of them. And I don't think I could give much of a description. They were a good distance away and I saw them only through the chinks between the branches, and wasn't taking very much notice. However, I will see what I can remember."

With this he embarked on a description of the three persons, rather vague and general though helped out by questions from the officer, who jotted down the answers in his notebook.

"Yes," the latter remarked as Tom concluded, "not so bad. But yet, Mr Pedley, I feel that you must have seen more than that. You are not an ordinary observer. You are a painter. Now, a painter's eye is a noticing eye and a remembering eye. Supposing you were to try to paint the scene from memory – "

"By Jove!" Tom interrupted, "I'm glad you said that, for it happens that that is just what I did do, and on the very day, while my memory was fresh. I thought the incident might make the subject for a picture, 'The Eavesdropper", and that evening I roughed out a trial sketch. I will show it to you."

From a collection of unfinished works on a shelf he produced the sketch and set it on the easel beside the larger picture, from which the background had been copied.

"Ha!" said the officer. "Now you see that I was right. The brush is mightier than the word. This tells us a lot more than your description. It shows us what the people really looked like. This figure is evidently Mr Montagu, hat and coat quite correct, and you have even shown the ivory handle of the umbrella. And the other two are not mere figures; they look like particular persons."

"Yes," agreed Polton, who had been gazing at the sketch with delighted interest, "Mr Blandy is quite right. But it is really very wonderful. Those two men have their backs to us, and the woman's face has practically no features; and yet I feel that they are real persons and that I should know them again if I were to meet them. Can you explain it, Mr Pedley?"

"Well," Tom replied, "I can only say that this is an impression of the scene at a particular moment, and that is how these people looked at that moment. You identify a person not only by his face but by his size, shape, proportions, and characteristic posture and movements. You can often recognize a man by his walk long before you can distinguish his features."

"Exactly," said Blandy, "and that is why our recognizing officers like to watch the remand prisoners in the exercise yard. They can often spot a disguised man by his general make-up and the way he walks or stands, and I am inclined to think that this sketch might be useful to a specialist of that kind. Would it be possible to borrow it and have a photograph made to accompany your description?"

Before Tom could reply, Polton broke in eagerly.

"Why not let me do the photograph for you, Inspector? I could bring my camera here so that you wouldn't have to borrow the sketch. I should like to do it, if you'd let me."

Inspector Blandy beamed on him with ineffable amiability.

"How very good of you, Mr Polton," said he. "Always so helpful. But it would be a good photograph, and you would have a copy to add to your little collection. I am inclined to accept gratefully if Mr Pedley will grant us permission."

Mr Pedley granted his permission without demur, whereupon the inspector, having arranged a date of delivery with Polton, prepared to take his leave.

"By the way," said he, picking up his hat and putting it down again, "there are two little points that we may as well clear up. First, as to the stature of the unknown man and the woman. The man looks distinctly shorter than Mr Montagu, who was about five feet ten. What do you say?"

"Yes," replied Tom. "I should put him at about five feet seven. The woman looked taller, but then women do. I should say that she was about the same height."

The inspector made a note of the answer and then said:

"When you met the carter, you seemed to be coming from the bottom of the wood.

"I was. As one of the men had not come back, it seemed that the path, which I had supposed ended at the bottom of the wood, must continue beyond, so I went down to see if it did. When I saw that it crossed the farmyard I came back and started homeward."

"Then you must have passed the cart shed. Isn't it rather remarkable that you should not have noticed the body, or, at any rate, the umbrella?"

"Not at all. There is an old hayrick between the path and the cart shed. I never saw more than a corner of the shed, and it was the wrong corner. Whiffin, you remember, was coming from the farmyard."

"Yes," said the inspector. "I had forgotten the rick; but I suspect the lady found it useful for stalking purposes. Well," he added, once more taking up his hat, "I think that is all; excepting that it remains for me to offer my most humble and hearty thanks for your invaluable help. It has been a great privilege for me to listen to your very illuminating observations and to be made the beneficiary of your remarkable technical knowledge and skill."

With this final flourish he made his way to the door escorted by Tom, who conducted him to the gate and launched him into the outer world.

"Rather an oily customer, that, for a police officer," Tom remarked when he returned to the studio, to find Polton still gloating over the sketch. "Don't you think so?"

Polton crinkled knowlingly, as he replied:

"Mr Blandy is an exceedingly polite gentleman. But he is a very able detective officer; as sharp as a needle and as slippery as an eel. You've got to be very careful with Mr Blandy. I hope, sir, that you didn't mind my offering to do the photograph. You see, sir, I thought it best that a valuable thing like that should not go out of your possession."

"That was very good of you, Polton. But, bless you, it isn't a valuable thing. It is practically a throw-out."

"Oh, don't say that, sir. I have been admiring it and thinking what a charming little picture it is and how wonderfully full of interest. When will it be convenient for me to come and take the photograph?"

"You needn't trouble to bring the camera here. Take the canvas with you and do the job in your own place; and, as it seems to have taken your fancy, you had better keep it and let me have a photograph, in case I should decide to paint the subject. The photograph will do just as well for me."

Polton was disposed to protest, but Tom stolidly wrapped the canvas in paper and handed it to him, and a few minutes later he departed, crinkling with pleasure and gratitude, with the little parcel under his arm.

CHAPTER THREE
Mrs Schiller

In all the busy town that seethed around him, there can have been but few persons whose lives were as untroubled as was that of Thomas Pedley. He had, in fact, not a care in the world. His work yielded a modest income which was more than enough to supply his modest needs, and the doing of that work was a pleasure that time could not stale. He never tired of painting. If he had come into a fortune, he would still have gone on painting for the mere joy of the occupation, and might then have missed the added satisfaction of living by his industry. At any rate, he craved no fortune and envied no one, except, perhaps, those artists whose work he considered better than his own.

Thus, through the uneventful years, Tom pursued "the noiseless tenor of his way" in quiet happiness and perfect contentment, up to the period at which this history now arrives, when we have to record the appearance of a cloud upon his usually serene horizon. It was only a small cloud; but its little shadow was enough to cause a sensible disturbance of his habitually placid state of mind.

The trouble was not connected with the Gravel-pit Wood incident. That had never occasioned him any anxiety, even though he had been aware – with a slightly amused interest – that the police had by no means forgotten his existence. But as the weeks had passed and the "Unsolved Mystery" had gradually faded from the pages of the daily papers, so had it faded from his own memory and ceased to be of any concern to him.

The cloud was, in fact, a feminine cloud. His troubles, like those of Milton Perkins, were connected with the female of his species. For Tom, as the reader has probably inferred, was a bachelor; and it was his considered intention to remain a bachelor. Wherefore, though he liked women well enough, he avoided all feminine intimacies and kept a wary eye on any unattached spinsters who came his way, and as for widows, he viewed them with positive alarm.

Now it happened that, on a certain afternoon, Tom was working with great enjoyment at a subject picture which his dealer had commissioned when the jangling of the studio bell announced a visitor. With a snort of annoyance he laid down his palette and brushes and went forth to confront the disturber of his peace; when he discovered on the threshold a rather tall woman, dressed – and painted – in the height of fashion, who turned at the sound of the opening gate, and greeted him with a smile that made his flesh creep.

"You are Mr Pedley, I think," said she.

Tom was of the same opinion, and said so.

"I hope you won't consider me troublesome," she said in a wheedling tone, "but I should be so grateful if you would lend me a sheet of Whatman. I have a piece of work to do, and I want to start on it at once, but I have run out of paper."

Now, if the smile had made Tom's flesh creep, the request positively made it crawl. For he knew – and so must she if she were a painter – that there was an excellent artists' colourman's shop within five minutes' walk of the place where they were standing, from whence, indeed, Tom got most of his supplies. It looked suspiciously like a pretext for making his acquaintance.

"Perhaps I should explain," she continued, "that I am your next-door neighbour – Mrs Schiller."

Tom bowed. He had observed the recent appearance of a brass plate bearing this name, and was now slightly reassured. At least, she was a married woman – unless she was a widow! In any case, he couldn't keep her waiting on the doorstep.

"I'll let you have a sheet with pleasure," said he. "Won't you come in?"

She complied with alacrity, and, as he conducted her along the passage, he asked: "What sort of surface would you like? I generally use 140, Not."

"That will do perfectly, if you can spare me a sheet. I will let you have it back; at least, not the same sheet, you know, but an equivalent."

"You needn't," said Tom, with a view to heading her off from another visit. "I have a good stock. Just laid in a fresh quire, and I don't use a lot as I work mostly in oil. This is my show."

He indicated the open door, and, as she stepped into the studio, his visitor looked around with a little squeak of surprise.

"But how enormous!" she exclaimed. "And how magnificent! I do envy you. My studio isn't really a studio at all. It is just my sitting room, though it is quite a good room, with a nice big window. You must let me show it to you, sometime."

Tom groaned inwardly. A very pushing young person, this. He began to suspect that she must be a widow, and decided that he must "mind his eye".

"Well," he replied, "you don't really need a place of this size to paint in, though, of course, it's a convenience to have plenty of elbow room."

He went to a set of wide shelves and, drawing out the imperial size portfolio in which he kept his stock of paper, opened it on the table and selected a sheet, which he rolled slightly and secured with a turn of string. Meanwhile, his visitor had taken her stand before the easel and was inspecting the nearly finished picture; a simple, open-air subject such as Tom liked to paint, showing a group of gipsies on a heathy common, tending their fire, with a couple of vans in the background.

"But how wonderful!" she exclaimed. "And how curious and interesting."

Tom paused in the act of tying the knot and looked round suspiciously.

"Why curious?" he asked.

"I mean," she explained, "the extraordinary representationalism. It might almost be a photograph. Do you always paint like this?"

Now Tom held privately the opinion that the comparison of a finished, realistic painting to a photograph was the hallmark of the perfect ignoramus. But he did not say so. He merely answered the question.

"I try to get as near as I can to the appearances of nature; but, of course, the best of us fall a long way short."

"Exactly," said she. "Imitative painting must be very difficult, and after all, you can't compete with the photographer. That is the advantage of abstract art. You are not trying to imitate anything in particular; you just let your personality express itself in terms of abstract form and colour. Have you ever experimented in the new progressive art?"

"No," replied Tom. "This is the way I paint, and it seems to me to be the right way; and I suppose my dealers and private clients take the same view, as they are willing to buy my pictures at a fair price. At any rate, such as it is, I had better get on with it."

By way of enforcing this blunt refusal of the attempted discussion, he held out the roll of paper and glanced wistfully at his palette.

"Yes," she agreed, taking the paper from him with an engaging smile, "I mustn't waste your time now, though I *should* like to talk this question over with you some day. But now I will take myself off, and thank you so much for the loan of the paper. I promise faithfully to repay it."

Once more Tom assured her that no repayment was necessary, though he now realized, hopelessly, that the promise would certainly be kept. Nevertheless, as he bade her adieu on the doorstep and watched her trip round to her own door, he resolved afresh to "mind his eye" and ward off any attempt to establish more definitely intimate relations; an admirable resolution but one which, to a scrupulously polite gentleman such as Tom Pedley, presented certain difficulties in practice, as he was very soon to discover. For, of course, the loan of the paper was repaid promptly; on the following day, in fact; and Tom's efforts, as he received the rolled sheet, to "close the incident" failed ignominiously. He did not on this occasion invite his fair visitor to come in. But though he conducted the transaction on the doorstep, the closure of the incident was but the prelude to the opening of another.

"I won't detain you now," said she with a smile that displayed between her scarlet lips a fine set of teeth, "but I do want you to see my studio, and especially I want you to tell me what you think of my work. A few words of criticism from an experienced artist like you would be so helpful. Now, you will come, won't you? Any time that suits you, This afternoon if you like, say about four o'clock. How would that do?"

Of course, it wouldn't do at all if there were any possibility of escape. But there was not. Tom looked at her helplessly, mumbling polite acknowledgments and thinking hard. But what could he say? Obviously he could not refuse; and this being clear to him, he decided to get the visit over at once and take precautions against its repetition.

"Very well," said she, "then we will say four o'clock; and if you are very good and don't slate my pictures too much, I will give you a nice cup of tea."

With a friendly nod and a further display of teeth she tripped away briskly in the direction of Hampstead Road, and Tom, muttering objurgations, retired to bestow the sheet of paper in the portfolio.

It need hardly be said that the afternoon's visit did nothing towards "closing the incident". As she opened the street door in response to his ring at the bell, removing a cigarette to execute a smile of welcome, his hostess received him as though he had been "the companion of her childhood and the playmate of her youth". She shook his hand with affectionate warmth, and, still holding it, led him into a large front room where a brand new easel, flanked by a small table, stood close to the window. Tom cast a comprehensive glance around and rapidly assessed the occupant in professional terms. Apart from the easel and the colour box, brushes and water pot on the table, it was just a typical woman's sitting room, in which the tea table with its furnishings seemed more at home than the easel.

"This is my humble workshop," said his hostess; "a poor affair compared with your noble studio, but still – "

"It would probably have been good enough for Turner or De Wint," said Tom. "It's the painter that matters, not the studio. Shall we have a look at some of your work?"

"Yes, let's," she replied brightly, leading him towards the easel. "This is my latest. I am not quite satisfied with it but I don't think I will carry it any further for fear of spoiling it. What do you think?"

Tom stared at the object on the easel and gibbered inarticulately. A half-sheet of Whatman had been pinned untidily on a board and covered with curved streaks of bright colour, evidently laid, very wet, on damped paper, producing an effect like that of an artist's colourman's sheet of samples.

"Well," he stammered, recovering himself slightly, "I don't see what more you could do to it. Perhaps the – er – the subject is – er – just a little obscure. Not perfectly obvious, you know. Possibly – er –"

"Oh, there isn't any subject," she explained; "not in an imitative sense, that is. It is just an essay in abstract colour. I propose to call it 'A Symphony in Green and Blue'. Do you think it sounds pretentious to call it a symphony?"

"I wouldn't say pretentious," he replied, "but I don't much like calling things by wrong names. It isn't a symphony, you know. A symphony is a combination of sounds, whereas this work is a – is a – well, it's a painting."

Mrs Schiller laughed softly. "You were going to say 'it's a picture', and then you thought better of it. Now didn't you?"

"Well," Tom admitted with an apologetic grin, "it isn't quite what I should call a picture, but then I really don't know anything about this new form of art. I suppose it is an abstract picture."

"That is just what it is; an entirely non-representational abstraction of colour. Rather an extreme example, perhaps, so we will change it for something more representational."

She fished out a portfolio from under a settee and took from it a small mounted drawing which she stood up on the easel.

"The first one," she explained, "is a study of abstract colour. Now this one is an essay in abstract form. But it has a subject. I have called it 'Adam and Eve', How do you like it?"

Tom considered this new masterpiece with knitted, brows and a feeling of growing bewilderment. It represented two human figures such as might have been drawn by an average child of nine or ten with no natural aptitude for art, in a heavy, clumsy pencil outline filled in with daubs of colour. As the serious production of a sane adult, the thing was incredible.

"They are a good deal alike," Tom remarked, by way of saying something.

"Yes," she agreed, "but of course they would be, as they haven't any clothes, poor things. The bigger one would naturally be Adam, though it really doesn't matter. The title is only a convention. The picture is really a study in essential form."

"I see," said Tom, though he didn't; but he continued to gaze at the work with bulging eyeballs while the lady looked over his shoulder with a curious cryptic smile – which vanished instantly when he turned towards her. After a prolonged inspection with no further comment, he cast a furtive glance at the portfolio, whereupon his hostess removed the figure subject and replaced it by another painting, apparently representing a human head and shoulders, and, in character, very much like those "portraits" with which untalented schoolchildren adorn blank spaces in their copybooks. Such, in fact, Tom at first assumed it to be, but the artist hastily corrected him.

"Oh, no," said she. "It is not imitative. I have called it 'Madonna', but it is just a study in simplification based on the architectural structure of the human head, with all the irrelevant details eliminated."

"Yes," Tom commented, "I noticed that there had been a good deal of elimination. Those brown patches, I suppose, represent the hair?"

"They don't represent it," she replied. "They merely acknowledge and connote its existence. Perhaps, in a non-representational work, they are really superfluous, but they are useful in elucidating the pattern."

This explanation left Tom speechless as did the other selections from the portfolio. They were all much of the same kind; either meaningless streaks of colour or childish drawings of men and animals. Some of them he judged to be landscapes from the appearance in them of green, mop-like shapes, which might have "connoted" trees, and in one the simplified landscape was inhabited by abstract animals suggesting the cruder productions of a toy shop.

"Well," said Mrs Schiller as she returned the last of them to the portfolio, "that is my repertoire; and now that you have seen them all, I want you to tell me frankly what you think of them. You need not mind being outspoken. Candid criticism is what I want from you."

"But my dear Mrs Schiller," Tom exclaimed despairingly, "I am quite incompetent to criticize your work. I know nothing whatever about this modernist art excepting that it is a totally different thing from the art which I have always known and practised. And we can't discuss it because we are not speaking the same language. When I paint a picture I aim at beauty and interest; and since there is nothing so beautiful as nature, I keep as close to natural appearances as I can. And as a picture is a work of imagination and not a mere representation like an illustration in a scientific textbook, I try to arrange my objects in a pleasing composition and to make them convey some interesting ideas. But, apparently, modernist art avoids truth to nature and any kind of intellectual or emotional interest. I don't understand it at all."

"But," she objected, "don't you find beauty in abstract form?"

"I have always supposed," he replied, "that abstract form appertains to mathematics, whereas painting and sculpture are concerned with visible and tangible things. But really, Mrs Schiller, it's of no use for me to argue the question. We are talking and thinking on different planes."

"I suppose we really are," she agreed, "but it's rather disappointing. I had hoped to profit by your experience, but I see now that it has no bearing on modern art. But never mind, we will drown our disagreements in the teapot. Will you take this chair while I boil the kettle, or would you prefer a softer one?"

"I like a hard chair," replied Tom.

"So do I. Odd, isn't it, that women seem to want a chair stuffed like a feather bed and piled up with cushions? I could never understand why, seeing that they are lighter than men, as a rule, and better covered."

"Perhaps," Tom suggested, as he subsided on to the wooden-seated chair, "it is because they wear less clothes and want the cushions for warmth."

"Well, at any rate," said she, as she put a match to the gas ring on the hearth which supported a handsome copper kettle, "we are on the same plane in the matter of chairs, so we have one agreement to start with."

She drew up a light mahogany armchair, and, seating herself, gave her attention to the kettle; and while it was heating she continued the discussion with a whimsical mock seriousness that Tom found quite pleasant. In fact, there was no denying that Mrs Schiller's personality was distinctly attractive if one could forget the atrocities of her painting; and Tom, who liked women well enough so long as they did not want him to marry them, realized with some surprise that he was finding the little informal function quite agreeable (though he was still resolved that this visit should "close the incident"). The excellent China tea was brewed to perfection, the table appointments, including the kettle, were pleasant to look on, and his hostess' bright flippancies kept him mildly amused.

Presently the conversation reverted to the subject of painting, and Tom ventured to seek some solution of the mystery that had perplexed him.

"Have you always painted in the modernist manner?" he asked.

"Always!" she repeated with a smile. "I haven't always painted at all. It is a completely new venture on my part, and it came about quite by chance; a very odd chance it seems when I look back on it. A girl-friend of mine asked me to go with her to a show at a gallery in Leicester Square; an exhibition of works of modern masters. I didn't want to go, because I had never felt the least interest in pictures and didn't know anything about them, but she insisted that I must go because everybody was talking about these pictures, and the art critics declared they were the latest discoveries in art.

"So I went, and, to my surprise, I was tremendously impressed and interested. The pictures were so different from anything that I had ever seen before; so quaint and curious. They looked as if they might have been done by children. I was really charmed with them; so much so that I decided to try if I could do anything like them. And I found that I could. Isn't it strange? I had never drawn or painted before, and yet I found it quite easy to do. Don't you think it is very remarkable?"

"Very remarkable," Tom agreed quite sincerely, though not quite in the sense that she meant. For him the mystery was now completely solved, though there were other matters concerning which he was curious.

"Do you send in to the exhibitions?" he asked. "It is rather necessary if you expect to make a living by your work."

"I haven't actually exhibited," she replied, "but I am getting a collection together in readiness, and I go to see the modernist shows to see what sort of prices works of my kind fetch, or, at least, are offered at. They seem to me rather high, but I notice that very few of the pictures are sold."

"Yes," said Tom, "there are not many picture buyers nowadays, and the few picture lovers who do buy mostly prefer work of the traditional kind. But your best plan would be to try some of the dealers who specialize in modernist works. They would know what your pictures are worth in their market, and they might be able to give you some useful advice. They might even buy some of your works – at their own price, of course."

"That's an excellent idea," said she. "I will certainly try it. Perhaps you could give me the names of one or two dealers. Would you?"

Tom shook his head. "My dealers would be no good for you. They are old-fashioned fellows who deal in old-fashioned work. No modernist stuff for them. They'd be afraid of frightening away their regular customers."

"That doesn't sound very encouraging," she remarked with a wry smile.

"I suppose it doesn't," Tom admitted; and in the pause that followed it was suddenly borne in on him that these comradely confidences were not very favourable to the "closure of the incident". And then, in the vulgar but convenient phrase, he "put the lid on it".

"You appear," said he, "to work exclusively in water colour. Do you find that more suitable than oil?"

"The truth is," she replied, "that I have never tried oil painting because I don't quite know how to go about it; I mean as to mixing the paint and putting it on with those queer-looking stiff-haired brushes. But I should like to paint in oil, or at least give the medium a trial." She paused for a few moments. Then in an insinuating tone she continued, "I wonder whether my kind and helpful neighbour would come to my assistance."

Tom looked at her apprehensively. "I suppose I'm the neighbour," said he, "but I don't quite see what you want me to do."

"It is only a modest request," she urged, "but I should be so grateful if, sometime when you are at work, you would let me come and look on."

"But to what purpose?" he demanded. "My painting and your painting are not the same kind of thing at all."

"I know," she agreed. "But, after all, modernist painters use the same materials and implements as artists of the more old-fashioned type. Now, you know all about the methods of oil painting, and, if I could watch you when you are working, I should see how you do it, and then I should be able, with a little practice, to do it myself. Won't you let me come once or twice? I promise not to waste your time or interrupt you by talking."

Tom looked at the smiling, wheedlesome face and realized that he was cornered. It would be churlish to refuse, and indeed, utterly unlike him to withhold any help from a fellow artist, no matter how bad. But still it was necessary for him to "mind his eye". It would never do to give this enterprising young woman the run of his studio.

"When I am at work," he said at length, "I like to be alone and concentrate on what I am doing, but I shall be very pleased to give you a demonstration of the technique of oil painting. What I would suggest is that you bring in one of your pictures, and that I make a copy of it in oil, while you look on. Then you can ask as many questions as you please and I will give you any tips as to the management of the medium that seem necessary. How will that do?"

"But it is the very thing that I would have asked for if I had dared. I am delighted, and more grateful than I can tell you. Perhaps you will let me know when I may come for the demonstration."

"I will," he replied. "It won't be for a day or two, but when I have finished the picture that I have in hand, I will drop a note into your letter box giving one or two alternative dates. And I hope," he continued as he rose to depart, "that you will like the medium and do great things in it."

As he re-entered his studio and occupied himself in cleaning his palette and brushes and doing a few odd jobs, he cogitated profoundly on the events of the afternoon. One thing was plain to him; the "closure of the incident" was "off". The good lady had fairly taken possession of him. Already she had established herself definitely as an acquaintance, and he saw clearly that the next interview would put her on the footing of a friend. It was an unfortunate affair, but he must make the best of it and continue to "mind his eye" – if the word "continue" was strictly applicable.

As to the woman herself, he was completely puzzled. He could make nothing of her. Was she simply an impostor or did she suffer from some extraordinary delusion? The plain and obvious facts were that she could not draw at all, that her watercolour painting was that of an untalented child and that she seemed to have no artistic ideas or the capacity to invent a subject. But was it possible that she had some kind of artistic gifts which he was unable to gauge? The supposition seemed to be negatived by her own admission that she had never felt any interest in pictures. For the outstanding characteristic of real talent is the early age at which it shows itself. Pope "lisped in numbers, for the numbers came"; Mozart and Handel were accomplished musicians, and even composers, when they were small children; John Millais was a masterly draughtsman at the age of five; Bonington died in the twenties with a European reputation; and so with Fred Walker, Chantrey, and a host of others. No, a person who reaches middle age without showing any sign of artistic aptitude is certainly not a born artist.

The only possible conclusion seemed to be that Mrs Schiller was either a rank impostor or the subject of some strange delusion; and at that he had to leave it. After all, it was not his affair. His concern was to see that he was not involved in any entanglements; and the lady's masterful ways promised to give him full occupation in that respect without troubling about her artistic gifts.

CHAPTER FOUR
Mr Vanderpuye

There are persons, unfortunately too common, who seem to be incapable of doing anything well. Impatience to get the job finished and inability to concentrate on the doing beget slipshod work and faulty results. Conversely, there are some more happily constituted who cannot bring themselves to do anything badly. Of this type Tom Pedley was a representative specimen. To the simplest task he gave his whole attention and would not leave it until it was done to a finish, even though the task was no more than the washing of a teacup or the polishing of a spoon. Hence the demonstration of oil technique, though he secretly regarded it as a waste of time, was carried out with as much thoroughness as if Mrs Schiller had been a pupil of the highest promise.

"I have brought two of my pictures," the lady explained when she made her appearance on the appointed day; "the Symphony in Green and Blue and the Adam and Eve subject. Which do you think will be the more suitable?"

"May as well do them both," replied Tom, "as one has some sort of shape in it and the other hasn't. We'll begin with the Symphony. You seem to have used mighty big brushes and kept the paper uncommonly wet."

"Oh, I didn't use any brushes at all. I just soaked the paper in water, mixed up some emerald oxide and French ultramarine in separate saucers and poured it on in long streaks. When I tilted the board, of course, the streaks ran together and produced those subtle gradations of colour that I have tried to express by the word Symphony."

"I see," said Tom with an appreciative grin. "Deuced good method. Labour-saving, too. Well, you can't do that sort of thing in oil. Got to do the blending with the brush unless you work with the knife. I'll show you."

He set up the "Symphony" on the easel with a fourteen by twelve canvas by its side. Then, on a clean palette, he squeezed out three blobs of colour, emerald oxide, French ultramarine and flake white, and, taking up the palette knife, mixed one or two tints to match those of the "Symphony".

"We'll follow your methods as far as we can in oil," said he. "We begin with streaks of the deepest colour, add lighter tints at the edges, and then paint them into one another to produce the subtle gradations. Like this."

He fell to work with a couple of large brushes, keeping an attentive eye on the "Symphony" and giving from time to time a few words of explanation as to the management of the brush and the mixing of the tints. At the end of a quarter of an hour's work he had produced a copy of the "Symphony" which might have been a facsimile but for the difference in the medium. His pupil watched him and listened to his explanations without saying a word until he had finished. Then, as he stepped back and laid down his palette, she exclaimed:

"How extraordinary! You've made a perfect copy; and so quickly, too. It is really wonderful; and it looks so easy."

"Easy!" Tom repeated. "Of course it's easy. Any – er – anyone" (he had nearly said "any fool") "can put streaks of colour on a canvas and paint their edges into one another. But, of course," he added hurriedly, "you've got to invent the streaks. Now we'll have a go at Adam and Eve."

This, however, presented more difficulty. Try as he would, he could not quite attain the childish effect of the original. His figures persisted in looking slightly human and even in differentiating themselves into a recognizable man and woman.

"There," he said as he stepped back and regarded his performance with a grim smile, "I think that will do, though it isn't a fair copy. I seem to have missed some of the 'essential form', but that doesn't matter. You see the method. And now, as a wind up, I'll just show you how to work with the knife. That may suit you better than the brush."

He placed on the easel a slab of millboard, and, taking a couple of small, thin-bladed, trowel-shaped knives, rapidly executed another rendering of the "Symphony", while his pupil watched with delighted surprise. Finally, he showed her how to clean the palette and wash the brushes, admonishing her that a tidy worker takes care of his tools and doesn't waste his materials.

"And now," he concluded, "you know all about it. Facility will come with practice, and the ideas you have already, so all you've got to do is to provide yourself with the materials and fire away."

"I will certainly do that," said she. "But I can't tell you how grateful I am." She came close up to him, looking earnestly in his face and laying her hands on his arms (and for one awful moment he thought she was going to kiss him) and exclaimed: "It was so kind of you to take all this trouble for a mere stranger. I think you are a perfect dear. But we aren't really strangers, are we?"

"Well," Tom admitted cautiously, "I've certainly seen you before."

"Now, don't be an old bear," she protested smilingly. "Seen me before, indeed! But never mind. You haven't done with me yet. I want you to come with me to the artists' colourman and show me what I must get for a start. You will do that for me, won't you? Say yes, like a duck."

"Can't very well do that," objected Tom, "as I've never heard a duck say yes; but I'll come to the shop with you and see that you don't waste your money on foolishness. Might as well nip along now and get it done with. Shop's close by. Only take us a few minutes. What do you say?"

She said "yes" with a sly and very understanding smile; and Tom realized too late that his studied gruffness, so far from fending her off, had only put her on a more intimate footing. So they went forth together, and when Tom had superintended her purchases and seen her provided with the bare necessaries for a beginning, he took up the bulky parcel and escorted her home; and as he handed her the parcel and said "goodbye" on her doorstep, the effusiveness of her gratitude made him thankful that the farewells were exchanged in a public thoroughfare.

He turned away with a troubled face and a sinking heart. No self-delusion was now possible. He had failed utterly to "mind his eye" and had been definitely adopted, willy-nilly, by this remarkable young woman as her special friend and comrade. And there seemed to be no escape. A coarser and less genial man would have administered an effective rebuff; but Tom was a kindly soul, courteous and considerate by nature and habit and with all the old bachelor's deference to women. Unwillingly, he had to accept the conviction that this unwanted friendship was an established fact to which, henceforth, his old simple, self-contained way of life should be subject.

And so it proved. His new friend was not actually intrusive. She recognized that he was a solitary man who liked to work alone. But somehow it happened that hardly a day passed in which she did not make some kind of appearance. Of course, he had to go in to see her experiments in the new medium (at which he gazed stolidly, his capacity for astonishment having been exhausted) and give her further purely technical advice. Then she would drop in at the studio now and again to ask a question, to offer some little service or to bring some small gift, and the number of chance meetings in the neighbouring streets was such as to confound all the known laws of probability. Thus, insensibly, the intimacy grew and with it the space which she occupied in his life.

Tom observed the process with anxious foreboding and cursed the ill luck that had brought her into his orbit. But presently he began to realize that things were not so bad as he had feared. In the first place, she was not a widow. There was a husband in the background – apparently a German background; a shadowy figure, but still an undeniable bar to matrimony. So the principal danger was excluded. Then certain other reassuring facts became evident. At first her astonishing familiarity had horrified him, and the endearing phrases and epithets she used had seemed positively alarming, but he soon grew accustomed to being addressed as "Tom" or even "Tommy"; and as to the endearments, they appeared to be no more than a playful habit. He realized this as he noted the essential correctness of her conduct when they were together. Never was there the slightest tendency to sentimentality or philandering. She might call him "my dear" or "duck" or even "Tommy, darling", but the mere words seemed harmless enough – though foolish – in view of her perfectly matter-of-fact behaviour; and Tom, now reassured and satisfied that no real entanglement threatened, made shift to put up with what he regarded as a "damn silly and rather objectionable habit".

As to the woman herself, her personality was not unpleasing. Sprightly, humorous and amusing, she might have been a quite acceptable companion if he had wanted one – which he emphatically did not – and if she had shown any glimmer of sensibility to art as he understood it. But, though she soon dropped the art-journalist's jargon and tried to interest herself in his work, she really knew nothing and cared nothing about normal art; and lacking that interest, they had nothing in common.

Her appearance, on the other hand, rather interested him, and, in his capacity as an occasional portrait painter, he gave it some attention. He would have described her as a luridly picturesque woman; blonde, showy, and made up in the height of an ugly fashion, with vermilion lips, rouged and powdered cheeks, pencilled eyebrows, and a remarkable mass of fuzzy hair, which had apparently once been bobbed and was now in process of being unbobbed. That hair interested him especially. He had never seen anything quite like it. In colour it was a very light brown, approaching flaxen, but there was something unusual in its texture; something that gave it a peculiar shimmering character when it caught the light and seemed to make the colour variable. Considering the problem of rendering it in a portrait, Tom studied its changing lights and compared it with the greenish hazel eyes and as much of the complexion as he could make out; finally reaching the conclusion that it was some sort of fake, but what sort of fake he could not imagine.

For the rest, she was a rather tall woman, perhaps five feet seven without her high heels, fairly good-looking, with rather small features but a prominent chin and a strong lower jaw. Her most attractive aspect was undoubtedly the profile, and Tom, studying this with a professional eye, decided it would make quite a good medallion. He even made one or two trial sketches from memory in his notebook with a half-formed intention of offering to paint a medallion portrait, but abandoned the idea as he realized that the necessary sittings would tend further to cement a friendship that was already too close.

By which it will be seen that Tom was still, so to speak, fighting a rearguard action; still seeking to limit this unsought intimacy. Although he now knew that she could have no matrimonial designs on him, and he no longer feared any attempt to establish a questionable relationship, he disliked the association. He had never wanted a female friend and he resented the way in which this woman had attached herself to him. An eminently self-contained and rather solitary man, his principal wish was to be left alone to live his own life, and, as time went on, he found it more and more irksome to have that life pervaded by another personality, and not even a sympathetic one at that. But he saw no prospect of escape, short of a definite snub, of which he was incapable; and in the end he gave up the struggle, and, with a sigh of regret for the peace and freedom that were gone, resigned himself to making the best of the new conditions.

But the hour of his deliverance was at hand, little as he could have foreseen it, and little as he suspected the benign character of the agent when he arrived bearing, all unknown, the order of release. And as the darkest hour is that before the dawn, so the beginning of his emancipation occurred at a moment when he felt that the nuisance of this forced intimacy was becoming intolerable.

It was about four o'clock in the afternoon and the lady had just dropped in at the studio with an invitation to tea, which he had firmly declined.

"Oh, rubbish," she protested. "You are always too busy to come and have tea with me; at least you say you are, and I don't believe you. It's just an excuse. Is it my tea or my society you that don't like?"

"My dear Mrs Schiller – " Tom began, but she cut him short.

"Oh, not Mrs Schiller! Haven't I told you again and again not to call me by that horrible name? Call me Lotta. I'm sure it's a very nice name."

"It's a most admirable name. Well – er – Lotta – "

"Well, my dear, if you won't come to have tea with me, I shall stay here and make yours for you and help you to drink it; and then I'll take myself off and leave my darling old bear to the peaceful enjoyment of his den. You'll let me stay, Tom, dear, won't you?"

It was at this moment that the studio bell, jangling imperatively out in the yard, broke into the discussion.

"Shall I run out and see who it is?" asked Lotta.

"No. I'd better go. May be able to settle the business on the doorstep."

He strode out along the passage, hoping that it might be so. But when he opened the door and discovered on the threshold his old friend, Mr Polton, accompanied by a stranger, he knew that no evasion was possible. He would have to invite them in.

"Good afternoon, sir," said Polton, greeting him with a cheerful and crinkly smile. "I have taken the liberty of bringing you a client who would like you to paint his portrait. Am I right in using the word 'client'?"

"Well, we usually call them sitters, though that does sound a little suggestive of poultry. But it doesn't matter. Won't you come in?"

They came in, and as they walked slowly along the passage, Polton completed the introductions. The prospective sitter, a light-coloured, good-looking African gentleman, was a Mr William Vanderpuye, a native of Elmina on the Gold Coast, who was attending a course of lectures on Medical Jurisprudence at St Margaret's Hospital.

"He is also doing some practical work in our laboratory," Polton explained further, "as Dr Thorndyke's pupil. That is how I came to have the pleasure of making his acquaintance."

At this point they reached the studio door, which Tom threw open, inviting them to enter. Accordingly they entered, and then, becoming aware of the other occupant of the studio, they both stopped short, and, for a moment, three inquisitive pairs of eyes made a rapid mutual inspection. Sweating with embarrassment and cursing under his breath, Tom hastened to introduce his three guests, and then, by way of giving the lady an opportunity to retire, explained:

"Mr Vanderpuye is going to do me the honour of sitting to me for his portrait."

"Oh, how interesting!" she exclaimed. "But now I expect you will want to arrange about the sittings, so I suppose I had better run away and leave you to your consultation."

As she spoke, she directed a subtly appealing glance at Mr Vanderpuye, who replied instantly and with emphasis:

"Not at all, Mrs Schiller. You mustn't let me drive you away. We are not going to talk secrets but just to arrange about the portrait. Besides," he added, a little ambiguously, "it seems that you paint yourself, so you may be able to advise us."

"That is very gracious of you," said she; "and if you would really like me to stay, I should be delighted to hear all about the portrait; and I will make you a nice cup of tea as a thank offering for the invitation."

She began, forthwith, to set out the tea things while Polton filled the kettle and put it on the gas ring. Tom looked on with mixed feelings which changed from moment to moment. He could easily have dispensed with Lotta's company; but noting the way in which his new patron's eyes followed her movements, he began to suspect it might be all for the best. Apparently, he was Lotta's only male friend. It would be a great relief to him if she should get another.

With this idea in his mind, he observed the trend of events while tea was being consumed (as also did Mr Polton, to whom the lady was a startling mystery) and found it encouraging. Of a set purpose, as it seemed, Lotta kept the ball of conversation rolling almost entirely between herself and Mr Vanderpuye, addressing him in a tone of deference which he evidently found flattering. Indeed, the African gentleman was obviously much impressed by the fair Lotta, and openly admiring; which was not unnatural, for she was a good-looking woman (if one did not object to the "abstract colour"), who could make herself extremely agreeable when she tried. And she was obviously trying now.

"I am inclined to envy Mr Pedley his opportunity," said she. "You are such an admirable subject for a portrait."

"Do you really think so?" he exclaimed, delighted. "I was rather afraid that the complexion – and the hair you know – "

"Oh, but that is what I meant by the opportunity. Your warm olive complexion creates all sorts of possibilities in the way of colour harmonies; so unlike the pale, relatively colourless European face. Perhaps," she continued reflectively, "that may account for the fact that the African peoples seem to be born colourists. Don't you think so?"

"It may be so," Vanderpuye agreed. "They certainly like colour, and plenty of it. My steward, at home, used to wear a scarlet flannel suit and green carpet slippers."

"But what a lovely combination!" exclaimed Lotta. "Such a subtle and delicate contrast! Don't you agree with me?"

Mr Vanderpuye was prepared to agree to anything, and did so with a genial smile; thereby revealing such a set of teeth as seldom gladdens the eye of the modern European.

"But, of course," he added, "I don't know much about the matter except that I like bright colours myself, whereas you are an artist and have, no doubt, studied the subject profoundly."

"I have," she admitted. "Colour is the engrossing interest of my life. So much do I love it that I am often impelled to paint pictures consisting entirely of colour without any other motive. Symphonies and concertos in colour, you know."

"They must be very beautiful, I am sure," said Vanderpuye, "though I don't quite understand how you can make a picture of colour alone. Perhaps, some day, I may have the privilege of seeing your works."

"Would you like to? If you would, I should be only too proud and delighted to show them to you. I live next door to Mr Pedley, so you could easily drop in sometime after one of your sittings."

"It would be better to make an appointment," suggested Vanderpuye. "What time would you like me to attend for the sitting, Mr Pedley?"

"I should prefer the morning light," replied Tom; "say from nine to twelve. How would that suit you, Mr Vanderpuye?"

"Admirably," was the reply. "And as to the date? When would you like to begin?"

"The sooner the better, so far as I am concerned. How would tomorrow do?"

"It would do perfectly for me. Then we will say tomorrow morning at nine. And as to you, Mrs Schiller; if I should look in at your studio shortly after twelve, would that be convenient?"

"Quite," she replied. "I shall have just finished my morning's work. And now," she added, "as we have emptied the teapot, and I expect that you have some further arrangements to discuss, I had better make myself scarce."

She rose and, having shaken hands with the two visitors and announced that she would let herself out, bestowed a parting smile on Mr Vanderpuye and bustled away.

The sound of the closing outer door brought the conversation back to the portrait and the "further arrangements"; but with the details of these we are not concerned. Finally it was decided that the portrait should be a three-quarter length presenting the subject in his barrister's wig and gown, standing with a brief in his hand as if addressing the court; and having settled this and the question of costs, the two visitors rose to depart.

"Au revoir, then," said Mr Vanderpuye, "or, as the Hausa men say in my country, *Sei Gobe* – 'Until Tomorrow'. Nine o'clock sharp will see me on your doorstep."

"And twelve o'clock sharp on Mrs Schiller's," added Tom, with a sly smile.

Mr Vanderpuye smiled in return. Whether he also blushed there was no means of judging.

CHAPTER FIVE

A Trivial Chapter, but not Irrelevant

The vague hopes which Tom Pedley had conceived that a friendship between his new patron and Lotta Schiller might relieve him to some extent of the lady's society were more than fulfilled. For very soon it began to appear that Mr Vanderpuye was not merely to share the burden of that intimacy; he had in effect stepped into the reversion of Tom's status as Lotta's sole male friend. Not that Tom was totally discarded by her. She still made occasional appearances in the studio; but those appearances tended in a most singular manner to coincide with the presence there of Mr Vanderpuye.

There was no mistaking the position, nor, indeed, was there any concealment of it. The impulsive and susceptible African gentleman made no secret of his admiration of the fair and sprightly Lotta or of the fact that they spent a good deal of time together; while, as to the lady herself, she was at no pains whatever to disguise the new relationship. Thus Tom, guided by the light of experience, watched with grim amusement the development of the familiar symptoms; noted that Mr William Vanderpuye had been promoted to the style and title of Billy – with or without the customary enrichments – and that Mrs Lotta Schiller had ceased to command a surname.

The portrait progressed steadily, but, being a nearly complete life-size figure with some accessories, its execution involved a considerable number of sittings, though Tom often saved time by working at the

51

accessories in the intervals; and as it grew towards completion its quality began to show itself. It was a tactful and sympathetic portrait. There was no flattery. The likeness was faithfully rendered, but it was an eminently becoming likeness, presenting the sitter at his best; and if there was any tendency to stress the more favourable points, that merely reflected Tom Pedley's ordinary attitude towards his fellow creatures.

From time to time Lotta dropped in at the studio (usually about twelve) to inspect and criticize, and Tom listened to her with delighted amusement. Gone was all the claptrap about representationalism and imitative art. She was now the frank and honest Philistine. Unlike the art critics from whom she had borrowed her "highbrow" phrases, who dismiss the "mere resemblance" in a portrait as a negligible irrelevancy, she was out for the likeness and nothing but the likeness; and as it approached the final stage, even she was satisfied.

"Do you think it is like me, Lotta?" Vanderpuye asked anxiously as they stood before the canvas. "I hope it is, but it seems a little flattering."

"You are a silly, self-deprecating little ass, Billy," said she (Billy stood a trifle over six feet in his stockings). "You don't realize what a good-looking fellow you are."

"Well, my dear," he rejoined, regarding her with a fond smile, "I am always willing to learn, especially from you."

"Then," said she, "you can take it from me that the handsome legal gentleman in the picture is a faithful representation of my friend Bill, and not flattered in the least. Isn't that so, Tom?"

"I think so," he replied. "I have painted him as I see him and as his friends see him, and I hope I have done him impartial justice."

Tom's view was confirmed by another of "Bill's" friends, to wit, Mr Polton, who made occasional visits and followed the progress of the work with the deepest interest; a sort of proprietory interest, in fact, for it transpired that it was at his instigation that the portrait had been commissioned when photographs had been tried and found wanting (photographs of coloured people tend to be eminently unflattering). The confirmation came on a certain occasion when the four interested parties were gathered around the portrait, now practically finished, to discuss its merits.

"The art of painting," Mr Polton moralized, "seems to me almost like a supernatural power. Of course, I can do scale drawings to work from, but they are only diagrams. They don't look like the real objects; whereas with this picture, if I stand a little way off and look at it with one eye closed, I seem to be actually looking at Mr Vanderpuye."

"Yes," Lotta agreed, "it is a perfect representation; almost as perfect as a photograph."

"I beg your pardon, ma'am," Polton objected, "but it is a good deal more perfect. You can't do this sort of thing by photography."

"Not the colour, of course, but I meant the representation of form."

"But, ma'am," Polton persisted, "there is something more than form in this portrait; something that photography can't do. I tried one or two photographs of Mr Vanderpuye when I was teaching him the technique, but they were quite a failure. The form was perfectly correct and they would have been excellent for identification; but there was something lacking, and that something was what we might call the personality. But that is just what the portrait has got. It is Mr Vanderpuye himself, whereas the photographs were mere representations of his shape."

Tom nodded approvingly. "Mr Polton is right," said he. "Photography can give a perfect representation of an object, such as a statue or a building, which is always the same. But a living person changes from moment to moment. A photograph can only show the appearance at a given instant, but the portrait painter must disregard the accidents of the moment and seek out the essential and permanent character."

This seemed to be quite a new idea to Lotta, for she exclaimed:

"Really! Now I never thought of that; and I am rather sorry, too, because I had meant to ask Mr Polton to take a photograph of Bill just as he is posed for the painting. But if it would not be a true likeness, I shouldn't care to have it. Still, it's very disappointing."

"There's no need for you to be disappointed, ma'am," Polton interposed. "If Mr Pedley would allow me to take a photograph of the painting, you would have a portrait with all the qualities of the original except the colour. It would be a true copy."

Lotta was delighted, and most profuse in her thanks. She even informed Mr Polton, much to his surprise, that he was a duck.

"What size, ma'am," he asked when the permission had been obtained, "would you wish the photograph to be?"

"Oh, quite small," she replied, "so that I could have it mounted in a little case that I could carry about with me, or perhaps in a brooch or pendant that I could wear. Would that be possible, Mr Polton?"

"Oh, certainly, ma'am; but, if you will excuse my mentioning it, a brooch or a pendant would not be so very suitable for your purpose because, when you were wearing it, the portrait would be visible to everybody but yourself."

Lotta laughed. "Of course," said she. "How silly of me; and exhibiting the sacred portrait to strangers is just what I don't want to do. But what would you suggest?"

"I think," he replied, "that the old-fashioned locket would answer the purpose best."

"A locket," interposed Vanderpuye. "What is a locket? You will pardon me, but I am only a poor ignorant African."

"A locket, sir," Polton explained, "is a sort of pendant, usually of gold, forming a little flat case which opens by a hinge, and displays two little frames. Sometimes there used to be two portraits, one in each frame, but more commonly one frame contained a portrait and the other a lock of the – er – the selected person's hair either plaited and made up into a tiny coil or arranged in a flat spiral."

Vanderpuye chuckled gleefully. "I like the idea of the locket," said he, "but I am afraid you would get into difficulties with my hair."

"Not at all, sir," replied Polton. "Each of your hairs forms a natural spiral like a little watch spring. That is one of the African racial characteristics. Shall I show you?"

He produced from his pocket a pair of watchmaker's tweezers and a pair of folding scissors, and, having picked up a single hair from Vanderpuye's wool, cut it off neatly, laid it on a white card, and passed it round for inspection.

"How perfectly lovely!" Lotta exclaimed. "It is, as you say, exactly like a tiny watch spring. Yes, I will certainly have a locket."

"If you wished to extend the spiral," Polton suggested, "so as to fill the frame, it could easily be done by using two or three hairs."

"Oh, but that would spoil it," she protested, "and it is so beautiful. No, just one perfect little watch spring in the middle of the space. Don't you agree with me, Bill?"

"Certainly, my dear," he replied with a broad smile, "especially as it would exhibit a racial characteristic. But how are we going to get the locket? Are they still to be obtained in the shops?"

"I expect they are. But I don't want a shop locket. It would be a soulless, machine-made thing, unworthy of my beloved Bill and his charming little watch spring. What do you suggest, Mr Polton? I suppose you couldn't make a locket for me, yourself?"

"So far as the mere construction is concerned, of course, I could make a locket. But I am not a goldsmith. The design would have to be made by an artist. If Mr Pedley would make the design, I would carry it out for you with great pleasure."

"Oh, but how kind of you, Mr Polton! You are really too sweet. I think I have already remarked that you are a duck."

"I think you have, ma'am," he replied with a somewhat wry crinkle, "and I beg to thank you, for the − er − for the compliment."

"Not at all, Mr Polton. And now, Tom, about this locket. Can you design it?"

"Yes," he replied. "I have done some designing for goldsmith's work and a simple locket would present no difficulty, especially as I should be collaborating with Mr Polton. If you like, I will make one or two sketches for you to see, and we can then discuss the question of ornament."

"Yes, that would be very nice of you, Tom; and you must let me know what it will cost."

"That is not your concern, Lotta," said Vanderpuye. "It is to be a gift from me."

"How very noble of you, Bill. Of course that will make it much more precious, and I accept gratefully on one condition; which is that you have a locket, too, and that you let me give it to you."

"But men don't wear lockets, do they?" he asked.

"They used to," said Tom, "before the arrival of the wristwatch. The locket was usually suspended from the watch-chain."

"Well," said Vanderpuye, "as you see, I carry a pocket watch on a chain, as a wristwatch is not very suitable for the Tropics, so I am eligible for a locket, and I should very much like to have one with a portrait of Lotta and a lock of her beautiful golden hair. Would you two gentleman accept the commission?"

The two gentlemen agreed that they would, whereupon Lotta objected:

"But you have no business to offer the commission. That is my affair, seeing that the locket is to be a gift from me."

Vanderpuye smiled blandly. "The commission," said he, "was offered and accepted without prejudice as we say in the law. The other question is for separate consideration. Now we have to arrange details. The locket is to contain a portrait and a lock of golden hair. The hair presents no difficulty, as it is obviously available. But what about the portrait? Should we ask Mr Polton to do us a little photograph?"

"No you don't," exclaimed Lotta; "and I am surprised at you, Bill, when you've just heard what these two experts said about portrait photographs. No, it shall be a real painted portrait. I will paint it myself; and then I shall ask dear Mr Polton to make a little photograph of the painting, and I am sure he won't refuse."

"Certainly not, ma'am," said Polton. "It will give me great pleasure, and I think it a most excellent idea. It will be a memento in a double sense; a portrait of the giver and a specimen of her handiwork."

Vanderpuye, however, was less enthusiastic. (He had seen "the giver's handiwork" and Polton hadn't.) "Why not let me commission Mr Pedley to paint a portrait?" he suggested.

"You'll do nothing of the kind," she replied. "The locket is to be my gift and I want the portrait to be my very own work."

There was nothing more to be said. Vanderpuye looked a little glum, and Tom, too good-natured to be simply amused, was regretful. A vivid recollection of "The Madonna" suggested breakers ahead and a disappointment for Mr Vanderpuye. But he made no comment. Perhaps the future might develop some way out of the dilemma.

A few days later at the last of the sittings a few final touches were added; and the portrait being now entirely finished, Tom escorted the sitter to the frame-maker's to advise him as to a suitable frame. When this business had been disposed of, Tom produced one or two sketches which he had roughed out in the interval showing alternative designs for the two lockets. The one for the standing figure was a rather long ellipse, while the other, to hang on the watch-guard, was considerably smaller and circular in shape. Both forms were shown with alternative designs of decoration, in simple embossed metal, in coloured enamel, and with set stones.

"If you will be seeing Mrs Schiller you might show her the sketches," said Tom, "and talk them over with her; and if you both approve of the circular shape for the smaller one, you might remind her to design her portrait to fill the circular space so that the head is not too small."

"I shall be seeing her in about half an hour's time," said Vanderpuye. "We are lunching at a place which she has discovered in Soho, so we shall have an opportunity to discuss the designs. But I think we should both like to take your advice on the matter."

"Yes," Tom agreed, "a little discussion and explanation might be useful as the sketches are rather slight. Perhaps, when Mrs Schiller has finished her portrait, we might all four meet at the studio and make the final arrangements."

"I will suggest that to her," said Vanderpuye, "and I will let you and Mr Polton know when the portrait is ready. I wish," he added, confidentially, "that she had agreed to your painting it. Her style of work doesn't seem to me very suitable for a portrait; but, of course, I am no judge. What do you think?"

Tom's opinions on the subject were perfectly definite; but his reply was discreetly evasive.

"I have never seen a portrait by her, so I can hardly judge; but we will hope for the best."

With this, by way of avoiding a dangerous topic, he shook Vanderpuye's hand cordially and the two men went their respective ways.

The meeting took place about a week later, the day and hour having been decided by Polton, and, somewhat before the appointed time that cunning artificer made his appearance and forthwith set to work. From one of his numerous and capacious pockets he produced a small folding camera which, when it was opened, was seen to be fitted with a level and a sighting frame.

"I haven't brought a stand," said he, "as I thought that an easel would be more convenient and more rigid. Can you lend me one?"

"Yes," replied Tom. "I have one unoccupied; a heavy one with a lifting screw, which will answer your purpose perfectly. It is as steady as a rock."

He drew it out from its corner and trundled it across to a place opposite the portrait, when Polton took charge of it, placing his camera on the tray, and, with the aid of the sighting frame, adjusting the relative positions of the camera and the portrait until the latter exactly filled the space of the frame. Then he made the exposure, and was in the act of winding on the exposed film when the sound of the studio bell announced the arrival of the other two parties to the symposium. As they entered and Polton made his bow, it seemed to him that Vanderpuye's expression lacked its usual geniality; in fact, the African gentleman looked undeniably sulky. On the other hand, the fair and volatile Lotta was in the best of spirits, and apparently quite pleased with herself.

"Why," she exclaimed as she bounced into the studio, "here is my dear Mr Polton, improving the shining hour like a pre-punctual duck and all ready to begin work." She shook his hand warmly and continued, "And what a darling little camera. But isn't it rather small for that big portrait?"

"It is going to be quite a small photograph, you will remember, ma'am; not more than an inch and a half high."

"Yes, of course. How silly of me. Are you going to take the photograph now?"

"I have taken it already, ma'am, and I shall have great pleasure in taking your own when it is available."

"It is available now," said Lotta, opening her handbag and taking out an envelope about eight inches by six. "I made it quite a small painting as you see, but I dare say it will be big enough."

"The size is amply sufficient," Polton replied, "as it has to be reduced so much."

He took the envelope which she handed to him, and, opening the flap, tenderly drew out a small mounted watercolour, which he regarded with a reverential smile. It emerged with the back uppermost, but, as he quickly turned it over, the smile faded from his countenance and gave place to an expression of astonishment and dismay. For some moments he stood speechless and rigid, staring incredulously at the thing which he held in his hand. Then he cast a furtive glance at the artist and was reassured to find her watching him with a sly smile. Obviously it was a joke, he decided, but he was too discreet to say so. He would lie low and let the situation develop.

"Well, Mr Polton," said Lotta, "how do you like it?"

"Since you ask me, ma'am," he replied with a cautious crinkle, "I really don't think you have done yourself justice."

"You wouldn't have me flatter myself, would you?" she demanded.

"Oh, no, ma'am," he replied. "But there was no need to. You had only to represent yourself exactly as you are to produce a very charming portrait."

Lotta laughed gaily. "Thank you, Mr Polton, for a very neatly turned compliment."

"It's no compliment at all," Vanderpuye burst in. "Mr Polton is perfectly right. What I wanted was a likeness; but this portrait isn't like you a bit. I should never have recognized it. What do you say, Mr Pedley?"

But Tom, who was looking at the portrait over Polton's shoulder, emulated the latter gentleman's caution.

"Of course," said he, "it is not a literal representation. But then it isn't meant to be."

"Exactly," Lotta agreed. "The mere physical resemblance is not what I was aiming at. This portrait is not a work of imitative art. It is a work of self-expression."

The argument between Lotta and Vanderpuye was pursued for some time with some heat, not to say bitterness. But it led nowhere. Lotta was immovable, and Vanderpuye had at length to retire defeated. Meanwhile Polton, having realized to his amazement that this preposterous thing had to be taken seriously, took it seriously, and, without further comment, stuck it up on the easel beside the other portrait and gravely proceeded with the photograph. When he had finished and handed the portrait back to its creator, the sketches for the lockets were produced and discussed at some length; the conclusion reached being that both should be decorated with a simple design in *champlevé* enamel and that the details should be left to the designer and the executant.

"And that appears to be all," said Lotta, bestowing the "self-portrait" in her handbag.

"Excepting the hair, ma'am," Polton reminded her. "If I may be permitted to take a sample for each locket I shall be able to get on with the work without troubling you further."

From his inexhaustible pockets he brought forth a couple of seed envelopes, a pair of tweezers, and a pair of folding scissors, all of which he laid on the table. Then, beginning with Vanderpuye, he separated one of the little crisp curls and cut it off flush with the skin, putting it at once into one of the envelopes, on which, having sealed it, he wrote, "W Vanderpuye, Esq."

Lotta watched him with a smile and commended his caution.

"It would be a bit awkward if you had two unlabelled envelopes and didn't know which was which. Now, how much of mine do you want? Be thrifty, if you please. I can't have you leaving a bald patch."

"Certainly not, ma'am," Polton assured her. "A dozen hairs will be enough, and they will never be missed."

By way of confirmation, he counted them out one by one, and then, gathering up the little strand, cut it through close to the roots. Having twisted the strand into a loose yarn, he coiled it neatly and slipped it into the envelope, which he sealed and inscribed with the name of "Mrs Lotta Schiller".

This brought the proceedings to an end, and, when Polton had put the two precious envelopes into a stout leather wallet and stowed the latter in a capacious inner pocket, Lotta and Mr Vanderpuye rose together to take their departure, and, having shaken hands with Polton, went out escorted by their host.

When the latter returned to the studio, he discovered his collaborator seated opposite the clock, apparently regarding it with intense concentration. He looked round as Tom entered, and, gazing at him with wrinkled brows, exclaimed solemnly:

"This is a most extraordinary thing, sir."

"What is?" asked Tom, looking at the clock and not perceiving anything unusual about it.

"I am referring, sir, to this portrait of Mrs Schiller's. I am utterly bewildered. At first, I took for granted that it was a joke."

"Vanderpuye didn't," Tom remarked with a grin.

"No, indeed. But do you understand it, sir? To me, it looked exactly like the sort of portraits that I used to draw when I was a boy of ten, and that other little boys used to draw. But I suppose I must have been mistaken. Was I, sir?"

"No," replied Tom. "You were perfectly right."

"But," Polton protested, "Mrs Schiller is a professional artist, as I understand. Can she really paint or draw?"

"Since you ask me, Polton, I should say that she can't. She draws in that way because she can't draw in any other."

"But what an amazing thing, sir. If she can't draw or paint, how does she manage to practise as an artist?"

"I don't know," replied Tom, "that it is quite correct to describe her as practising as an artist She has never sold any of her work and never exhibited any. By the term 'practising artist' one usually means an artist who gets a living by his work. Still, there are painters whose work is no better than hers who exhibit and even sell. You can see their stuff in the various freak exhibitions that appear from time to time in London. That is how Mrs Schiller got her ideas. She went to one of these freak shows which was being boosted by the art journalists, and she thought that the stuff looked so easy to do that she decided to try whether she couldn't do something like it. So she tried, and found that she could. Naturally. Anyone could; even a child; and some children can do a good deal better."

"But does anyone take these works seriously?"

"Seriously!" exclaimed Tom. "My dear Polton, you should read the art critics' notices of them and then see the mugs, who want to be thought 'highbrow', crowding into the galleries and staring, open-mouthed, at what they believe to be the last word in progressive art. But, to do them justice, they don't often buy any of the stuff."

"And the painters, sir, who produce them; are they impostors or only cranky?"

"It is difficult to say," replied Tom. "The early modernists were, I think, quite sincere cranks. Some of them were admittedly insane. But nowadays it is impossible to judge. For the mischief is, you see, Polton, that if once you accept incompetent, childish, barbaric productions as genuine works of art, you have thrown the door wide open to impostors."

"And what about Mrs Schiller, sir?"

"Well, Polton, you have seen her. She certainly isn't mad, and she certainly can't paint; and my impression is that she knows it as well as you and I do. But what her motive may be for keeping up the pretence is known only to herself."

Polton pondered awhile on this answer; then he raised another question.

"I am rather puzzled, sir, as to her relations with Mr Vanderpuye. She is, I understand, a married woman, so those relations are not very proper in any case. But there seems to me something rather unreal about them. From their behaviour you would take these two persons for very devoted friends, if not actually lovers, and that, I feel sure, is genuinely the case with Mr Vanderpuye. But I have my doubts about the lady; and if she is an impostor in one thing, she can be in another. But I am like you; I can't imagine a motive for imposture. Of course, Mr Vanderpuye is a rich man, but I don't, somehow, suspect her of trying to get money out of him. And yet I can't think of any other motive. In fact, I can't make it out at all."

"Is there any need to make it out?" asked Tom. "It isn't our affair, you know."

"Excepting that Mr Vanderpuye is my friend, and a very worthy, lovable gentleman. I shouldn't like him to get involved in any unpleasantness."

"Quite right, Polton," Tom agreed, "but I don't see what you can do beyond keeping your weather eyelid lifting; and that you seem to have been doing."

Which observation having closed the discussion, the two parties to it transferred their attention to the sketches and the consideration of the technical details connected with the goldsmith's art.

CHAPTER SIX

The Forest of Essex

On a certain evening early in November Tom Pedley, having put down his canvas carrier to free one hand, inserted his latchkey and pushed the gate open. Then, according to his invariable custom, he withdrew the key and pocketed it before entering; and as he did so, happening to glance up the street, he perceived Lotta Schiller and her friend Billy just turning the corner and approaching. He had not seen either of them for more than a fortnight; not, in fact, since the frame-maker had carted away the portrait and the two lockets had been delivered to their respective owners. So he thought it proper to pause at the open gate to exchange greetings, especially as they had already seen him and notified the fact.

"Where have you been all this time, Tom?" exclaimed Lotta as they met on the doorstep. "I haven't seen you for ages."

"Well, I haven't been in the same place all the time," Tom replied. "Today I have been in Epping Forest. Doing a bit of landscape painting for a change after the portrait."

"Epping Forest," repeated Lotta. "How delightful. I've never been to Epping Forest. May we come in and have a look at what you've been painting?"

"Do, by all means," Tom replied heartily. "The picture isn't finished, but it will give you an idea of the place."

They entered together, and Tom, having unstrapped the carrier, placed the canvas on the easel at an angle to the great window.

"The light isn't very good," said he, "but you can see what the forest is like."

"Yes, indeed," she exclaimed enthusiastically, "and it is perfectly lovely. It looks like a real forest."

"It is a real forest," said Tom. "It is a surviving remnant of the primeval forest of Britain; and there is quite a lot of it, still."

"But how thrilling! A primeval forest! Have you ever seen a primeval forest, Bill?"

"Yes," said Vanderpuye. "I have seen the great forest that covers Ashanti, and it is something like this painting. The African forest trees are probably a good deal more lofty than these, but it is difficult to judge from a picture."

"It is almost impossible," said Tom, "without figures or animals to give a scale. I think of putting in one or two deer."

"But there aren't really any deer there, are there?" asked Lotta.

"Bless you, yes," he replied. "Deer, foxes, badgers, and all sorts of wild beasts. It is a genuine forest, not a mere park. And there are two ancient British camps. I pass one of them on the way to my pitch."

"It sounds like a most heavenly place," said Lotta. "And to think that I have never seen it, though it is so near London. It would be delightful to spend a day there. Don't you think so, Bill?"

Bill agreed with enthusiasm, as he usually did to Lotta's suggestions.

"Then that is settled. We will have a day rambling and picnicking in the forest, and Tom shall show us the way. Oh, you needn't look like that. We shan't hang about and hinder you."

"I wasn't looking like that," Tom protested. "I shall be very pleased to show you the way there and start you on your ramble. My picture will be ready to go on with in three or four days; say next Thursday. How will that suit you?"

"It will suit me perfectly," she replied; and Bill having concurred, she added: "I suppose we shall have to take some food with us. How do you manage, Tom?"

"I take my lunch with me, but you needn't. There is an excellent inn near High Beach called the King's Oak, where you can get refreshment for man and beast."

"I don't quite like that expression," said Lotta, "as only one of us is a man. But never mind. Now let us settle our arrangements. I think we had better meet and start from here, as I am here already and Bill isn't a Londoner. Give us a time, and then we will go and leave you in peace."

Tom suggested nine o'clock on Thursday morning, and, this having been agreed to, his visitors departed; whereupon, having cleaned his palette and washed his brushes and himself, he proceeded to lay the table – including in its furnishings Polton's incomparable tankard – opened the haybox, and settled himself with deep satisfaction to the disposal of his evening meal.

Punctually, on Thursday morning, the two ramblers made their appearance at the rendezvous, and a few minutes later the party set forth for Fenchurch Street, Vanderpuye carrying the strapped stool and easel. An empty first-class compartment being easily obtainable at this time in the day, they took possession of one, and, having deposited Tom's impedimenta on the hat rack, lit pipes and cigarettes and prepared to enjoy the journey. And a very pleasant journey it was (excepting the stop at Stratford, when mephitic fumes from some chemical works poured into the compartment and caused them hastily to pull up the window glasses). Lotta was in buoyant spirits and rattled away gaily between the puffs of her cigarette, while the two men smoked their pipes and allowed themselves to be entertained.

"For a painter, Tom," she remarked, as the train drew out of Woodford Station, "I consider you extraordinarily unobservant. You actually haven't noticed my beautiful new locket."

As a matter of fact he had, and thought it slightly unsuitable to the occasion.

"You are quite wrong, Lotta," said he. "My eyes have been glued to it ever since we started, and I have been thinking what a remarkable genius the fellow must have been who designed it."

"Now listen to that, Bill," said she, selecting a fresh cigarette from her case. "Isn't he a conceited fellow? Brazenly fishing for a compliment; and he won't get one."

"I knew that," retorted Tom, "so I supplied the compliment myself. But it really does look rather fine, thanks to the brilliant way in which Polton carried it out."

Lotta laughed scornfully. "Now he's pretending to be modest. But it's no use, Tom. We know you. Still, I agree that the little man did his part beautifully, and I am grateful to both of you, to say nothing of the generous giver."

Here she bestowed an affectionate smile on the gratified Vanderpuye, who smiled in return as a man can afford to smile who has such a magnificent set of teeth. There followed a brief interlude in Lotta's babblings while she lit and smoked the fresh cigarette. A few minutes later the train slowed down, and Tom, reaching down his property from the rack and slipping the strap of the satchel over his shoulder, announced: "This is our station," and prepared to open the door.

As the train came to rest, Vanderpuye once more relieved Tom of the folded easel and the three emerged on to the platform. Passing out of the station, they walked up the rather dull village street until they came to a large pond on the border of the forest. Here Tom turned off into a path which skirted the pond and presently entered a broad green ride. A short distance along this he entered a narrow green ride that led off to the left up a gentle incline and then down across the end of a little valley, the marshy bottom of which was covered with beds of rushes.

"This hollow," Tom announced, "is called Debden Slade. May as well remember the name in case you have to ask the way. This path – what they call in the forest a green ride – leads, as you see, up the hill and directly to the corner of the ancient British fortification, called Loughton Camp, and passes round two sides of it."

"But you are going to show us the way to it," Lotta stipulated.

"Yes, I am coming with you as far as the camp, and, when you have seen it, I will set you on your road before we separate."

"I suppose," said Vanderpuye, "you know your way about the forest quite well?"

"Yes," Tom replied. "I have done a lot of sketching and painting here in the last few years. It is quite easy to find your way about the forest after a little experience, but at first I always used to bring a large-scale map and a compass. This is the camp that we are approaching; the south side. We shall pass round it to the north-west side, and there our roads diverge."

"But I don't see any camp," said Lotta, looking vaguely into the dense wood which seemed to close the green path that they had been ascending. "I can only see a high bank covered with a mass of funny little trees that look as if they wanted their hair cut."

"It isn't very distinct," Tom admitted, "except on the map. But you must bear in mind that it was built two or three thousand years ago or more, and that it has probably not been occupied since the Roman invasion. In all those centuries the forest has grown over it and more or less covered it up. But you can make it out quite well if you climb up the bank through the trees and let yourself down into the enclosure. Then you can see that there is a roughly four-sided space enclosed by high earth walls or ramparts. But as it is all covered by a dense mass of those small trees, you can only see it a bit at a time."

"But why are the trees so small?" Lotta asked. "There doesn't seem to be a single full-grown tree among them, though, from what you say, they have had plenty of time to grow."

"They are not young trees," said Tom. "They are old dwarfs. The people of this manor used to have lopping rights. Consequently all the trees, as they grew up, were pollarded, and, every year the new branches that sprouted from the crown were lopped off for firewood, with the result that the trees became gnarled and stunted. They are rather uncanny in appearance, but not very beautiful."

"No," agreed Lotta, "uncanny is the word. They look like little witches with their hair standing on end. But the whole place is rather weird and solemn, especially when one thinks of the dead and gone Britons and the centuries that the camp has been lying desolate and forgotten. Those holes in the bank, I suppose, have been made by animals of some kind."

"Yes. The small holes are usually rabbit burrows; the larger ones are fox earths."

As they had been talking they had walked slowly along the green path in the deep shade cast by the pollard beeches that crowded the high bank of the old rampart. Presently they turned the corner of the camp and passed along the north-western side, until they reached a more open space where the green ride grew broader and turned sharply to the left while a narrower path led on straight ahead. At the point where the two paths separated Tom halted and held out his hand for the easel which Vanderpuye was still carrying.

"This is where we part company," said he. "My way is by the little green path to Great Monk Wood, about three-quarters of a mile farther on. Yours is by the green ride along the crest of the hill; a pleasant walk with a delightful view all the way."

"Yes," said Lotta, looking across the open forest that stretched away from the foot of the hill, "it is a lovely view; and it seems a relief to be out in the open, away from that gloomy old camp and those unearthly, weird little trees. And yet, somehow, I find a curious fascination in that ancient fortress. I should like to get inside the walls and see what a British camp was really like. Wouldn't you like to explore it, Bill?"

The amiable and accommodating Bill expressed the strongest desire to explore the camp and the profoundest interest in the Ancient Britons and their works.

"Well," said Tom, "you can't explore it today, because you would want a map and a compass and you ought to have a copy of the plan that was made when the Essex Field Club surveyed the camp. I have one filed away somewhere, so, if you propose to make a serious exploration, I can lend it to you with a map of the forest and a compass. But now you had better stroll across to High Beach and learn to find your way about."

"Yes," agreed Vanderpuye, "that will be best, especially as we have brought no refreshment, and you say that there is an inn at High

Beach where we can get some lunch. But we shall want you to direct us."

"It is perfectly plain sailing," replied Tom. "You see that clump of elms in the distance?"

"I see a clump of trees, and I take your word for it that they are elms."

"Well, they are at High Beach, so, if you keep your eye on them you can't go wrong. You have to follow this green ride along the crest of the hill. About half a mile from here you will cross the Epping Road and half a mile farther on you will come to a green ride at right angles to this. Turn to the left and go along it and you will come to the King's Oak inn, where you can stoke up if you want to. High Beach is only a few minutes' walk from the pub along the same ride. So now you know all about it."

He put the easel and canvas carrier down on the turf and shook hands with the two ramblers, wishing them adieu and a pleasant journey. Lotta smiled slyly as she shook his hand and remarked to her companion: "That means that he has had enough of our society, so we had better make ourselves scarce. Come along, Bill."

The pair turned away to start on their walk, but Tom did not immediately resume his journey: His hands being free, he took the opportunity to fill his pipe in a leisurely fashion. But when it was full and ready for lighting, he still stood at the parting of the ways, following with a meditative eye the progress of the two adventurers as they stepped out briskly along the broad green ride. Once more Polton's question recurred to him. What were the relations of these two persons? They had the manner of an engaged couple which they certainly were not; but were they lovers or only friends? In his own case, Lotta's behaviour – apart from the verbal endearments – had been scrupulously correct. True, he had given her no opening for anything different, but still the fact remained that she had never made the slightest approach. Were her relations with Vanderpuye of the same platonic order? It seemed doubtful, for the conditions were not the same. Vanderpuye was no unwilling partner to this intimacy. From the first he had been Lotta's ardent admirer; but from admiration to passion is but a short step; and passion, in his case and hers, could but lead straight to disaster.

Thus Tom cogitated as he stood looking at the two receding figures. Many a time in the months that followed did that scene recur to him; the long, straight, grassy ride with the figures of the man and woman stepping forward gaily and now growing small in the distance. And still his eyes followed them with an interest which he could not explain, until they reached a point where the ride described a curve; and here Lotta, glancing back and seeing him still standing there, waved her hand to him, and Vanderpuye executed a flourish with his hat. Tom returned their farewell greeting, and a few moments later they entered the curve and vanished behind the roadside bushes; whereupon he lit his pipe, picked up his fardels, and set forth along the little green path for his pitch in Great Monk Wood.

He had told himself, and Polton, that the nature of Lotta's relations with her African friend was no affair of his. And it was not. Nevertheless, as he strode along the narrow track through the silent and lonely forest, the question still occupied his thoughts; especially the question as to what was to be the end of it. For neither of the pair – and certainly not for Lotta – had he any strong personal regard; but he was a kindly man and it irked him to think of these two, heading, as he feared, for trouble. Particularly was he concerned for Vanderpuye; who, as an African, probably passionate and impulsive, and inexperienced in European ways, was the more likely to get himself into difficulties and to bear the brunt of any unpleasant consequences. For he was a barrister with a position to maintain and a future to consider. It would be a grievous thing if he should be involved in a scandal at the very start of his career.

At this point in his reflections he arrived at the forest opening which was the subject of his painting. He laid down his burdens, took off his satchel, and, having identified the holes in the ground made at his last sitting by the feet of his stool and easel, unpacked the latter and set them up in the old position. Then he fixed up the canvas, set his palette, made a careful and critical survey of his subject and compared it with the half-finished painting; and straightway Lotta Schiller and her African friend faded from his thoughts and left him to the untroubled consideration of his work.

It was a lovely day despite the lateness of the month, and a beautiful scene. The noble beeches still bore many of their leaves, though these had now exchanged the tender green of summer for the gorgeous tints – all too fleeting – that marked the waning year. For four delightful hours Tom worked industriously, painting at the top of his form and enjoying every moment. Not a human creature came near him in all that time, though he received occasional visits from the non-human people of the forest, as the landscape painter commonly does. An inquisitive squirrel played peep-bo with him round a tree and then came down and danced around him within a few feet of the easel. A pair of friendly blackbirds pursued their business close by, and once or twice a couple of the dark-coated forest deer stole across the opening, apparently oblivious of his presence.

At the end of the second hour he took what workmen call a "beaver"; a modest meal of bread and cheese (whereby the squirrel benefited to the extent of some morsels of bread and a piece of cheese rind), with a draught of beer from a large flask. Then once more he took up his palette and brushes and worked away steadily until the changing light told him that it was time to go; when he packed up tidily, lit his pipe, picked up his kit, and started back by the way he had come. At the junction of the two paths he paused to look along the green ride, though the afternoon was still young and his friends would hardly be returning so early. Nevertheless, as he took his way round the camp and back past the pond, he kept a half-unconscious look-out for them, and even at the station as he paced the platform they were still in his mind until the train came in and bore him away alone.

During the next few days his thoughts turned occasionally to his two friends, with vague speculations as to how they had fared in the forest. He had rather expected a visit from Lotta, and, on the strength of that speculation, had looked out the map, the compass, and the plan of the camp to hand to her when she should call. But to his surprise – almost to his disappointment – she made no appearance, and, eventually he decided that she had given up the project of exploring the camp, and, having put the things back in their usual receptacles, he dismissed the matter from his mind.

Yet, as the days passed without the expected visit or even the customary chance meetings in the street, her complete disappearance from his orbit impressed him as a little odd. He was even faintly displeased; a state of mind which he, himself, recognized as rather strange and perverse. For it was only a few weeks ago, when he had been the unwilling *cher ami*, that his chief desire in life had been to be rid of her; whereas now, though he felt no great concern, still, he would have been quite pleased to find her on his doorstep. Once he had even contemplated calling to make inquiries, but discretion prevailed. He had no desire to revive that troublesome intimacy.

It is probable that, if nothing further had happened, the passing of Lotta out of his life would have been accepted and presently ceased to be noticed. But a new circumstance tended to revive his curiosity. Returning one day by way of Cumberland Market, and thus passing her house, he noticed that her brass plate was not in its usual place. It was not a fixed plate permanently secured to the wall, but was held in place by removable fastenings, and it had been Lotta's custom to take it down in the evening and replace it in the morning. Thus, when he noticed its absence, he assumed that she had merely forgotten to fix it up, and thought no more about it. But, happening on the following day to glance at her door and again noting the absence of the plate, he gave the matter more attention; with the result that, after several daily observations, he decided that the plate had disappeared for good. Then, again, he had thought of calling, but now he was restrained by a fresh consideration. Possibilities which he had dimly envisaged might have become realized, and if so, it were well for him not to meddle in Lotta's affairs. On the other hand, he was now definitely anxious and a little disturbed, particularly on Vanderpuye's account, and it seemed to him that a few discreet inquiries through a third party might elicit the facts without committing him in any way.

Now the obvious third party was Mr Polton. He was in touch with Vanderpuye and was certainly keeping an eye on the course of events. But the question was, how to get at Mr Polton. Tom had never ventured to call on him as he resided on the premises of his employer, Dr Thorndyke, and an uninvited visit would have seemed somewhat of an intrusion. Of course, he could have written to Mr Polton, but that would have involved a direct inquiry, which he wished to avoid. His idea was that if he could contrive a meeting with his ingenious friend, the required information could be made to transpire naturally in a judiciously managed conversation, without his asking any questions at all.

The problem was, therefore, to find a pretext for a visit to Polton; a convincing pretext which would account for his having called rather than written. To the solution of this problem Tom addressed himself, and, being an eminently straightforward man, little addicted to pretexts of any kind, he had to give it a disproportionate amount of attention. And then the problem solved itself. Happening to pull out a drawer in which he kept miscellaneous oddments, he discovered in it the pedometer which he had been accustomed to carry on his expeditions in search of landscape subjects. For years it had served him well, but latterly it had become erratic in its action and so unreliable that he had ceased to carry it. So he had put it aside, intending some time to take Mr Polton's opinion on it. But out of sight had been out of mind and the matter had been forgotten. Now, however, it gave him not a mere pretext but a reasonable occasion for the visit.

Accordingly he dispatched a short note to Polton, announcing his intention to call, and, if an interview should not be convenient, to leave the pedometer for a diagnostic inspection; to which Polton replied by return with a cordial invitation and the necessary directions to his domain in the premises.

CHAPTER SEVEN
Of a Pedometer and a Tragedy

At four o'clock precisely, on a bright December afternoon, Tom Pedley arrived at the entry of Number 5A King's Bench Walk, having made his way thither very pleasantly through the old-world courts of the Temple. For a few moments he paused to examine with an artist's appreciation the fine red brick portico (commonly attributed to Wren), then he entered, and, following Polton's directions, ascended the stairs to the landing of the "Second Pair". As he reached it a door opened and his host came out to meet him.

"This is very pleasant, sir," said Polton, shaking hands warmly. "I don't often have a visitor, being a solitary worker like yourself, so your visit will be quite a little treat for me. Will you come into the laboratory? We are going to have tea in my room upstairs, but I am boiling the kettle here to avoid smoking it on the fire."

As they entered the large room Tom glanced about him curiously, noting that some of the appointments, such as a joiner's bench, a lathe, and a large copying camera, hardly accorded with his conception of a laboratory, and that a handsome copper kettle, mounted on a tripod over a Bunsen burner and a fine old silver teapot seemed to have strayed in from elsewhere.

"Perhaps, sir," suggested Polton, "we might have a look at the pedometer while the kettle is getting up steam."

Tom fished the instrument out of his pocket and handed it to him, whereupon, having opened the glass back, he stuck a watchmaker's eyeglass in his eye and examined the visible part of the mechanism.

"There doesn't seem to be much amiss with it," he reported, dancing the instrument up and down to test the lever; "just a matter of wear. The little spring click has worn short and tends to slip over the teeth of the ratchet wheel. That is a fatal defect, but it's easily mended; and I may find some other faults when I come to take it down, as we say in the trade — that is, take it to pieces. At any rate it will be none the worse for a clean up and a touch of fresh oil."

"I am afraid I am giving you a lot more trouble than I expected," said Tom.

Polton looked up at him with his queer, crinkly smile.

"Trouble, sir!" he exclaimed. "It is no trouble; it isn't even work. It will give me several hours' pleasant entertainment, and I am much obliged to you for bringing me the instrument."

In confirmation he produced from one of his innumerable pockets a small portable screwdriver and seemed about to attack the pedometer forthwith, when the kettle intervened by blowing out a jet of steam; whereupon he replaced the cap of the screwdriver, returned it to his pocket, and proceeded methodically to make the tea.

As he led the way upstairs, carrying the teapot while his guest followed with the kettle, Tom remarked on the comeliness of the latter.

"Yes, sir," replied Polton, "it's a fine old kettle. They don't make them like that nowadays. I found it in a marine store in Portugal Street. Came from some old lawyer's chambers in Lincoln's Inn, I expect; and very shabby and battered it was, but I put a bit of work into it and made it as good as new. You see, sir, I rather take after you; I like the common things that I use and live with to be good and pleasant to look at."

His statement was borne out by the aspect of the spacious room on the "Third Pair" which they now entered, where a tea table, flanked by two easy chairs, stood before the fire. Tom, having deposited the kettle on a trivet, out of reach of the smoke or flame, sat down in the chair allocated to him and surveyed the prospect, while Polton did the honours of the tea table; noting the well-filled bookshelves, the one or two pictures on the walls (including his sketch for "The

Eavesdropper", simply but tastefully framed) and a fourfold screen which he suspected of concealing a bed. It was all simple and plain, but the room and everything that was in it appealed quietly to Tom's rather fastidious taste, even to the quaint old cottage clock that hung on the wall and hardly disturbed the silence by its homely tick.

"This is my private domain, sir," said Polton, "but I don't spend much time in it. The laboratory is really my home. I am an inveterate mechanic, always happiest at my bench. That pedometer of yours is quite a windfall for me. May I ask how long you have had it?"

"I should say about a dozen years," replied Tom.

"And do you find it fairly accurate? The experts on surveying dismiss the pedometer as a mere useless toy. What is your experience of it?"

"It is accurate enough for my purpose," Tom replied. "I'm not a surveyor. I don't deal in inches, but I find that it agrees pretty closely with maps and milestones, and that is enough for me."

"The reason that I asked is that I had thought of getting one for Mr Vanderpuye to take back with him. There won't be many milestones in his country."

"Is Mr Vanderpuye going back to Africa soon?" Tom asked with suddenly awakened interest.

"Not very soon," replied Polton, "because he has joined the Bar Mess at the Central Criminal Court and is attending the court regularly; that is, he has been since Mrs Schiller went away."

"Oh, she has gone away, has she?" asked Tom, considerably startled.

"Yes, sir; and I hope she will stop away, for, before she went, he used to neglect his work terribly. I am very much relieved that she has gone."

"Do you know whether she has gone for good?"

"I am afraid not, sir. Of course, I couldn't ask any questions, but I gathered from Mr Vanderpuye that she had gone to stay with some friends at Birmingham. How long she will be away I have no idea, and I don't believe he has."

"I suppose you don't know whether he corresponds with her?"

"I don't actually know, sir, but I think not. My impression is that he doesn't even know her address. Queer, isn't it? But then she's a queer woman. With all her flighty ways, she is uncommonly good at keeping her own counsel."

This last observation rather impressed Tom; for now, reflecting on it, he suddenly realized how very little he knew about this strange woman. However, she was not his concern now that his anxieties on Vanderpuye's account had been dispelled; and, as he had obtained the information that he had come to seek, he began to consider whether it was not time for him to go. Polton had duties of some kind, and a prolonged visit might be inconvenient. But when he made tentative signs of departure, his host protested:

"You are not going on my account, sir, I hope; because the Doctor is dining out tonight and I've got the evening to myself. Besides, now that he has given me an understudy to carry on in my absence, I am much freer than I used to be. Of course, I mustn't detain you if you can't spare the time, but – "

In effect, Tom was very glad to stay, and said so, and, accordingly, having filled his pipe (at Polton's invitation), settled down to spend a very pleasant and interesting evening. For his host, although "an inveterate mechanic", possessed a wealth of information on all sorts of curious and unexpected subjects; and when they had examined the remarkable technical library, the pictures on the wall, and the picturesque old clock (Polton's chiefest treasure; a relic of the home of his childhood, which had come to him on the demise of a certain Aunt Judy), they subsided into their respective chairs to gossip discursively on the various subjects in which they had a common interest, with a general leaning towards "antiques".

"To return to your pedometer, sir," said Polton, when Tom finally rose to depart, "I shall look it over in my spare time, but it won't take long. When it is done I will bring it round to your studio, if you will tell me when I shall find you at home".

"It's very good of you, Polton, but I think you had better settle the time. I can always stay in if I want to."

"Then, sir, I would suggest next Thursday, about three o'clock if that will suit you."

"It will suit me perfectly," said Tom, taking up his hat and stick; and, having thus made the assignation, he shook hands with his host who, nevertheless, escorted him as far as the laboratory floor where they parted, Tom to make his way homeward and Polton, probably, to launch the attack on the pedometer.

During the next few days Tom gave only an occasional passing thought to Lotta. He was completely reassured. There had been no elopement or scandal of any kind, and that was all that mattered to him. As to the woman herself, he could only echo Polton's wish that she might stay away as long as possible; and if she should never come back, her absence would create a void not entirely unacceptable. In fact he began to hope that she had passed out of his life, that he had, at last, really finished with her; and from vaguely hoping came gradually to believe that it might be so.

The disillusionment was sudden and violent. It synchronized with the arrival on the appointed day of his pedometer-bearing friend. At three o'clock to the minute on Thursday afternoon the studio bell rang, and Tom, hurrying out at the summons, found Mr Polton on the wide doorstep. But he was not alone. Sharing the doorstep with him was an anxious-looking woman whom he recognized as his next-door neighbour, Mrs Mitchens, who was also Lotta's landlady. He had been on bowing terms with her for some years but had never spoken to her except to wish her good morning, and he now wondered what her business with him might be. But he was soon enlightened, for almost as he appeared at the door she asked in an agitated tone:

"Could I have a few words with you, Mr Pedley?" (On which Polton tried to efface himself and prepared to slink in by the half-open door.) "It's about Mrs Schiller, sir."

As she spoke the name Polton halted suddenly, and tried to look as if he were not listening.

"I have come to you, Mr Pedley," Mrs Mitchens continued, "because you were a friend of hers and I thought you might know what has become of her. I haven't seen or heard of her for quite a long time."

"Oh, that's all right, Mrs Mitchens," Tom answered cheerfully. "She has just gone away to stay with some friends at Birmingham."

But Mrs Mitchens did not look satisfied. "It's very strange," she objected. "She never said anything to me about going away, and the rent hasn't been paid, though she was always so punctual. You are sure she has gone to Birmingham?"

Tom reflected for a moment and then, turning to Polton, asked: "What do you say? Are we sure?"

"Well, sir," was the reply. "I wouldn't put it as high as that. I was told by Mr Vanderpuye that Mrs Schiller had told him that she was going to stay with friends at Birmingham. That is all. We don't actually know whether she has or has not gone."

"Then," said Mrs Mitchens, "I am afraid she has not gone."

"Why do you say that?" Tom asked.

Mrs Mitchens appeared to be in difficulties. "I hardly know how to express it," she replied, "but there's something wrong in her rooms. My husband and I have both noticed it, and it seems to be getting worse."

"I don't quite understand," said Tom. "What is getting worse?"

"It is difficult to explain," she replied, "but if you will be so good as to step into the hall, you will understand what I mean."

Tom showed no eagerness to accept this invitation, but Polton, now all agog, requested the lady to lead the way and followed her with a purposeful air while Tom brought up the rear, and watched her gloomily as she inserted her latchkey.

But Mrs Mitchens was right. No sooner had they entered the hall and shut the outer door than they both understood perfectly what she had meant. But the realization affected them differently. Tom shrank back with an expression of horrified disgust towards the outer door, whereas Polton, having sampled the air by a little diagnostic sniff, took the definite initiative.

"I presume, madam," said he, "that this door is locked?"

"Yes," she replied. "Locked from the inside."

"Well," said Polton, "that room ought to be entered; at once."

"That is what my husband said, and he tried it with one of our keys, but unfortunately the key is in the lock, and he didn't like to break the door open."

"No," Polton agreed, "it is better to use a key if possible. May I ask whether the lock has been used much?"

"Yes," she replied, "constantly. Mrs Schiller always locked the door at night and whenever she went out."

"Ha," said he, "then it should turn pretty easily. It is sometimes possible," he continued reflectively, with his hand in an inner pocket, "to persuade a key round from the outside if it isn't too stiff. Now, I wonder if I happen to have anything in my pocket that would answer the purpose."

Apparently he had; for as he stooped to peer into the keyhole, his hand came out of the pocket holding an object that looked somewhat like a rather unusual pocket corkscrew fitted with some stout angular wire levers. One of these he inserted into the keyhole and pried about the interior of the lock while Mrs Mitchens gazed expectantly at his hand, which concealed both the keyhole and the instrument.

"Yes," said he, "the very thing"; and, as he spoke, the lock clicked, the instrument was withdrawn (disappearing instantly into the pocket whence it had come), and Polton turned the handle and tried the door, shutting it again immediately.

"It isn't bolted, you see, madam," said he, stepping back to make way for her.

She showed a natural reluctance to enter that mysterious and ominous room, but after a few moments' hesitation she grasped the knob, turned it softly, opened the door and stepped in. But even as she entered she uttered a low scream and stood stock-still with the door-knob in her hand, staring before her with an expression of horror.

"Oh, the poor thing!" she exclaimed. "She has made away with herself. Do, please, come in and look at her."

On this, Polton entered the room followed by Tom, and for a while both stood by the door gazing at the tragic figure sitting limply with dropped head in a little elbow chair that had been drawn up to the table. The right arm hung straight down while the left lay on the table, and, close to the discoloured hand was an empty tumbler, and, a few inches away, a small glass water jug and a little bottle containing white tablets.

"Poor creature!" moaned Mrs Mitchens. "I wonder why she did it, so bright and cheerful as she always seemed. And how dreadful she looks, poor dear. I should never have recognized her."

Polton, meanwhile, had cast a keen glance round the room, and now, stepping forward, leaned over the table to scrutinize the tumbler and the bottle of tablets.

"What is in that bottle?" Tom asked.

"Cyanide of potassium," was the reply.

"That is a strong poison, isn't it?"

"A most deadly poison," Polton replied, "and extremely rapid in its action; quite easy to obtain, too, as you see from the label on this bottle – 'Photographic Tablets'; easy to get and hard to trace."

"The tracing of them won't be of much importance in this case," remarked Tom, "as she poisoned herself. The question is, Why on earth did she do it?"

From the poison Polton turned his attention to the corpse; and, as he stood gazing at the dead woman, an expression of surprise and perplexity stole over his face. At this moment a beam of pale autumn sunlight shone in through the window, lighting up the fair hair to the brightness of burnished gold. This appearance seemed further to surprise Polton, for, with a distinctly startled expression, he stepped close to the corpse, and, delicately picking up a small tress of the golden hair, held it close to his face and scrutinized it intently. Then as if still unsatisfied, he gently raised the bowed head and looked long and intently into the poor bloated, discoloured face. Tom and the landlady both watched him in astonishment, and the former demanded:

"What is it, Polton?"

Polton, still holding the head erect, replied impressively:

"This woman, sir, is not Mrs Schiller."

"Not Mrs Schiller!" the landlady echoed. "But she must be. Who else could she be, locked in here in Mrs Schiller's room?"

"This is certainly not Mrs Schiller," Polton persisted. "I ask you, sir, to come and see for yourself. You knew her better than I did. You will see that the hair is the wrong colour and the features are different."

"I noticed the hair when the sun shone on it," said Tom, "and it struck me as being somehow changed. But as to the features, I should say that they are quite unrecognizable."

"Not at all, sir," replied Polton. "The skin is bloated, but there is the nose. That is unchanged, and so, more or less, is the chin. And there are the ears; they are hardly affected at all. You had better come and have a look at her as the identification is most important."

Thus urged, Tom plucked up courage to make a close inspection; and as Polton held the head up, he examined first the profile and then the ears. A very brief scrutiny satisfied him, for, as he backed away from the corpse, he announced:

"Yes, Polton, you are right. This is not Lotta Schiller. The nose and chin look the wrong shape, but the ears are quite conclusive. They are of an entirely different type from Lotta's, and differently set on the head."

"You really think, sir," said the landlady, "that this poor creature is not Mrs Schiller?"

"I feel no doubt whatever," he replied; "and very much relieved I am that she is not."

"So am I, for that matter," said Mrs Mitchens. "But how on earth does she come to be here? Locked herself in, too. It's an absolute mystery."

"It certainly is," Tom agreed. "But it isn't our mystery. It will be for the police to solve it."

"That is true, sir," said Polton, "though perhaps it may be more of our mystery than you think. But, of course, the police will have to be informed at once, and it will be for them to find out who this poor woman is, and how she came to be here. But there is one question that I should like to settle now; that is whether she took the poison herself, or whether it was given to her by someone else."

"But," Tom objected, "the police will deal with that question. It isn't our affair."

"It is not, sir," Polton admitted. "But I should like to know, just for my own satisfaction. Do you happen to have a piece of fairly stiff smooth paper about you?"

With a rather puzzled air Tom brought out of his pocket the artist's notebook that he always carried.

"Will that do?" he asked. "If it will, you can tear a leaf out, but don't take one with a drawing on it."

"I won't tear the leaf out," said Polton. "It will be handier in the book, and I shan't want to keep it."

He took the little canvas-bound volume, and, watched curiously by Tom and the landlady, went over to a small writing table on which lay, beside the blotter, a rubber stamp and an inking-pad.

Taking up the latter, he carried it across to the table at which the dead woman was sitting, when he once more examined the tumbler as well as he could without touching it.

"The fingermarks," he observed, "look like those of a left hand; and as the left hand is near the tumbler we will try that first."

Very gently, to avoid disturbing the body, he raised the hand, and, grasping the thumb, pressed it on the inking-pad. Then, laying down the pad and taking up the book, he brought the inked thumb over a blank page, pressed it down lightly and withdrew it. In the same way he took an impression of each of the four fingers, the group of prints being arranged in a line in their correct order, and, as soon as he had finished, he carefully wiped the traces of ink from the fingertips with his handkerchief. Softly laying down the hand, he placed the open book by the side of the tumbler and carefully compared the prints on each.

"Well," said Tom, "what do you make of it?"

"The prints on the tumbler are her fingerprints all right," replied Polton. "Would you like to see them?"

Tom's principal desire now was to escape from the charnel-house atmosphere of this room, but, as Polton evidently wished him to see the prints, he went over to the table.

"My prints are very poor, smeary impressions," said Polton, "but you can see the patterns quite well. Look at the thumbprint with that spiral whorl on it, and compare it with the one on the tumbler. You can see plainly that it is the same pattern."

"Yes," Tom agreed, "I can make that out quite clearly; but the patterns of the fingers don't seem so distinctive."

"No," Polton admitted, "they are rather indistinct for some reason, especially in the middle of each print. But still, if you compare them with the tumbler, you can see that the patterns are the same."

"I'll take your word for it," said Tom, "as you know more about it than I do. And, after all, it isn't our affair whether she took the poison herself or not. Of course, the police will settle that question, and if you take my advice, you will say nothing about these fingerprints. The authorities don't much like outside interference."

"I think Mr Pedley is right," said Mrs Mitchens. "We don't want to appear officious or meddlesome, and we certainly don't want to offend the police."

"No, ma'am," Polton agreed, "we do not. It will be much better to keep our own counsel; which, in fact, is what I had intended to suggest. I made the trial just to satisfy my curiosity as to whether it was a case of suicide or murder."

"Well," said Tom, edging towards the door, "now we know; and the next question is, who is to inform the police?"

As he raised the question he looked significantly at Mrs Mitchens, who replied gloomily, as they retired to the hall:

"I suppose, as I am the householder and Mrs Schiller's landlady, I had better go. But I can't tell them much, and I expect they will want to question you about Mrs Schiller."

"I expect they will," said Tom, "but, meanwhile, I think you are the proper person to give the information."

With this view Polton agreed emphatically, and, by way of closing the discussion, softly drew the key out of the lock, closed the door, and, having locked it, withdrew the key and handed it to the landlady. Then he and Tom, after a few words of condolence with Mrs Mitchens, took their leave and made their way to the studio.

"Pah!" exclaimed Tom, taking several deep breaths as they emerged into the open air. "What a horrible affair! But I suppose you are used to this sort of thing."

"To some extent, sir," replied Polton. "I have learned from the Doctor not to allow my attention to be distracted by mere physical unpleasantness. But what a mysterious affair this is. I can make nothing of it. Here is a woman, apparently a stranger, locked in Mrs Schiller's room with Mrs Schiller's key. All sorts of questions arise. Who is she? How did she get that key? Why did she come to that place to commit suicide – if she really did commit suicide? And where is Mrs Schiller? The police will want to find answers to those questions, and some of them will take a good deal of answering, I fancy."

"Yes," Tom agreed gloomily, "and they'll look to us to find some of the answers. It's going to be an infernal nuisance."

When they had washed – which Tom did with exhaustive thoroughness – in a big bowl in the studio sink, they resumed the discussion while they laid the table for tea and boiled the kettle. But nothing came of it beyond bringing to light the curious difference in their points of view. To Tom, the tragedy was repulsively horrible and his connection with it profoundly distasteful. Interest in it or curiosity he had none. Polton, on the other hand, so far from being shocked or disgusted, seemed to savour the details with a sort of ghoulish relish and fairly to revel in the mystery and obscurity of the case; so much so that Tom's repeated efforts to divert the conversation into more agreeable channels failed utterly, and, for the first time in his experience, he was almost relieved when the time came for Polton to return to his duties.

"Well, sir," the departing guest remarked as he wriggled into his overcoat, "this has been an eventful afternoon. I have enjoyed it immensely." Here he paused suddenly in his wrigglings, gazing at Tom in ludicrous consternation. "God bless me, sir," he exclaimed, "I had nearly forgotten the pedometer. I have cleaned it up and put it in going order, and I have fitted a new regulator with a micrometer screw and attached a watch-key to turn it with. You will see at once how it works, but I have written down a few directions."

He produced the instrument, wrapped in tissue paper, and laid it with the little document on the table. Then, deprecating Tom's grateful acknowledgments, he shook hands and bustled away, en route for the Temple.

Chapter Eight

Revelations

When Polton's departure had left him to the peaceful enjoyment of his own society, Tom Pedley tried to dismiss from his mind the gruesome experience of the afternoon and settle down to his ordinary occupations. But try as he would to forget it, that dreadful figure, seated at the table, intruded constantly into his thoughts and refused to be dislodged; and when, later in the evening, the studio bell announced a visitor, he resigned himself to the inevitable, and went out to the gate, where, as he had expected, he found a police officer waiting on the threshold.

"You'll guess what I have come about, sir," the latter said, genially, as Tom conducted him to the studio; "just to make a few preliminary inquiries. I am the coroner's officer and it is my job to find out what evidence is available for the inquest."

"Well, Sergeant," said Tom, "I will give you all the help I can, though I am afraid it will be mighty little. However, if you will take a seat and tell me what you want to know, I'll do my best. Perhaps a glass of beer might be helpful."

The sergeant agreed that it might; and when he had been settled in an easy chair by the fire with a jug of beer and a couple of glasses on a small table by his side, and had – by invitation – filled and lighted his pipe, the inquisition began.

But we know what Tom's information amounted to. Of the material facts of the case he knew nothing. The dead woman was a stranger to him, and even Lotta Schiller was little more; indeed, as he strove vainly to answer the sergeant's questions, he was surprised to find how completely ignorant he was of her antecedents, her position in the world, her friends and relations, of everything, in fact, concerning her except the little that he had gathered from direct observation.

"Seems rather a mysterious sort of lady," the sergeant remarked as Tom refilled his glass. "Pretty discreet, too; not given to babbling. Is there anybody that knows more about her than you do?"

Tom suggested Mr Vanderpuye, but as the latter's address was unknown to him, he referred the sergeant to Mr Polton.

"That's the gentleman who unlocked the door from the outside," commented the sergeant. "Handy gentleman he must be. Yes, I'd like to have a word with him if you would tell me where to find him."

"He is a laboratory assistant to Dr Thorndyke of 5A King's Bench Walk, and he lives on the premises."

At the mention of "The Doctor's" name the sergeant pricked up his ears.

"Oh, that's who he is," said he. "Would be a handy gentleman, naturally. I'll just pop along and see what he can tell me. Do you think it is too late to call on him tonight?"

Bearing in mind Polton's intense interest in the case, Tom thought that it was not; whereupon the sergeant, having finished his beer and reloaded his pipe, prepared to depart.

"We shall want his evidence," said he as he moved towards the door, "to prove that the door was really locked from the inside; and as to yourself, sir, although you don't seem to have much to tell, I expect you'll get a summons. Something new might arise which you could throw light on. However, the inquest won't be opened for some days as time has to be allowed for the analysis after the post-mortem."

Events justified the sergeant's forecast. In due course the summons was served, and, at the appointed place and time Tom presented himself to give evidence if called upon. He arrived a little before time and thereby secured a reasonably comfortable Windsor armchair, in which he sat at his ease and observed the arrival of the other witnesses, among whom were Mrs Mitchens, his friend, Dr Oldfield, Polton and Vanderpuye – who arrived together – and last, no less a person than his old acquaintance, Detective-Inspector Blandy.

"Hallo, Pedley," said the doctor, taking the adjoining chair, "sorry to see you mixed up in a disreputable affair like this. Extraordinary business, though, isn't it? Ha, here comes the coroner and the jury; they've been to view the body, I suppose, and look as if they hadn't enjoyed it. Well, how are you? I haven't seen anything of you for quite a long time; not since you took up with that painted Judy that I have seen you gadding about with."

Tom reddened slightly. He had, in fact, rather neglected his friends since Lotta had taken possession of him. However, there was no opportunity to rebut the accusation, for the coroner, having taken his seat and glanced round at the witnesses and the reporters, proceeded to open the inquiry with a brief address. It was a very brief address; no more than a simple statement that "we are here to inquire into the circumstances in which a woman, whose name appears to be Emma Robey, met with her death. I need not," he continued, "go into any particulars, as these will transpire in the depositions of the witnesses; and by way of introducing you to the circumstances I will begin by taking the evidence of Sergeant Porter."

On hearing his name mentioned, Tom's new acquaintance took up his position at the table and stood at attention while he disposed of the preliminaries with professional swiftness and precision and waited for the next question.

"I think, Sergeant," said the coroner, "that you had better just tell us what you know about this affair"; whereupon the officer proceeded, with the manner of one reading from a document, to recite the facts.

"On Thursday the 30th of December 1930 at 3.46 p.m., Mrs Julia Mitchens came to the police station and reported that she had found in a room in her house the dead body of a woman who was a stranger to her, and who had apparently committed suicide by taking poison. She stated that the room had been let to, and was ordinarily occupied by, a Mrs Schiller, but that the said tenant had been absent from her rooms for some time and that her present whereabouts was unknown. In answer to certain questions from me, she gave the following further particulars" – here the sergeant gave a more detailed account of the events, including the unlocking of the door by Mr Polton "with some kind of instrument", which we need not report since they are already known to the reader.

On receiving these particulars, he had accompanied Mrs Mitchens to her house and had been admitted by her to the room, where he found the corpse and the other objects as she had described them. Having given a vivid and exact description of the room, the seated corpse, the tumbler and the poison bottle, he continued:

"As the circumstances were very remarkable, I decided to make no detailed examination without further instructions, and, accordingly I came away, having locked the door and taken possession of the key, and returned to the station, where I made my report to the Superintendent. When he had heard it, he decided that it would be advisable to inform the authorities at headquarters of the facts so far known and directed me to telephone to the Criminal Investigation Department at Scotland Yard, which I did, and was informed in reply that an officer was being dispatched immediately. I also telephoned to the Divisional surgeon, acquainting him with the facts and asking him to attend as soon as possible.

"In about twenty minutes, Inspector Blandy of the CID arrived by car, and, almost at the same moment, the Divisional Surgeon, Dr Oldfield. Acting on instructions, I conducted them to the house, number thirty-nine Jacob Street, and admitted them to the room. When the doctor had made his examination he went away, but I stayed for about ten minutes to assist the inspector with his examination. Then I handed him the key and came away, leaving him to continue his investigations."

At this point the sergeant made a definite pause, looking inquiringly at the coroner, who said, in answer to the implied question:

"Yes, Sergeant; and, as Inspector Blandy is here to give evidence, I don't think we need trouble you for any further particulars, unless the jury wish to ask any questions."

The jury did not, and accordingly, when the depositions had been read and signed, the sergeant retired to his place behind the coroner, and the name of the next witness, Dr Oldfield, was called.

The doctor, like the sergeant, made short work of the preliminaries, and, having been accommodated with a chair and started by the coroner, reeled off his evidence with similar ease and precision. But we need not report it verbatim. The general description of the corpse and its surroundings merely repeated that of the previous witness, but from this the doctor continued:

"I examined the body carefully as I found it, especially in relation to its position in the chair. It seemed very insecurely balanced, in fact it appeared to be supported almost entirely by the arm which was extended on the table. When I lifted this clear and let it hang down, the body slipped forward in the chair and would have slid to the floor if I had not propped it up."

"You seem to attach some significance to this condition," said the coroner: "What did it suggest to you?"

"I think it is a fact worth noting," the doctor replied cautiously, "but I would rather not go beyond that, except to say that it seemed somewhat against the probabilities. I should have expected that at the moment of death, when all the muscles suddenly relaxed, the body would have slipped forward out of the chair."

The coroner pondered this careful answer for a few moments and then asked:

"Could you judge how long deceased had been dead?"

"Only approximately. I would say about three weeks."

"Did you discover anything further?"

"Not on this occasion, but I examined the body very thoroughly at the mortuary and drew up a detailed description, mainly for use by the police. Do you wish me to give those details?"

"It is not actually necessary," the coroner replied, "but perhaps it would be as well to put the description on record in the depositions. Yes, let us have the full details."

The witness accordingly proceeded: "The body was that of a woman of about thirty, apparently married, as she was wearing a wedding ring, but there were no indications of her having borne a child. Her height was five feet six and a quarter inches, weight one hundred and twenty-four pounds – eight stone twelve. Figure spare, in fact definitely thin. Complexion fair, hair flaxen or golden. Its length suggested that it had been bobbed some time ago; now a little below the shoulders. Eyes apparently grey, but it was impossible to judge the exact tint owing to the condition of the body. For the same reason, the features were a little obscure but it could be seen that the nose was rather small, of the concave type with a slight prominence on the bridge. The mouth medium sized and apparently well shaped. The ears were more distinctive and less changed; they were slightly outstanding, thin in all parts with hardly any lobule, and set obliquely on the head. The line of the jaw was also markedly slanting and the chin was pointed and slightly receding.

"As to the identity of deceased, I was present when the clothing was removed from the body and I examined each garment. Two of them were marked in ink with the initials 'E R'; one was marked in ink 'E Robey'; and a small fancy handkerchief in the skirt pocket bore the name 'Emma' embroidered in white silk. That completes the description of deceased."

"Yes," said the coroner, "and a very full and clear description it is. There ought not to be any difficulty in getting the body identified. And now we come to the question of the cause of death. Were you able to ascertain that?"

"Yes. The cause of death was poisoning by potassium cyanide. The dose taken was very large, fully sixty grains, and death probably occurred almost instantaneously, or, at most, within a minute or two."

"Is potassium cyanide a very powerful poison?"

"Yes, very. It contains prussic acid in a concentrated form and acts in the same way and with the same violence and rapidity."

"What is the lethal dose?"

"It is usually given as less than five grains, probably as little as two and a half grains, but, as in the case of most poisons, the effects vary in different individuals. But a dose of sixty grains is enormous."

"Did you make the analysis yourself?"

"Yes, in conjunction with Professor Woodfield. When I made the post-mortem, I removed the organs and took them in sealed and marked receptacles to the laboratory of St Margaret's Hospital, where the professor and I made the analysis together."

"The poison was derived, I suppose, from the tablets of which we have heard?"

"So one would have assumed, and analysis proved that the tablets were really composed of potassium cyanide. But when we came to make the examination, a very curious fact transpired. The quantity of the poison taken was at least sixty grains; the tablets were shown by the label on the bottle to contain five grains each, and we verified this by analysis. The quantity taken was therefore equal to twelve tablets. But there were not twelve tablets missing from the bottle. The label showed that the bottle, when full, had contained fifty tablets of five grains each, so that if twelve had been consumed there should have remained thirty-eight. But there were forty-three, or five more than there should have been."

"That doesn't seem to me very conclusive," the coroner objected. "There might have been some error in filling the bottle. Don't you think so?"

"No, sir," Oldfield replied firmly. "We excluded that possibility. I purchased two fresh bottles from the makers, and the professor and I each counted the tablets. There were exactly fifty in each bottle; and the important fact is that each bottle was quite full. Neither would hold another tablet. Then we tried the bottle that was found on the deceased's table, and the result was the same; it would hold fifty tablets and not one more. A single extra tablet prevented the complete insertion of the cork."

The coroner appeared deeply impressed. "It is a most extraordinary thing," said he, "but there seems to be no doubt of the facts. Can you suggest any explanation?"

"The only explanation that occurs to me is that the poison taken was not derived from the tablets at all. Part of it certainly was not, and if a part came from another source it is most probable that the whole of it did. The facts suggest to me that a solution of the cyanide was prepared in advance, and that it was this solution which was swallowed by deceased. But that is only my opinion."

"Exactly. But if your view is correct, why were the tablets there?"

"That," Oldfield replied, "is not strictly a medical question."

"No," the coroner agreed with a smile, "but we needn't be too pedantic. You have considered the question, I think, and we should like to hear your conclusion."

"Then I may say that the tablets appeared to me to have been put there designedly to support the idea of suicide."

The coroner apparently considered this a rather lame conclusion, for he did not pursue the subject, but returned to the analysis.

"Did your chemical examination bring out anything more?"

"Yes, another very significant fact. At my suggestion, Professor Woodfield tested the material for morphine, and I assisted him. The result was that we discovered undoubted traces of the drug, though the condition of the body did not admit of anything like a reliable estimate of quantity. But morphine was certainly there, and in an appreciable amount, as was proved by our getting a positive reaction. A very small quantity would not have been discoverable at all."

"Can you give us any idea as to the amount that had been taken?"

"We agreed that our results suggested a full, but not very large dose; not more than a third of a grain, or at the outside, half a grain."

"But isn't half a grain rather a large dose?"

"It is a very large dose if given hypodermically, but not so excessive if swallowed. Still, one doesn't usually give more than a quarter of a grain."

"You said just now that the morphine test was made at your suggestion. What made you suspect the presence of morphine?"

"It was hardly a suspicion. The possibility occurred to me, and it seemed worth while to test it."

"But what suggested the possibility?"

"The idea arose from a consideration of the extraordinary circumstances of this case. Taken at their face value, the appearances point definitely to suicide. But yet it is impossible to rule out the alternative of homicide by the forcible administration of poison. It is very difficult, however, to compel a person to swallow even a liquid against his will, and the attempt would involve considerable violence, which would leave its marks on the body. But if the victim could be given a full dose of morphine beforehand, he would become so lethargic and passive that the poison could be administered quite easily.

"In this case, I searched carefully for bruises or other signs of violence but I found none; which seemed to exclude the suggestion of homicide, but only on the condition that no narcotic had been taken. It was then that I decided to test for the most likely and most suitable narcotic – morphine."

"And having found it, what do you infer? You seem to imply that its presence suggests homicidal poisoning."

"I would not put it as high as that; but if there should be other evidence creating a presumption of homicide, the presence of the morphine would be strong corroboration."

This completed the doctor's evidence, and, when the depositions had been read and signed, he was informed that he was free to go about his business. He elected, however, to return to his seat to hear the rest of the evidence, and to jot down a few notes.

"I think," said the coroner, "that if we take the inspector's evidence next, we shall have all the known facts of the case and can fill in details later from the evidence of the other witnesses."

Accordingly, Inspector Blandy, having, at the coroner's invitation, taken possession of the vacated chair, bestowed a benevolent smile on the jury and ran off the preliminaries with the air of one pronouncing a benediction. Then, in reply to the opening question, he introduced his evidence by a general statement which, in effect, repeated those of the preceding witnesses. Having described the room, the corpse, the table, and the various objects on it, he continued:

"When the doctor had finished his examination, I proceeded with my own, beginning with the tumbler and the water jug. On these were a number of fingerprints, mostly very distinct, and apparently, all made by the same hands. Those on the water jug were from a right hand and those on the tumbler were from the left. I took the finger-prints of deceased on small cards and compared them with those on the tumbler and the water jug, and I can say, positively, that they were the same. All the prints on the jug and the tumbler were certainly those of deceased's fingers, and there were no others."

"Would you regard that as conclusive evidence that deceased took the poison herself?"

"No, certainly not. Anyone having control of the dead body could easily have taken the fingerprints of deceased on the jug and the glass. The evidential value of the fingerprints is dependent on the other evidence."

"You have heard that deceased was locked in the room and that the key was on the inside."

"Yes," the inspector agreed, beaming benignly on the coroner, "but I have also heard that the door was unlocked from the outside by Mr Polton; and he could as easily have locked it from the outside, leaving the key inside. In fact, the thing is frequently done by criminals, especially by hotel thieves, who have a special instrument made for the purpose, somewhat like a dentist's root-forceps. With this they can grasp the key from the outside, unlock the door, commit their robbery, and, when they go away, relock the door from outside, leaving the key inside."

"Have you any reason to believe that the door of the deceased's room was locked from the outside in this way?"

"Not with the instrument that I have mentioned. That instrument, having roughened jaws, usually leaves little scratches on the key. I examined the key for scratches, but there were none. Nevertheless, I believe that the door was locked from the outside and that a very simple improvised apparatus was used. Perhaps I had better explain the method before giving the reasons for my belief. The procedure – which is well known to the police – is this: The key is placed in the lock so that a quarter turn will be enough to shoot the bolt; then a small rod such as a thick match, a skewer, or a lead pencil, is passed through the bow, or handle, of the key and a loop at the end of a length of string is hitched on to the rod. The string has to be kept fairly tight to prevent the loop from falling off. The operator now goes out, closing the door after him, keeping the tightened string in the space between the edge of the door and the jamb, and well above the level of the key; then he gives a steady pull at the string with the result that the leverage of the little rod turns the key and shoots the bolt of the lock. When the key has made a quarter turn and locked the door, the loop slips off the rod, the string is pulled out through the crack of the door, and the little rod either drops on the floor or is flicked out of the key and falls some distance away."

The coroner looked a little dubious. "It sounds very ingenious," said he, "but rather risky for a person who has just committed a murder. Suppose the plan should fail."

"But it couldn't fail, sir," the inspector replied. "If it did not work the first time, all he would have to do would be to open the door and try again. Perhaps a demonstration will make it clear."

He opened the attaché case that he had brought with him and took out a flat slab of wood to which a lock had been attached and a through keyhole made. Inserting a key, he produced a thick match and a length of string with a loop at the end. Passing the match through the bow of the key, he held it there while he slipped the loop over it and drew the string fairly taut.

"Now," said he, "observe what happens. The key is towards you and I am on the outside of the door."

He held the slab firmly on the table, brought the tightened string round to the back, and gave a steady pull. Instantly, the key was seen to turn, the bolt shot out, the loop slipped off the match, and the latter, flicked out of the key, flew along the table.

The effect of the experiment was unmistakable. The jurymen smiled and nodded, and even the coroner admitted his conviction.

"And now, sir," said the inspector, picking up the match and viewing it through a lens, "I will ask you to examine this match. Near the middle you will see a little indented curved line on one side, and, on the opposite side, about half an inch nearer the head, a smaller, less distinct mark. Then, at the other end of the match, where the loop of the string caught it, you will see four little dents, one at each corner; and if you place the match in the key, as it was when I pulled the string, you will see that the two dents on the side correspond exactly with the sharp edges of the key-bow."

He illustrated the method and then passed the match together with his magnifying glass to the coroner, who examined it with intense interest and then passed it to the jury.

"Well, Inspector," said the coroner when the match had gone the round, "you have given us a most conclusive demonstration, and I am sure that we are all convinced of the practicability of the method. The next question is, Have you any evidence that it was actually used?"

The inspector's answer was to open once more his attaché case and take from it a corked glass tube containing a single large match, the end of which bore a spot of red sealing wax. Then from his pocket he produced a key, and, taking the match from its tube, laid it and the key on the table before the coroner.

"This match," said he, "which I have marked with sealing wax to prevent mistakes, is, as you see, a large-size Bryant and May. I found it on the floor of the room (which I will call 'deceased's room') under a small cabinet, two feet three inches from the door. This is the key with which that door was locked. On the match are six indentations exactly like those on the other match, which you have. The two side indentations correspond exactly with the sharp edges of the key-bow. I have no doubt that this match was used to lock that door; and I am confirmed in this by having found on the arris, or sharp corner of the edge of the door, an indented mark at exactly the spot where the string would have passed round, as proved by actual trial. I can't produce the door, but I have here a heelball rubbing which shows the mark distinctly."

He handed the sheet of paper to the coroner, who, having examined the rubbing, and passed it to the foreman of the jury, turned once more to the witness.

"You have given us, Inspector, a very complete and convincing demonstration; and there now arises from it another question. This key which you have shown us apparently belongs to the door of the room in which the body of deceased was found. But whose property is it? The presumption is that it belongs to the tenant of the room, Mrs Schiller. But is it actually her key, or only one similar to hers? Can you tell us that?"

"Only by hearsay. I am informed by Mrs Mitchens that this key is the actual key that she gave to Mrs Schiller. She can identify it by a mark that was made on it. As she is one of the witnesses, she can give you the particulars first-hand; but I think there is no doubt that this is Mrs Schiller's own key."

"Then the next question is, Where is Mrs Schiller?"

The inspector smiled a pensive smile. "I wish," he replied, "that I could answer that question. Ever since the discovery, we have been trying to get into touch with her, but we cannot learn anything as to her whereabouts. She is said to be in Birmingham, but that is a rather vague address even if it is correct. We have advertised in the papers, asking her to communicate with us, but there has been no reply."

"In effect, then, she has disappeared?"

"That is what it seems to amount to. At any rate she is missing."

"The importance of the matter is," said the coroner, that if this is her key, there must have been some kind of contact between her and deceased."

"Precisely, sir," Blandy agreed. "That is why we are so anxious to get into touch with her."

This was the inspector's final contribution, and, when he had signed the depositions and retired to his seat, the name of Julia Mitchens was called, and that lady proceeded to give her evidence, which was largely negative. She had never seen or heard of a person named Emma Robey. Of her tenant, Mrs Schiller, she knew practically nothing. The lady had engaged the ground-floor rooms, furnished, but had added some furniture. No references were given but the rent was paid – in cash – monthly, in advance. She had said that she needed no attendance but wanted to be left alone to do her work, which was that of an artist. Witness seldom saw her excepting when she paid the rent. She was pleasant in manner but not intimate. She had a separate electric bell with a small brass nameplate under it, and a removable brass plate on the wall, which she took down every evening. She had her own latchkey and keys of the bedroom and the sitting room. The bedroom door was kept locked, and she always locked the sitting-room door when she went out.

Witness never saw any visitors except Mr Pedley and a coloured gentleman, and them very rarely. Had known Mr Pedley by sight for some years. Does not know whether Mrs Schiller ever stayed away from home. Had noticed the absence of the plate from the wall for about three weeks, and, later, had become aware of an unpleasant odour in the hall.

"To come back to the subject of the keys," said the coroner. "A key was found in the lock of the sitting-room door. If Inspector Blandy will lend us that key for a moment, can you tell us for certain whether it is the one that you gave to Mrs Schiller?"

"I am sure I can, sir," was the reply.

Here the inspector produced the key, and, having taken the precaution to tie a small piece of string round the bow, passed it to the coroner who handed it to the witness.

"Yes, sir," said Mrs Mitchens after a single glance at it, "this is Mrs Schiller's own key."

"You speak quite confidently," said the coroner.

"How are you able to distinguish this key from all other keys?"

"It is this way, sir," she replied. "When Mrs Schiller engaged the rooms there was a big old-fashioned lock on the sitting-room door with a large clumsy key. Mrs Schiller found this very inconvenient, so I got the locksmith to fix a more modern lock with a smaller key. He supplied two keys with the lock and I decided to keep one in reserve in case the other should be lost; but I thought it better to mark the two keys to prevent mistakes, so my husband filed a nick on the handle of the one that Mrs Schiller was to have, and two nicks on the other to show that it was the duplicate. This key has one nick, so it must be Mrs Schiller's, and here is the duplicate with the two nicks on it."

As she spoke, she took a key from her handbag and laid it, with the other, on the table.

The coroner took up the two keys and having rapidly compared their bows, passed them to the jury, from whom they presently found their way back to their respective owners.

"This evidence," said the coroner, "is very important and perfectly conclusive. We now know for certain that the key which was found in the door was Mrs Schiller's own key. How it came there, Mrs Schiller alone can explain. I suppose," he added, turning to the witness, "you cannot give us any hint as to where she may possibly be?"

"No, indeed, sir," was the reply. "I had no idea that she had gone away; and when I first noticed the – er – unpleasantness, I thought she was lying dead in her room."

"By the way, you had the duplicate key. Why did you not try to enter that room?"

"We did try, sir; but the other key was in the lock."

"Yes, of course. Well, Mrs Mitchens, you have given us some very important evidence, and now, if nothing else occurs to you I think we need not detain you any longer."

The next witness was Tom Pedley. But Tom knew nothing about anything, and said so. To his relief no questions were asked about Lotta's artistic abilities and the only contribution that he made was a brief history of his acquaintance with Lotta, a very definite statement of his relations with her and a rather sketchy description of the expedition to Epping Forest, that being the last occasion on which he had seen her. He was followed by Nathaniel Polton, who testified that the door was undoubtedly locked when he tried it, and, from the smoothness with which the key turned, he inferred that the lock had been kept oiled. He had had no difficulty in unlocking it with a simple bent wire appliance (which he had unfortunately forgotten to bring with him) and could with equal ease have relocked it. He knew nothing of Mrs Schiller, who was virtually a stranger to him.

The evidence of the last two witnesses had been "harkened to" by the jury with somewhat languid interest; but when the name of the next witness was called and the rather commanding figure of Mr William Vanderpuye arose, attention was visibly sharpened. Realizing this, the new witness, striking in appearance and faultlessly "turned out", seemed, naturally, a little self-conscious as he walked across to the table; but, having been sworn, he stated his personal particulars – as a barrister of the Inner Temple – confidently enough and thereafter gave his evidence clearly and with perfect dignity and composure.

Of the tragedy, itself, he knew nothing and had heard of it first from the coroner's officer. He had never seen or heard of a person named Emma Robey, and the circumstances connected with her death were entirely unknown to him. This closed the first part of his examination and the rest of his evidence was concerned exclusively with Lotta Schiller. Having described the opening of his acquaintance with her in Tom Pedley's studio, he answered the coroner's questions frankly and fully though he volunteered nothing.

"Did you see much of Mrs Schiller?" the coroner asked.

"Yes; for a time I used to see her almost daily, and we often spent whole days together."

"And how did you spend your time on these occasions?"

"Principally in seeing the sights of the town: theatres, concerts, cinemas, museums and picture galleries. We took our meals at restaurants."

"Did you usually meet by appointment?"

"No, I nearly always called for her at her rooms, and saw her home at night."

"When you saw her home, did you go into the house?"

"No, never. I just saw her to her door. When I called for her I used sometimes to go in for a few minutes, but never at night."

"I am going to ask you a question which you are not bound to answer if you have any reasons for objecting. It is this: What were your exact relations with Mrs Schiller? Were you just friends, or were you on affectionate terms, or were you, in effect, lovers? Remember, I am not pressing you for an answer."

"There is nothing that I need conceal," Vanderpuye replied calmly. "We were rather more than ordinary friends. I may say that our relations were affectionate, at least on my side; I can't answer for her, though she seemed rather devoted to me. But we certainly were not lovers."

"You were not, for instance, on kissing terms?"

"No, I never kissed her. She made it quite clear that kissing was not permissible."

"Reference has been made to certain lockets that were exchanged. You would not regard them as love tokens?"

"No. They were made at her suggestion to serve as souvenirs when I should have gone back to Africa."

"When did you last see Mrs Schiller?"

"On the eighteenth of November, the day of our trip to Epping Forest which Mr Pedley has spoken of."

"Would you give us some particulars of what happened after you parted from Mr Pedley?"

"We walked across to High Beach, as he had directed us, and had lunch at the King's Oak. Then we went for a ramble in the forest and soon lost our way. After wandering about for a long time we met a forester who directed us to Loughton, and, with some difficulty, as it was then getting dark, we found our way there and eventually caught a train to London. I saw her home and said goodnight to her on her doorstep at about half past nine. It was in the train that she first told me that she was going to stay with some friends at Birmingham."

"Did she give you her address there?"

"No. She said that it would be best that no letters should pass between us and that she might be visiting friends elsewhere; but she promised to let me know when she would be returning, though she did not know when that might be. Since then I have neither seen her nor heard from her."

This was the substance of Vanderpuye's evidence, and, after one or two further questions, which elicited nothing new, the coroner glanced through his notes, "I think the witness has told us all that he knows about this strange affair, and, unless the members of the jury wish to put any questions, we need not detain him any longer."

He glanced inquiringly at the jurors, and, as no one made any sign, the depositions were read, the signature added, and the coroner, having thanked the witness for the frank and helpful way in which he had given his evidence, released him; whereupon he retired to his chair beside Mr Polton.

The next witness – who proved also to be the last – was a small elderly woman of somewhat foxy aspect who advanced to the table with a complacent smirk and gave her evidence readily and with obvious enjoyment. Her name was Jane Bigham, address, 98 Jacob Street, no occupation except that she supplemented the small income left to her by her late husband by knitting socks and other articles for sale. She usually sat at the window, partly for the sake of the light, but principally because, being an expert knitter who had no need to keep her eyes on her work, she could entertain herself by observing what was going on in the street. She knew all her neighbours by sight and a good deal about their habits and doings; and as her house was exactly opposite that of Mrs Mitchens, she had often seen Mrs Schiller. She remembered that lady moving in with her little bits of furniture about six months ago, and the brass plate being fixed up ("which I went across the very same day to read the name on it").

"You seem to have taken an interest in Mrs Schiller," the coroner remarked with a smile.

"I did, sir. I wondered what a woman like her was doing in our quiet street with her paint and her powder and her high-heeled shoes; in fact I suspected that she was no better than she ought to be."

"Very few of us are, Mrs Bigham," said the coroner, "but it is not a crime to wear high-heeled shoes or to paint and powder. Most women do nowadays."

"So they do, sir, the more shame to them. At any rate, within a week of her coming, I saw her go to Mr Pedley's door and ring the bell, and when he opened the door I could see that he didn't know her, and looked as if he didn't want to. But she went in and stayed half an hour. After that she often used to go there, and once or twice Mr Pedley went to her rooms about teatime, and sometimes they used to come home together as if they'd met somewhere.

"Then, a month or two later, a coloured gentleman appeared on the scene – the one that has just given evidence, Mr Vanderboy. At first he used to go to Mr Pedley's, and she seemed to know that he was there for she would slip round and ring the bell and then she and Mr Vanderboy would come out together. Then he took to calling for her and they would go off together and not come back until night – sometimes quite late."

Here an intelligent juryman protested that "we've had all this before", and the coroner agreed that "we had better get on. Will you kindly tell us," he continued, "when you last saw Mrs Schiller."

The witness directed a baleful glance at the juryman and replied after a resentful sniff:

"About three weeks ago, it would be. I saw her come home with Mr Vanderboy about half past nine at night, and, by the look of her I reckoned she'd had a drop too much."

"What made you think that?" the coroner demanded.

"Well, sir, she looked a bit unsteady on her legs, and she held on to his arm, which was not her 'abit. And then when they came to the door, it was him that put in the latchkey and opened it and helped her in."

"Did he go into the house?"

"Yes, and he stayed there about an hour and a half, for I saw him come out at a few minutes past eleven. I just chanced to go to the window at that time" (the coroner smiled grimly at the coincidence) "and there he was coming out carrying a bag – or a small suitcase it might have been – which he hadn't got when he went in; and mighty careful he was not to make a noise, for, instead of slamming the door, he put in the latchkey and closed the door without a sound. Which was curious, for it seemed as if he had a latchkey of his own."

"Did you ever see Mr Vanderpuye go into the house on any other occasion?"

"Well, I can't say that I ever did. But if he had a latchkey – "

Here the intelligent juryman interrupted with the question:

"Can the witness swear, sir, that the man she saw was Mr Vanderpuye?"

"What do you say, Mrs Bigham?" the coroner asked. "Are you perfectly certain that the man was Mr Vanderpuye?"

"Well, sir, he certainly looked like him. Besides, who else could he have been?"

"The question is, did you clearly and definitely recognize him as Mr Vanderpuye?"

"Why, as to clearly and definitely recognizing a person across the street on a dark December night, and no street lamp near, it's hardly possible. Of course, I couldn't see the colour of his features, but he looked to me like Mr Vanderboy. Besides, who else could he – "

"Never mind who he might be. Can you swear that he was Mr Vanderpuye and not some other man; Mr Pedley, for instance?"

"Lord! I never thought of that. Perhaps you're right, sir, being next door, too. But no, it couldn't have been, because I saw him walk away towards Hampstead Road."

"I was not suggesting that the man *was* Mr Pedley. I was merely giving an instance. The fact is that you did not actually recognize him at all. You assumed that he was Mr Vanderpuye. Is that not so?"

The witness reluctantly admitted that it was; and the coroner then proceeded to the identification of the woman with a similar result. There had been no actual recognition. The witness had taken it for granted that she was Mrs Schiller because "she certainly looked like her, and then who else could she be?" etc.

By this time the coroner and the jury had had enough of Mrs Bigham, who was, accordingly, dethroned and sent back regretfully to her chair. Then Mrs Mitchens and Vanderpuye were recalled and briefly re-examined, but neither could throw any light on the incident. Mrs Mitchens and her husband were early birds and usually retired to their bedroom in the second-floor back at ten o'clock; and Vanderpuye repeated his statement that he had never entered the house at night. This completed the evidence and the coroner proceeded at once to his brief but lucid summing up.

"I need not, members of the jury," he began, "weary you with a recapitulation of the evidence which you have listened to so attentively, but merely suggest to you the conclusions which seem to emerge from it. Our function is to ascertain when, where, and how deceased, a woman of whom we know nothing but that her name was

Emma Robey, came by her death. The place we know was 39 Jacob Street; the exact date is less certain; but the death occurred about three weeks before the discovery of the body on the thirtieth of December, that is approximately on the ninth of December. The cause of death was a very large dose of potassium cyanide either taken by deceased herself, or given to her by some other person. If she took the poison, herself, she may have done so inadvertently, or with the deliberate intention of taking her own life. If it was given to her by some other person, that person is guilty of wilful murder.

"There are thus three possibilities: accident, suicide, and murder. Accident we may dismiss since there is no evidence suggesting it; and we are left with the alternatives of suicide and murder. Now what evidence is there to support the theory of suicide? There are two facts which, taken together, seem at the first glance to point conclusively to self-destruction. First, the fingermarks on the tumbler and water jug were undoubtedly those of deceased's own fingers. Secondly, deceased was found alone in a locked room with the key on the inside of the door. These two facts, as I have said, seem to furnish convincing evidence of suicide. Nevertheless, it is worth noting that an experienced police surgeon and an experienced detective-inspector both appear to have suspected from the first and in spite of that evidence that this was a case, not of suicide but of murder; and when they came to give evidence, they gave substantial reasons for their suspicions. Let us consider first the evidence of Inspector Blandy. From him we learn that the evidence of the fingerprints is practically worthless since they could easily have been made by a murderer from the victim's fingers after death.

"Then we come to the locked door. Now, the fact that Mr Polton unlocked that door from the outside and could as easily have locked it destroys at once the conclusive significance of that item of evidence. It proves that it was possible for the door to have been locked from the outside. But the inspector's evidence goes further. It goes to prove that the door was, in fact, locked from the outside. I need not remind you of his convincing demonstration, but I must impress on you the enormous evidential value of the match which he found. That match bore marks that exactly fitted the bow of that particular key and also the clear impression of a loop of string. It was found close to the door in the position in which one would have expected to find it if it had been used in the way which he described and demonstrated; and the door, itself, bore a mark of the exact kind and in the exact place in which it would have been made by a taut string used in that way. On the supposition that the door had been locked from the outside with a match and string, all those appearances are perfectly consistent and understandable. On any other supposition they are completely incomprehensible. I submit that there is no escape from the evidence of that match. We are compelled to believe that the door was locked from the outside and therefore that it could not have been locked by deceased.

"The doctor's evidence concerning the morphia – or morphine, as it is now usually called – which he found in the body, and the significance which he attached to it, was very striking; but it became much more so when we had heard the evidence of Mrs Bigham. We may disregard her identification of the two persons whom she saw as a mere guess, and probably wrong at that. But what her evidence did prove was that on a certain dark night about three weeks before the discovery of the body (which had been dead about three weeks), a man and a woman entered that house by means of a latchkey.

"Now, who were these two persons? Let us first consider the woman. Mrs Bigham assumed that she was Mrs Schiller, from which we may infer that she either was Mrs Schiller or a woman who might have been mistaken for her. But deceased was actually mistaken for Mrs Schiller by Mrs Mitchens and Mr Pedley, both of whom knew the latter well. It is thus possible that the woman seen by Mrs Bigham was Emma Robey; and it is here that the doctor's evidence is so important. The woman looked to Mrs Bigham as if she were the worse for drink; and the medical witness swore that deceased had taken a considerable dose of morphia. But a person under the influence of morphia might easily be mistaken for one under the influence of alcohol. So that the evidence establishes a rather strong probability that the woman Mrs Bigham saw was actually the deceased.

"Now let us consider the man. Of his personal appearance we can say no more than that Mrs Bigham took him to be Mr Vanderpuye and that there was probably some general resemblance as to age and figure. That, however, is a mere surmise. But there are three facts which seem to be profoundly significant. This man opened the door with a latchkey; but as he might have received it from the woman, that circumstance has no great importance. The three strikingly significant facts that I allude to are: first, that he still had the key in his possession when he came out; second, that he took extraordinary precautions against noise by easing the door to with the key; third, that when he came out he was carrying a bag or suitcase which he was not carrying when he went in.

What was he doing with that latchkey, which was certainly not his, whoever he was? The strong suggestion is that he had kept it for the express purpose of shutting the door silently. But why that strange, stealthy exit? Why was he so anxious that his departure should not be known to the inmates of the house? Finally, whose bag was it that he was carrying, and what was in it? When we ask ourselves those questions, remembering that this man had been in the house, apparently alone with the woman, for an hour and a half, the answer seems to be that his behaviour is singularly suggestive of that of one escaping from the scene of a crime and taking with him certain incriminating objects connected with it. That, I say, is the suggestion. It is nothing more, taken alone. But taken together with the evidence of the doctor and the inspector, it is, perhaps, more than suggestion. That is for you to judge. When you consider your verdict you will have to decide between two alternatives: did deceased meet her death by her own act or by the act of another; did she commit suicide or was she murdered? That is the issue, and I leave you to consider it."

The silence that settled down on the court as the coroner concluded his address was of short duration; so short as to suggest that the jury had already made up their minds; for within a couple of minutes the foreman announced that they had agreed on their verdict.

"We find," said he, in answer to the coroner's question, "that deceased died from the effects of poison, administered to her by some person unknown."

"Yes," said the coroner, "that is a verdict of wilful murder. I shall enter it as such, and I may say that I am in full agreement with you."

This brought the proceedings to an end. The witnesses, spectators, and reporters rose and began to file out of the court: Dr Oldfield bustled out to his waiting car with the inspector, and Tom Pedley, Polton, and Vanderpuye went off together en route for the studio.

CHAPTER NINE
Where is Lotta?

The inquest and the events which had preceded it had broken in on the quiet current of Tom Pedley's life leaving him somewhat unsettled, and as the day following the inquiry found him disinclined for regular work he devoted it to a survey of his stock of materials and the drawing up in his notebook of a list of deficiencies. The process disclosed the fact that the book which he was using was nearly full and that he had no other to replace it. Now, Tom's notebooks were no mere ready-made productions which could be bought when required. They had been designed by him with careful thought as to suitability of size, shape, thickness, and binding, and were specially made for him, of a selected paper which was good for pen or pencil, or, at a pinch, a wash of colour, by the artists' colourman in the Hampstead Road. He usually ordered a dozen at a time, and each one, as it became used up, was provided with a date label on the back and was stowed away on a shelf with its predecessors to form part of an ever-growing series.

It was an admirable plan; for not only did the series furnish a store of material for reference, but, since Tom invariably dated his sketches no matter how slight, and even the written notes, the collection served as a fairly complete diary and a record of his doings and his whereabouts on a given date. Accordingly, having added to his list a dozen of the indispensable notebooks, he set forth at once for the establishment of the provider.

As he turned the corner of Jacob Street into the Hampstead Road, he perceived, a short distance ahead, his old acquaintance Inspector Blandy in earnest conversation with Mrs Bigham; and as he had no desire for a meeting with either the inspector or Mrs Bigham (whom he privately regarded as an inveterate "Nosy Parker"), he mended his pace and assumed an air of intense preoccupation. But it was of no use. Both saw him at the same moment; and the inspector, hastily detaching himself from the lady, advanced to meet him, holding out his hand and beaming with benevolence.

"This is a stroke of good fortune for me," he exclaimed, pressing Tom's hand affectionately, "I have been wanting to have a word with you and now here you are."

Tom agreed, cautiously, that there he was and waited for developments.

"The matter is this," the inspector explained: "We have been trying to get into touch with Mrs Schiller but we haven't succeeded. Either she hasn't seen our advertisements or she is keeping out of the way; and, as she won't, or at least, doesn't come forward, we must take more active measures. To do that, we must have a full and exact description of her, and the question has arisen, how are we to get it? Now, as soon as that question arose, my thoughts naturally turned to you. Mr Pedley, I said, with his remarkable powers of observation and his wonderful visual memory, will be able to give us a description that will be as good as, or even better than, a photograph."

"Is Mrs Schiller under suspicion?" Tom asked, warily.

"Suspicion!" the inspector repeated in a shocked tone. "Certainly not. Why should she be? But she could give us invaluable information respecting that key, for instance, and perhaps about Mrs Robey and those other unknown persons. I trust you won't refuse us your help. It is to her interest as well as being a matter of public policy that this mystery should be cleared up."

"I shouldn't be prepared to give a description offhand," said Tom.

"Of course you wouldn't," Blandy agreed. "The visual memory must have time to operate – but not too much time, as the matter is urgent. I suggest that you think it over and jot down a few notes."

"And post them to you," Tom suggested, hopefully; but the inspector amended:

"Hand them to me, personally. You see, they might need some explanation and amplification. Would it be possible for me to call for them at your studio this evening?"

Deciding that it would be best to get the business over at once, Tom assented, and, when the hour of 7.30 had been agreed on, he shook the inspector's hand and left him to rejoin Mrs Bigham (who had been lurking observantly in the offing) while he hurried away to the shop of the artists' colourman.

Having transacted his business there, he came away, and turning northward, started on a brisk walk through the quiet squares to consider the situation. The whole affair was extremely distasteful to him. He had no love for Lotta Schiller, but she had been in a sense his friend, and his natural loyalty revolted against the idea of his aiding the police in their pursuit of her; for that was what it amounted to in spite of Blandy's indignant protest. Obviously, she was under suspicion; but to what extent and how justly Tom did not like to ask himself. However, he had no choice. A crime had been committed and it was his duty as a good citizen to give what help he could to the police in their investigation of it; and having reached this conclusion, he turned his face homeward to give effect to it.

Once embarked on the description, he carried it out with his customary thoroughness. On one of the few remaining pages of his notebook, he jotted down his recollections of Lotta, point by point, referring back to the memory sketches that he had made of her for details of the profile, and trying to visualize her as completely as was possible. The result rather surprised him; for though he had seen her often enough and observed her with a certain disapproving interest, he had not expected that his memory would have yielded a description so vivid and so full of detail.

When he had completed his notes, he took a sheet of paper and wrote out a fair copy, thereby making the production of the notebook unnecessary; and he had but just finished this when, punctually to the minute, the studio bell rang, whereupon he pocketed the notebook and went out to admit the inspector.

"This is extraordinarily kind of you, Mr Pedley," said Blandy as he entered and smiled a general benediction on the premises, "to let me take up your valuable time in this way. But I mustn't take up too much of it. Are these the notes?"

He picked up the copy which Tom had placed on the table, and, laying down a portfolio that he had brought (which Tom instantly recognized as Lotta's), glanced rapidly through the notes, while Tom speculated anxiously on the significance of the portfolio.

"Astonishing!" Blandy exclaimed as he finished the preliminary reading. "One might have thought that you had the lady before you as you wrote. What a wonderful thing is the artist's visual memory. You seem to have observed and remembered everything, even to the difference between the two ears. By the way, what exactly does a Darwinian tubercle look like? Perhaps a slight sketch on the back of this paper — "

Tom took the copy from him, and, turning it over, made a rapid but careful pencil sketch of a right ear, showing the feature in question.

"Oh, thank you," said Blandy, taking the paper from him. "I see. This little projection on the edge is the tubercle. But tell me; does this drawing represent that particular ear in other respects?"

"It does as nearly as I can remember."

"That is good enough for me. And now with regard to the hair; I am not quite clear about that. You say, 'Hair unusual in colour; between light brown and flaxen, but of a peculiar texture which makes the colour seem variable.' Could you amplify that description?"

"Well," said Tom, "I am not very clear about it myself, as I have never seen any other hair quite like it. I might compare it to shot silk. You know what that looks like; changes in colour when you move it about and let the light fall on it differently; green, it may be, in one position, and violet in another. Of course, Mrs Schiller's hair doesn't change to that extent, but it does seem to change; quite golden in one light and almost brown in another."

"You don't think it may have been dyed or faked in some way?"

"That is possible. Light hair dyed black sometimes looks red or purple when the light shines through it, but I never got the impression that her hair was dyed. However, I expect you know more about faked hair than I do."

The inspector admitted that it might be so, and, having entered the "amplification" on the back of the sheet, put one or two questions concerning the other items of the description. When these had been disposed of, he carefully put away the document, and, after a few moments' reflection, asked:

"By the way, Mr Pedley, when did you last see Mrs Schiller?"

"On the day of the Epping Forest jaunt, I parted from her and Vanderpuye close by the Ancient British camp, they taking the green ride towards High Beach and I going on to Great Monk Wood. We said 'goodbye' at the corner, and I never saw her again."

"Rather odd, that. Don't you think so?"

"I did at the time, but then I didn't know she was going away. In fact, I expected that she would look me up within a day or two, and I even got out a map of the forest and a large-scale plan of the British camp to show or lend her."

"Why did you do that?" asked Blandy.

"I thought she intended to make another visit there. She seemed greatly interested in the camp, and she proposed to Vanderpuye that they should come another day and explore it; and, as he agreed, I took it as a settled thing."

"You don't happen to know whether they did make another visit there?"

"They couldn't have done, as Vanderpuye never saw her again after that night. You heard him say so at the inquest. But what I can't understand is why she made the proposal when she had already decided to go to Birmingham."

THE JACOB STREET MYSTERY

"Yes," the inspector agreed, thoughtfully, "it does seem a bit inconsistent. I wonder – "

But what he wondered never transpired, as he left the sentence unfinished and Tom did not pursue the subject. A brief silence followed. Then the inspector said, taking up the portfolio:

"I am going still further to trespass on your forbearance. Would you be so very kind as to look at these paintings of Mrs Schiller's and give me your opinion of them?"

"I am not a critic, you know, Inspector," Tom protested. "My job is to paint pictures, not to judge other people's work."

"I know," said Blandy, "and I understand your delicacy. But the point is this: is Mrs Schiller an artist at all or is she an impostor? Now, look at that." He drew forth the painting of Adam and Eve and laid it on the table. "It looks to me like a child's drawing, and not a clever child at that."

Tom had to admit that it did, "but," he added, "there is a new fashion in art which accepts childish drawing as the real thing. I don't understand it, but the highbrow journalists do. Why not get an opinion from an art critic?"

Blandy shook his head. "That is no use to me, Mr Pedley. I don't want to hear a man expound theories or spin phrases. I am out for facts. Now you are a genuine artist. I can see that for myself. You know what a competent artist is like, and I ask you to tell me, in confidence, whether Mrs Schiller is a bona fide artist or only an impostor. Remember, I am a police officer seeking information, and I think you ought to be frank with me."

"Well, Inspector," said Tom, "if it will help you, I will tell you what I know, but I don't want to offer mere opinions. I know that Mrs Schiller can't draw and can't paint, and that she seems to have no natural aptitude for painting. Whether she is or is not an impostor, I can't tell you. If she honestly believes that she is an artist, she is suffering from a delusion; if she knows that she is not an artist, but pretends that she is, she is an impostor. That is all I can say."

"It's enough for me," said Blandy. "I can answer the other question for myself. And now I will just pop round and put this portfolio back where I found it; and I can't thank you enough, Mr Pedley, for the generous way in which you have placed at my disposal your vast stores of knowledge and experience and your really astonishing powers of memory."

With this final flourish, he shook Tom's hand affectionately and allowed himself to be escorted to the gate.

Having launched his visitor into the street, Tom returned to the studio breathing more freely and hoping that he had now heard the last of the unpleasant affair in which he had become involved. And, in the days that followed, that hope seemed to be justified. Gradually he drifted back into his ordinary ways of life, now working in the studio at a new subject picture and now going forth in overcoat and warm gloves to make a rapid winter sketch in some accessible country district. An occasional glance at a newspaper told him that the mysterious Emma Robey was still unidentified and that the search for the equally mysterious Mrs Schiller had yielded no results. But, beyond a faint curiosity as to what part Lotta had played in the crime and a hope that she was not in for serious trouble, he was not much interested. His principal desire was to be left alone to get on with his painting.

About three weeks later he made a fresh contact with the case, but it was such a slight one that, at the moment, it caused him no concern. It is true that when, in answer to the summons of the bell, he went out to the gate and found Inspector Blandy on the threshold, he was slightly disturbed until that officer announced his harmless mission.

"I am ashamed, Mr Pedley, to come pestering you in this way, but I won't detain you a minute. You were so kind as to mention, when I last called on you, that you had put out a plan of the British camp at Loughton to show or lend to Mrs Schiller. Now I have come to ask if you would be so very good as to let me see that plan."

"But, of course, Inspector," Tom replied, ushering him into the studio. "Do you want to look at it here, or would you like to take it away with you to study at your leisure?"

"That is a most generous suggestion, sir," said Blandy (who had obviously come to borrow the plan). "I didn't dare to make it myself, but if you would be so extremely kind – "

"Not at all," Tom replied, opening a cupboard and running his eye along the shelves. "Ah, here we are. It's really a pamphlet, you see, with a folded plan bound up with the text, so you've got all the information together. I hope you will find it useful, and you needn't be in any hurry about returning it."

He handed the little volume to the inspector, who, having glanced at it, slipped it into his pocket and then tactfully retired, discharging volleys of thanks on the way to the gate. When he had gone, Tom returned to the studio and prepared to resume his work; but, for once, his curiosity was definitely aroused. It had really been a rather odd transaction. For what purpose could the inspector require the plan? And why had he suddenly developed this curious "interest" in the British camp? These questions Tom continued to revolve in his mind at intervals for the rest of the evening, but answer there was none. He could make nothing of it, and at last put it away with the reflection that he could only wait and see what came of it.

He had not long to wait. On the following morning when he went forth to do his modest shopping, he was confronted with a staring poster outside the newsagent's announcing in enormous type: "Jacob Street Murder: Dramatic Development", and straightway went in and bought a paper. A single glance at the scare headlines on the front page enlightened him sufficiently as to the purpose of the inspector's visit and he folded up the paper and pocketed it for more leisurely perusal when he had finished his shopping.

At length, having completed his round, he re-entered the studio; deposited his parcels on the table, drew out the paper, and, subsiding into the easy chair, read through the account in all its detail. Omitting the typographical flourishes, it ran as follows:

"Yesterday morning a forester, making his round through that part of Epping Forest which constitutes Loughton Manor, made a startling discovery. Following the green path that skirts the

119

ancient British earthworks known as Loughton Camp, he noticed among the roots of the trees halfway up the bank, and nearly hidden by the fallen leaves, a lady's handbag. Climbing up the bank and brushing aside the leaves, he picked it up, and, having noted the initials, LS, on the outside, opened it to see if it bore any clue to the identity of the owner. Inside it he found, among other things, a leather card case containing a number of visiting cards, and on drawing one out he read on it, 'Mrs L Schiller, 39 Jacob Street, Hampstead Road, London.'

"Recognizing the name from the Press notices that he had read, he immediately realized the importance of the discovery and proceeded without delay to Loughton Police Station where he delivered the bag to the officer in charge and described exactly the place where he had found it. A preliminary inspection showed that the bag contained, in addition to the visiting cards, two objects of considerable interest. One was a small blue handkerchief bearing the name, 'Lotta', embroidered in blue silk in one corner, and closely resembling the handkerchief found on the person of the murdered woman, Emma Robey; the other was a leather key-pouch with a separate swivel for each key. There were six swivels but only four keys; and it could be seen, by the distinct impressions on the leather, that the two missing keys were, respectively, a latchkey and the key of a room door or the door of a large cupboard. Having made his inspection, the superintendent reported by telephone to headquarters at Scotland Yard, and meanwhile dispatched a detective officer to accompany the forester to the place where the bag was found, to mark the spot and to keep it under observation until he was relieved.

"In reply to the telephone message, the superintendent was informed that a CID officer was being sent down to conduct inquiries; and about an hour later a police car arrived bearing Detective-Inspector Blandy and Sergeant Hill, both of the CID. These two officers, having seen and taken possession of the bag, were conducted to the spot where the local detective was waiting, and, with his assistance and that of the forester, they made a systematic search of the immediate locality. As nothing further came to light there, they climbed the bank and descended into the area of the camp, where they separated and carried out a methodical search of the ground, which was covered by a dense growth of pollard hornbeams and a thick mantle of dead leaves.

"For some time the search was without result; but at length it was rewarded by a new and most significant discovery. Tucked away in a hollow between the roots of a small hornbeam, the sergeant espied a gold locket, whereupon he signalled to the inspector and meanwhile made a distinguishing mark on the tree. Examination of the locket showed it to be a handsome and valuable trinket, richly ornamented with enamel and bearing the engraved initials, 'LS', and when it was opened, one side was seen to be occupied by a portrait of a coloured gentleman in a wig and gown while the other held what at first looked like the hairspring of a watch but was in fact a single coiled hair of the African type, presumably from the head of the legal gentleman.

"The rest of the search yielded no further discoveries, but these two relics of the missing woman furnish abundant material for speculation; for instance – "

Here the writer illustrated the point by various speculative suggestions, which we need not quote, and to which Tom paid little attention as they contained nothing that he did not know. But as he reflected on the facts disclosed, certain uncomfortable questions presented themselves and demanded answers.

What had really happened to Lotta? Had she been lured to that solitary place and made away with? That was the plain suggestion; and it seemed to be the one adopted by the police, judging by the inspector's sudden interest in the plan – after the finding of the locket – which hinted at a further and more thorough exploration. But what could she have been doing in the forest? When and why had she gone there? Who was her companion, and what was the connection between the new tragedy and the murder of Emma Robey? That there was some connection seemed to be proved by the vanished keys and the curious resemblance of the two handkerchiefs; and this latter seemed to hint at some complicity on Lotta's part.

But it was all very obscure and confusing. Tom could make nothing of it and finally decided to wait for further developments, and meanwhile to avoid as far as was possible letting his thoughts dwell on it. Which was a decision more easily formed than carried out. For though he had never had any great liking for Lotta, it troubled him deeply to think that any mischance might have befallen her and still more to suspect her of a guilty connection with a most atrocious crime.

CHAPTER TEN

The Camp Revisited

Once again, Tom Pedley stood at the parting of the ways outside the ancient British camp looking thoughtfully along the broad green ride that leads towards High Beach. Under the grey winter sky the scene lacked the beauty and gaiety that had charmed him when he had last looked on it with the late autumn sunshine lighting up the gorgeous raiment of the beech trees and sprinkling the bushes with gold and the turf with emerald. Yet the picture came back to him, not for the first time, with singular vividness; the two figures stepping out gaily and babbling cheerfully as they went, dwindling to the eye with every pace, and at last, halting at the curve to make their farewells. Little had he thought as he returned Lotta's greeting that he was looking his last on her; that the wave of her hand was a final farewell and that as she turned and disappeared round the bend, she had passed out of his ken for ever.

His presence in the forest was not entirely voluntary. He had not wanted to come. But his friend, Polton, had entreated him so earnestly to seize this opportunity (which he, the said Polton, had secured), that Tom had not the heart to disappoint him. So here he was, taking as little advantage of the opportunity as he could decently manage with due regard to his friend's feelings.

The occasion was the complete and final exploration of the ten or twelve acres of land enclosed by the ramparts, with the object of clearing up the mystery of Lotta Schiller's disappearance. The prima facie appearances strongly suggested that she had been murdered and if she had, the overwhelming probability was that her body had been concealed in this enclosed space. Hence, the police, feeling that all doubts on the subject should be set at rest as soon as possible, had decided that the suspected area must be examined with such conclusive thoroughness as to settle the question finally.

But there was a difficulty. Since the camp was scheduled as an ancient monument, promiscuous digging was inadmissible. That difficulty, however, was easily disposed of. To an expert eye, any disturbance of the surface, no matter how artfully disguised, is instantly discernible, and there is no lack of expert eyes in the Criminal Investigation Department. Eventually it was arranged that the Office of Works should send a representative and that the CID officers, under Inspector Blandy, should be assisted by certain competent volunteers from the Essex Field Club, and by Mr Elmhurst, the eminent Kentish archaeologist, whose great experience in the excavation of ancient sites had commended him both to the police and the Office of Works. Thus was ensured a most complete exploration of the precincts with security against possible damage to the camp from an antiquarian point of view.

Now, it happened that Mr Polton got wind of the proposed investigation and was forthwith all agog to be present; for that cunning artificer had followed with eager, almost ghoulish, interest every phase of the crime whose discovery he had witnessed. And now the final act of the tragedy was about to be played with the possible exhumation of a corpse as its climax. It was too much for him. By hook or by crook he must manage to secure a front seat. And he did. By an artful and persuasive offer to his old acquaintance, Inspector Blandy, of assistance in the matter of photography and plaster moulding, he succeeded in extracting an invitation from that suave and polite officer. But more than this; representing to the inspector the invaluable service that Tom Pedley might render in identifying objects or remains (and really convincing him this time), he got the invitation extended, much more to his own satisfaction than to Tom's. So here they were with the assembled explorers, Polton following every movement with devouring interest while Tom browsed about in the neighbourhood of the camp and made occasional visits of inspection.

The examination was conducted with professional thoroughness. The precincts being marked out into sections by pencil lines on the plan, each section was pegged out on the ground and dealt with exhaustively before passing on to the next. No labourers were employed, the whole procedure being carried out by the skilled explorers, who tenderly removed the thick mantle of dead leaves, almost leaf by leaf, to ensure that the actual surface should be exposed quite undisturbed. And it was well that they did; for the very first section uncovered showed the traces, faint but quite recognizable, of two pairs of feet, those of a man and a woman.

"They are not very good prints," said Blandy when Polton offered to take casts and a photograph. "Made through the leaves, apparently. We'll cover them up for the present and see if anything better turns up."

Accordingly an empty sack was laid, carefully, on the footprints and the examination proceeded. The next section showed more prints, but these also were rather shallow and blurred, suggesting some thickness of dead leaves between the feet and the earth; and so it went on for two more sections, each showing faint impressions of the two pairs of feet, and all of them displaying the prints of those feet in parallel pairs, implying that the two persons were walking side by side.

At this point the inspector, who had been anxiously poring over the plan, called out to Sergeant Hill:

"Aren't we getting near the tree that we marked, Sergeant? I put a pencilled cross on the plan, but that was only guesswork, away from the place."

"I think you are right, sir," the sergeant replied. "It was somewhere about here. I'll just go on ahead and see if I can find it."

He walked forward, treading delicately on the russet carpet of leaves and peering among the weird-looking dwarf beeches and hornbeams that jostled one another in the precincts, like a crowd of fantastic hamadryads, and spread out their contorted roots over the surface. Then he disappeared into the miniature forest, and for a time, soft rustlings from the coppice announced his unseen activities. Suddenly, a louder sound, as of a falling body, with expletory accompaniments, was borne to the inspector's ears, and a few moments later the sergeant reappeared with a slightly uneven gait.

"Tripped over one of those damned roots," he explained, stooping to rub his right foot, "but I found the tree, sir, and I've laid my handkerchief at the foot of the trunk so that we can't possibly miss it."

Meanwhile the explorers went on steadily with their work, and, having at length uncovered the surface of the whole section and minutely examined every square inch of it, proceeded to peg out the next under the direction of Mr Elmhurst, who wielded a surveyor's tape and entered the particulars on his copy of the plan. In the course of his measurements he encountered the marked tree, which was contained in the new section and which, having been exactly located by means of the land-tape, acquired "a local habitation and a name" on the plan.

"Now," said the sergeant, "we ought to see what that locket meant. Something must have happened, and it must have happened just about here; and I think it would be as well to lay down some sacks for the workers to stand on."

This suggestion was adopted, and, when the sacks had been spread on the ground, the whole company of explorers concentrated on this region, clearing a broad track towards the tree and scrutinizing each handful of leaves as it was removed. The ground thus uncovered still bore the imprints, faint and blurred, of the two pairs of feet, which continued evenly side by side until they had been traced to a point within a few yards of the tree. Then there was a sudden change in two respects. No longer dim and faint, the footprints were now clear, sharp, and deeply impressed in the moist, clayey soil; and in place of the orderly, parallel lines, there appeared a confused welter of footprints pointing in all directions and overlapping and partially obliterating one another over a considerable area. From this a line of prints led in the direction of the tree, but although both pairs of feet could be distinguished, they were no longer side by side. Both led straight ahead and both had conspicuously deep toe-marks; but whereas the woman's footprints were in some places trodden into, those of the man were all whole and undisturbed.

"Seem to tell their story pretty plainly, don't they?" said the sergeant, viewing the whole group critically from his sack, and addressing Mr Elmhurst.

"So it appears to me," the latter replied. "My reading of them is that the couple walked together to this place, side by side and apparently quite amicably; then the man made a sudden attack and there was a struggle which ended in the woman escaping and running off, pursued by the man."

"That's about what it amounts to," the sergeant agreed; "and now the question is, what was the next act? For the Lord's sake be careful in uncovering the rest of the tracks."

But the caution was unnecessary, for all the explorers were now on the tiptoe of expectation, and the position of the tracks being known, they were able to work from the sides and avoid the risk of treading on the prints.

"It is a bit of luck for us, sir," the sergeant remarked to Blandy, "that the prints that matter most should happen to be the clearest. The ground here must have been uncovered at the time, and the leaves blown over it afterwards. I only hope the rest of the tracks will be as distinct."

"It's of no great importance," the inspector replied: "We know they were here, and we know who one of them was. The real question is, What has become of the woman?"

A couple of minutes later, that question seemed on the way to being answered; for, opposite the marked tree and extending several yards beyond it, was an area of heavily trampled ground on which the impressions of the two pairs of feet were so intermingled and confused that hardly a complete footprint was distinguishable. And the sergeant's hopes were realized. The imprints had evidently been made on bare ground and the few that were whole were deep and remarkably distinct.

"Well, sir," said the sergeant, "there seems to have been a pretty considerable dust-up. He didn't have it all his own way. I wonder how – "

He did not finish the sentence, for the inspector was not listening. His sharp eye had apparently noticed something ahead, for after one long and intent look accompanied by the inevitable smile, he advanced over the uncleared leaves with a sack in either hand to a spot beyond the tree where the clearance was still in progress. Here he laid down one sack, and standing on it, stooped low and pored over the ground at his feet. After a full minute's scrutiny, he stood up and looked significantly at the sergeant, who had followed him.

"Yes, sir," said the sergeant, "I see what you mean. This is where it ended. There's a clean-cut groove made by her heel as she slipped, and there are two marks that show, plainly, the heel ends of her shoes. She must have been lying down on her back to make those marks. And I seem to make out an impression of the body."

"'Seem'," the inspector repeated impatiently. "It's as plain as a pikestaff. She came down on that group of footprints and flattened some of them out. You can see where her shoulders came, and beyond them a faint mark where the head would have been; and right underneath us is a slight flattening of the footprints where the hips would have rested. It is not very clear but it is just in the right place."

He drew a spring tape from his pocket and, stooping down, measured the distance from the two heel impressions to the middle of the ill-defined flattening.

"Yes," he reported with his thumb on the tape, "thirty-three inches, and her height was about five feet seven. And now the question is, What happened next? She couldn't have got up without making some very characteristic footmarks; and there aren't any. But there are one or two very distinct prints of the man's feet and they seem to be on top of the others. Let us see where they go to."

He picked up his sacks, and, followed by the sergeant, moved forward over the heaped-up leaves by the side of the uncovered track, following eagerly with his eyes the footprints that the clearance had disclosed, until he reached the place where the work of clearing was still going on.

"Only a single line of footprints, you see," he remarked. "Not a sign of the woman, though, if she had come this way, her heels at least would have shown plainly. What do you think of these prints? Do they strike you as specially deep?"

"I was just wondering," the sergeant replied. "They ought to be if he was carrying a woman who might have been nearly as heavy as himself. But it's rather hard to judge."

"It is," Blandy agreed; "and when you have judged, it's only an opinion. What we want is an actual measurement. I wonder if Mr Polton has brought his plaster outfit."

"If he hasn't, we have," said the sergeant, who slightly resented the presence of the unofficial interloper; "and we are quite competent to do the job."

"Of course we are," said Blandy, tactfully using the first person, "but Polton isn't only competent, he is a first-class expert. We must see if he has brought his kit."

There was no difficulty in finding out, for Polton, thrilled by the discovery of the "signs of a struggle", had been unobtrusively following the inspector with a gloating eye fixed on the tell-tale markings. When the inspector broached the subject to him, his eyes glistened.

"Yes, sir," he replied eagerly. "I've got a good supply of the best sculptor's plaster and enough water to start with. As you want the moulds for measurement, it will be necessary to include the surface of the ground immediately surrounding the footprint."

"Exactly," replied Blandy; "that's the idea. Give us an edge that can be measured."

"And as to a control, sir? When I have made a mould of one of these prints, would you like me to do one of those where the two parties were walking together?"

"Certainly, if you will be so good. We must have the means of comparison to ascertain whether these prints are deeper than the others."

With these instructions, Polton hastened away to the entrance to the camp, where he had deposited his kit, and returned carrying a heavy suitcase and a three-pint can of water. The inspector selected a sample footprint, Mr Elmhurst marked its position on his copy of the chart, with a distinguishing letter, and Polton opened his case and fell to work. Meanwhile, the explorers, still following the tracks, had uncovered another fifty yards, along which the solitary walker could be traced, now with difficulty where he had apparently tramped over the thick coating of leaves, now quite easily where he had trodden on the bare earth. But for the moment the inspector let them work unheeded while he and the sergeant and Mr Elmhurst stood by and watched Polton's rapid and skilful manipulation of the plaster.

"Don't you usually spray some varnish into the footprint before pouring the plaster?" the inspector asked.

"Not in clay, sir," Polton replied. "Clay – moist clay like this – takes the plaster quite kindly and gives a beautifully sharp mould. Besides, sir, there are the measurements. They will be very delicate, and even a thin film of varnish might affect them."

"Very true, Mr Polton," Blandy agreed. "We must be correct to a hair's breadth."

Accordingly the moulder proceeded with his task, and having poured the plaster and put in the iron wire reinforcements was watching the surface as it solidified when one of the explorers approached hurriedly, holding some object daintily between his finger and thumb.

"We found this, Inspector, among the leaves just at the foot of the bank," he announced as he delivered the object – a painted wooden button – to Blandy. "I thought I had better bring it along at once."

"You are extremely kind," said Blandy, taking the button from him and regarding it with mild interest. "Then you have actually reached the bank?"

"Yes; and there are footmarks on it – rather indistinct but quite unmistakable – and there is a broken branch which seems to have given way when the man caught hold of it climbing up the slope."

"And the footmarks? Any trace of the woman?"

"No; unless that button belonged to her, which seems rather probable."

"It does," said Blandy, "but probability isn't much good." He looked at the button reflectively and then held it out towards Polton, who took it from him and, having examined it minutely, handed it back.

"I can't identify it, sir," he announced regretfully; "but then I shouldn't be likely to, having seen so little of the lady. But Mr Pedley might. He used to see her pretty often – and there he is, coming up the track at this very moment."

As Tom approached rather wearily along the uncleared border of the track, the inspector hailed him and held out the button; whereupon Tom quickened his pace.

"This button has just been picked up, Mr Pedley," said Blandy. "Can you tell us anything about it?"

Tom took it from him, and after one brief glance, replied,

"Yes. It is a button from Mrs Schiller's jacket."

"You speak quite positively," said Blandy. "Do you mean that she had buttons of this kind on her jacket or that you can definitely identify this button? To me, it looks like an ordinary trade button such as you can see at Woolworth's."

"That is what it was, originally," replied Tom; "just a plain wooden button covered with a pink cellulose glaze. But she had a fancy for decorating the set with a painted design, and she consulted me about the method of doing it. I recommended her to use ordinary oil paint varnished with copal; and when she had painted them, as she hadn't any copal varnish, she brought them to me and I put a coat of varnish over them. This is certainly one of those buttons. I recognized it at a glance by the material, the technique, and the design, which I think represents some sort of flower."

"Then," said Blandy, "you could swear, positively, in a court of law, that this button was actually on Mrs Schiller's jacket?"

"Certainly I could," Tom replied. "I saw the buttons on the jacket – which, by the way, was a green jacket; and here is a thread of green silk still sticking in the eye of the button."

"Yes," said the inspector, verifying the fact as Tom returned the button, "very complete, very conclusive. I wish some of the other evidence was as good."

He carefully wrapped the button in an envelope from his wallet, and having bestowed it in an inner pocket, turned to the volunteer who had brought it.

"I will come back with you and get you to show me exactly where you found this button. Have they completed the clearance of the bank?"

"No, Inspector. They had only begun; but we could see the footmarks on the slope as the leaves hadn't settled there very thickly."

"Then perhaps there may be something more to see by this time," said Blandy; and with that he started off along the edge of the track, accompanied by his informant and followed by the sergeant and Mr Elmhurst, but not by Polton, who dared not leave his half-made mould.

When the party arrived at the bank, the inspector's hopeful surmise was justified. The footmarks on the steep slope, indistinctive as they were, told their story plainly enough. The unknown man had climbed the bank more than once, apparently helping himself by the lower branches of a pollard beech, one of which had broken under his weight. In one place, an elongated mark showed where he had slipped, and in another, deep heel-marks furnished evidence that he had descended the bank into the camp at least once.

"Looks as if he had gone to the top of the bank to see if all was clear on the other side," the sergeant remarked, "and then come back to fetch something; and we can guess what that something was."

"There is no need to guess," said Blandy. "Look at this."

Standing on the swept-up leaves at the side, he pointed to two small and faint impressions on the cleared ground, each of which was accompanied by a little sharp-edged dent.

"You're right, sir," agreed the sergeant, craning forward eagerly. "Those are the prints of the back parts of a pair of feet, and those little sharp-edged marks show that they were a woman's feet. No man's heel would make a mark like that."

At this moment Polton came bustling up with his suitcase and water can. Setting the former down on the leaves, he opened it and took out a bundle of lint, from which he extracted the newly made mould, and offered it for inspection.

The sergeant looked at it and chuckled. "It's quite uncanny," said he; "looks just like the sole of a white shoe, and for purposes of comparison it is as good as the shoe itself. How would it be, sir, for Mr Polton to make a plaster mould of these two impressions?"

"Just what I was thinking, sergeant. What do you say, Mr Polton? Have you got a fair supply of plaster?"

"I've got enough for three or four more moulds if I'm careful," Polton replied; "and these little shallow impressions wouldn't take much. I should have plenty for those other prints that have to be done."

"Thank you," said Blandy. "It's rather important, as the moulds will probably show the forms of the heels more clearly."

Accordingly, Polton set to work at once while the inspector resumed his examination of the bank, climbing to the top and scrutinizing the ground narrowly. Here he found obscure traces of something having been dragged across the top, and, what was more significant, a tiny thread of green silk caught on the ragged end of a broken twig. This he put in the envelope with the button and wrote on the outside a short descriptive note. Then he descended the outer slope of the bank and anxiously surveyed the ground at its base. But here the appearances were unpromising in the extreme, for he was now on the green ride, the ancient and well-trodden turf of which yielded no impressions whatever, as he ascertained by walking a few paces and noting the total absence of any resulting footprints.

"Well," he said gloomily to Mr Elmhurst, who, with the sergeant, had followed him down, "this looks like the end of the trail. Can you see which way he went?"

Elmhurst shook his head. "Nothing lighter than a horse would leave visible traces on this turf. We shall have to try to pick up the tracks farther afield, if he really carried the body out of the camp. It isn't certain that he did. We haven't finished clearing the surface yet, and until the whole of the camp has been examined we can't be sure that the body is not concealed in it, after all."

But the inspector was not comforted by this faint encouragement. "No," he admitted, "but we've followed the tracks to the top of the bank and it's pretty clear that he came out that way. Still, you are quite right. We mustn't leave any possibility untested."

The pursuit was accordingly suspended for the moment. Elmhurst went back to the explorers and resumed the systematic examination of the camp; Polton, having finished the small moulds (which showed clearly the backs of a woman's high-heeled shoes), returned along the tracks and made a "control" mould of the man's footprints, where he was walking with his companion, one of the woman's at the same place, and one of the two feet of the prostrate figure near the tree; and in all these cases he photographed the impressions before making the moulds.

All this, with necessary adjournments for refreshment, took time, and the daylight was already failing when Mr Elmhurst sought out the inspector to make his report.

"Well, Inspector," said he, "she isn't here. Every inch of the camp has been examined, and there is no trace whatever of any disturbance of the surface. Of course, this elaborate procedure was hardly necessary, but it is all to the good. It settles the question beyond any possible doubt."

"It does," Blandy agreed gloomily. "But it is a disappointing result."

"I am afraid it is," Elmhurst admitted. "Still, it is conclusive, and it doesn't close the inquiry. If she isn't here, she must be somewhere else; and," he added encouragingly, "you've got all the rest of the forest, with the ponds and lakes, as a possibility."

Blandy smiled, less benevolently than usual. "The idea of a man," said he, "strolling about the forest, even at night, carrying the body of a good-sized woman, doesn't appeal to me. However, I suppose we shall have to consider the possibility."

Thus, unsatisfactorily, ended the exploration which had seemed in the morning so promising. It was not the end of the search. On succeeding days, the police, aided by the foresters and local members of the field club, roamed through glades and thickets, now carpeted with fallen leaves, seeking in vain some trace of the missing woman. The ponds at the Cuckoo Pits and various other sheets of water were dragged, the margins of streams searched for footprints, but nothing came of it. When all was done, and the search was at last abandoned, Inspector Blandy's verdict was justified. The marks on the summit of the rampart were "the end of the trail". There Lotta Schiller, dead or alive, had vanished; whither or in what state no man could tell. She had gone, taking with her the secret (if it had been known to her) of the mysterious death of Emma Robey and of the name of her murderer.

Doubtless the police kept her in mind and continued their inquiries; but if so, no faintest whisper of any discovery ever transpired. To Mr Polton with his dossier of newspaper cuttings, now tidily put away on its appropriate shelf, the failure was a deep disappointment which he hoped was not final. To Tom Pedley it was something of a relief; and as the weeks passed into months and the months into years, the memory of those tragic incidents faded by degrees until it was almost too dim to be painful.

PART TWO
THE UNKNOWN FACTOR

Narrated by Christopher Jervis, MD

CHAPTER ELEVEN
Mr Penfield Opens the Ball

The mountain that was in labour and brought forth a mouse is familiar to us all; but none of us, I suspect, and certainly not I, have ever heard of a mouse that was in labour and brought forth a mountain. Yet, since we are dealing with impossibilities, the one metaphor seems as good as the other. But I shall not argue the question. The second metaphor occurs to me only as illustrating the truth that trivial actions of unimportant persons may generate disproportionately momentous results; a proposition that is obvious enough to be grasped without any metaphor at all. And as to its application to the strange and tragic story that I have to tell, perhaps I had better leave that to develop in due course, merely remarking that the name of the super-prolific mouse was Nathaniel Polton, and that he happened to be our laboratory assistant and Dr Thorndyke's devoted henchman.

Our direct contact with the case occurred quite casually. The occasion was a visit of our old friend, Mr Joseph Penfield, of George Yard, Lombard Street, to our chambers at 5A King's Bench Walk. Ostensibly, it was a professional consultation, but conducted with Thorndyke's habitual informality; an informality which at once scandalized and delighted our legal friends. At the moment, Mr Penfield was seated cosily in an easy chair drawn up before the fire, with his toes on the kerb and his silver snuffbox and a glass of sherry on a small table by his side.

"Well," he said, "that seems to dispose of all my difficulties. Now I know all about it, or think I do, thanks to your learned and lucid exposition. I suppose that a solicitor of nearly forty years standing and experience ought not to have required it, but somehow, when I come here to discuss points of law with you, I feel like a mere schoolboy."

"It is a very misleading feeling," said Thorndyke. "The fact is that you usually consult us on problems that are outside your own special province and inside ours. On questions of property law or conveyancing you could probably make us feel like schoolboys, whereas on subjects such as survivorship or presumption of death, in which medical or scientific knowledge is helpful, the advantage is with us."

"That is true," Mr Penfield agreed, with more emphasis than the rather obvious explanation seemed to merit. "Very true."

He paused with a reflective air, looking steadily at the fire. Then, having refreshed himself with a delicate pinch of snuff and an infinitesimal sip of sherry, he continued:

"I am glad you mentioned the subject of presumption of death, because it happens to be one in which I am somewhat interested at the moment."

"Are you proposing to make an application?" Thorndyke asked.

"No," replied Penfield. "On the contrary, I am considering the expediency of contesting one. I have not quite made up my mind, but, as I am executor and trustee for the person whose death it is sought to presume, the onus seems to rest on me to contest the application. My duty is obviously to consider the interests of my client; and, since the presumption of death is not the same thing as the fact of death, there is always the possibility that the person who is presumed dead may be in fact alive. It would be exceedingly unpleasant if, when death had been presumed and the estate distributed, the client should turn up alive and demand an account of my stewardship. I should feel very unhappy if I had acquiesced passively in the application."

"I suppose," Thorndyke suggested, "there are substantial grounds for believing the person to be dead?"

"There must be. The case for the application is that there is good reason to believe that the person was murdered; and, though there is no direct evidence of the murder and the body was never found, the person has never been seen or heard of since the date of the presumed crime. As that date is so recent – only about two years ago – a substantial body of circumstantial evidence must be available to render the application possible. But I have not gone into that question."

"And as to the collateral circumstances; I suppose you know all about them?"

"Indeed I don't; and I am not much interested in them, since they can hardly be material to the issue. The question is whether this woman is or is not presumably dead. That is all that the court has to decide, and that is all that interests me."

"So," I remarked, "your client is, or was, a woman."

"Yes; a Mrs Schiller."

"Not Lotta Schiller!" I exclaimed.

"Ah. Then you know the name, and perhaps some of the circumstances?"

"We do, indeed. Polton was acquainted with the lady, and he took an almost morbid interest in the circumstances of her disappearance. He has collected every scrap of information bearing on it and he was actually present at the search for the body, making moulds and photographs of the footprints. He probably has the photographs still."

"Ha," said Mr Penfield, "very interesting; though a footprint seems rather to connote a living person. However, what you tell me puts an end to my hesitation. I shall contest the application if I can secure your support. What do you say?"

"I say, yes, certainly," replied Thorndyke. "The case is entirely within our province."

"It is more than that. You not only have the general knowledge and experience but you have the particular knowledge of the facts of this case, which should be invaluable in cross-examination. And then," he added with his queer wry smile, "you have the further attraction to me that you are able to prepare your own brief."

"Let us rather say, part of it," said Thorndyke. "We must depend on you for the general facts of the case. There is the motive, for instance.

Why does someone want to presume this woman's death? Who are the parties? Is the husband one of them?"

"He is not. No doubt he would be interested to know whether he is a husband or a widower, but he is not interested in the legal sense. He has nothing to gain, and he is not a party to the application. The motive is a sum of about twenty thousand pounds, and the applicant is the sole beneficiary under Mrs Schiller's will, who stands to gain that sum of money if the application succeeds. These facts do not seem very relevant to the issue, which is simply whether the woman is alive or dead; but I agree that you will want a general outline of the case. Perhaps a brief sketch of the history of my relations with Mrs Schiller might do for a start. The details could be filled in later."

Thorndyke having agreed to this suggestion, Mr Penfield took a pinch of snuff and began his narration.

"About five years ago – I can't give you exact dates or figures as I am speaking from memory – but a little over five years ago, Mrs Schiller came to my office to ask me to draw up her will and to take custody of it and of certain monies in her possession. She was a stranger to me, but she brought a letter of introduction from one of my clients – now deceased – and I agreed to undertake the business, though I was not very favourably impressed by the lady herself; a flashy, golden-haired baggage, painted like a clown and powdered like a miller, and very free and easy in her manners. However, it was a small affair and perfectly simple; a matter of about three hundred pounds, left by the will to one sole beneficiary; so I drafted a short will in her presence, read it over to her, and, at her request, appointed myself sole executor. Having made an appointment for the following morning, I got the will engrossed and made the necessary arrangements with the bank.

"When she arrived on the following morning, bringing with her the money in notes, some further arrangements had to be made. As she was in the habit of moving about a good deal and had no permanent address, she wished me to act as her man of business and manage her financial affairs, such as they were. I need not go into details. The arrangement constituted me her agent with power to receive and pay monies on her account; and when the will and the other document had been signed and witnessed in my office, the transaction was complete. She left my office immediately and I never saw her again or received any communication from her."

"She left you her address, I suppose?" said Thorndyke.

"Yes. She was then living in lodgings at a place called Linton Green – Corby Street, I think, was the exact address – and I remember that the landlady's name was Wharton. But that is of no consequence as she had left those lodgings when I made my inquiries and the landlady did not know where she had gone. She had promised to keep me informed of her whereabouts when she changed her address, but she never did; which, for a time, was no concern of mine, as I had no occasion to communicate with her.

"But then there came a new development. A certain rather wealthy man – a Mr Charles Montagu – died (I regret to say that he, also, was murdered. It is a distinctly unsavoury case altogether). Well, this man had bequeathed to a certain Miss Dalton a sum of about twenty thousand pounds. There was some delay in regard to the probate of his will owing to the fact that some large payments – over a thousand pounds – had been made in cash and not accounted for in the books. Another unsavoury detail; for there could hardly be a doubt that those payments represented blackmail, especially as the man was murdered. However, the will was eventually proved; but the probate was barely completed when Miss Dalton died.

"It then appeared that she had made a will leaving the bulk of her property to Mrs Schiller; who, as the residuary legatee, became entitled, also, to the twenty thousand pounds. But now there was a fresh difficulty. Not only was the whereabouts of Mrs Schiller unknown; it was not certain that she was alive, or even that she had been alive at the time of Miss Dalton's death. On this question I could, of course, give no information. I tried to get into touch with her through the usual channels but had no success; and so this matter remained in abeyance for a time.

"Then the position was clarified in a very startling manner. There was yet another murder (I must really apologize for these sordid details) and it appeared that Mrs Schiller was under some suspicion of being at least an accessory. That, however, does not concern us. The material fact is that she was proved to be alive, and, consequently, the bequest took effect; and I duly notified the claim on her behalf, disregarding the criminal details. But the astonishing thing that now transpired was that she had been living all this time at a place called Jacob Street within a short bus ride of my office.

"But the uncertainty which had just been cleared up was almost immediately succeeded by another; which is the one that concerns us. First, Mrs Schiller disappeared. Then traces of her were discovered which led the police to believe that she had been murdered. But no body was found and no actual proof of death was obtained. On the other hand, the woman has never been seen or heard of since the disappearance. It appears that the police have made all possible inquiries but have not been able to discover any traces whatever of her. Their attitude, I understand, is entirely non-committal; she may be dead or she may be alive, but there is no positive evidence either way.

"So that is the position; and our function − or perhaps I should say yours − will be to examine the known facts and assess the probabilities. If there are clearly good grounds for presuming death, it might not be worth while to do more than watch the case in my absent client's interest. We shall be better able to judge when we know exactly what facts the applicant relies on."

"Then," said Thorndyke, "I take it that you have not yet received copies of the affidavits?"

"No. I have had no formal notice of motion; only an informal, and quite friendly, notice of the proposed application. And, for my part, I am not going to be unnecessarily contentious. I don't particularly care whether the woman is alive or dead. I am only doing what I conceive to be my duty to an absent client, and I shall certainly not oppose the application if, when you have examined the facts, you think it ought to succeed. As soon as I receive the copies of the affidavits, I will let you have them, and you can then advise me as to our further proceedings."

This concluded the business, and, shortly afterwards, Mr Penfield rose, and having pocketed his snuffbox and waved away the proffered decanter, shook our hands and departed.

"Quite a promising case," I remarked when he had gone, "though Penfield does not seem enthusiastic. But he never is if there is any criminal element. It will be interesting to see what sort of case the applicant's lawyers have made out."

"I expect," said Thorndyke, "that they will take the same line as Penfield has taken."

"Yes," I agreed, "and, after all, it seems a perfectly logical view, though I suspect that you won't concur. But really all that the court has to decide is whether the probability that the woman is dead is so great as to justify the presumption that she is dead. The various collateral circumstances do seem, as Penfield maintains, to be irrelevant."

"The question is," Thorndyke replied, "what is meant by collateral circumstances? Penfield is assuming that facts and circumstances which appear to have no bearing on the main issue are irrelevant and may be disregarded. But until those facts are examined, it is impossible to say whether they are or are not relevant. It is a capital mistake to classify facts in advance as relevant and irrelevant, and to limit consideration of them to those which appear relevant."

"Still," I persisted, "there are the plain physical facts; and if they are such as to establish an overwhelming probability that the woman was murdered, the various other facts, such as her personal character and way of life, for instance, do really seem to have no bearing. The simple issue is whether she is dead or alive. If she is dead, that issue is settled. How she came to die or what were the factors that brought about her death are interesting questions, but not material to the issue. However, the known facts may not be conclusive enough to justify a decision. We shall be better able to judge when we have seen the affidavits."

"I don't expect that they will tell us anything new," said Thorndyke. "We have heard the whole story of the search from Polton and Elmhurst, and we read the account of what happened at the time. We probably know all the facts on which the applicant will rely, judging from what Penfield said."

"You may, but my recollection of them is rather dim. I am afraid I did not quite share Polton's enthusiasm. After all, it was no special concern of ours."

"Then," said Thorndyke, "let me refresh your memory. Put in a nutshell, the case amounts to this: A woman was murdered in Lotta Schiller's rooms at Thirty-nine Jacob Street. The person who committed the murder let himself in with Lotta Schiller's keys."

"Or perhaps with some similar, or skeleton keys," I suggested.

"No. One key was found in the lock and conclusively identified as Lotta's own key. At the time of the discovery of the murder, Lotta had already disappeared and could not be found or heard of by the police. Some time later – I have forgotten the dates – her handbag was found on the bank enclosing the British Camp in Epping Forest. It contained a key-pouch from which two keys were missing, one being the latch-key and the other the key of the room in which the murder seemed to have taken place. Inside the camp the police found a locket belonging to Lotta, and, incidentally, made by Polton, and containing a portrait of our friend, Vanderpuye."

"Yes, I remember that. Poor Vanderpuye! He will wish he had gone back to Africa when he hears that the scandal is going to be revived."

"Probably," Thorndyke agreed, "though his evidence will refer only to the date on which he last saw Lotta. But to continue: as the finding of these things indicated the probability that the woman had been murdered and her body disposed of in the neighbourhood, the police arranged an exhaustive search of the camp for further traces of her, dead or alive. The result of that search was the discovery of a series of footprints, apparently of a man and a woman, which proceeded side by side to a point near the place where the locket was found. Here the ground was trampled in a way that suggested a struggle, and there was a rather obscure impression of a woman's body lying in a supine position. From this point the footprints continued, but they were those of the man only. There were no further footprints of the woman;

and it is suggested that the impressions of the man's feet were somewhat deeper than they had been before.

"The single track of footprints crossed the camp to the north-west side until they reached the enclosing bank, and here some further discoveries were made. It was seen that the man had climbed up the bank twice – the first time apparently to reconnoitre. Near the foot of the bank was another, very obscure, impression of a woman's body lying on the ground. Near it a button was picked up. It was a very distinctive button, painted by hand, and was conclusively identified by a Mr Pedley as a button from Lotta's jacket. On a broken twig, half-way up the bank, a wisp of a green material was clinging, and this shred Mr Pedley identified as exactly similar to the material of her jacket and dress. Finally, at the top of the bank, the earth showed marks as if some heavy object had been dragged across the summit.

"That, as Inspector Blandy put it at the time, was 'the end of the trail'. On the outer side of the bank was the turf of the green ride, which would not have shown impressions in any case; but the fact is that no tracks or traces of any kind were found outside the camp, while inside the enclosure, there was no sign anywhere of the ground having been disturbed. It can be taken as certain that the body – if there was a body – was not buried in the camp; and no traces of either the man or the woman could be discovered anywhere else.

"Those are the facts that I think we shall find embodied in the affidavits, together with evidence that the woman has not been seen or heard of since her visit to the forest with Vanderpuye. On them will be based the application for the court's permission to presume that Lotta Schiller is dead; and I ask you, Jervis, as an experienced medico-legal practitioner, whether you still think that collateral facts, such as the woman's personal character and way of life, are not material to the issue."

"I still don't see that they are," said I, "though, as you apparently do, I suppose I am wrong. But it seems to me that the facts that you have stated point very strongly to the conclusion that the woman was murdered and her body concealed somewhere in the forest. There appears to have been an adequate motive for the murder; to get possession of the keys and to eliminate a person who might have been dangerous. For it is practically certain that Lotta Schiller would either have known or guessed who committed the murder in her rooms.

"The prima facie evidence that she was murdered seems to me extremely strong; and when we add to it the fact that she has never since been seen or heard of, the probability becomes overwhelming, and certainly enough, in my opinion, to warrant the presumption that she is dead."

"QED," Thorndyke commented with an appreciative chuckle. "You have put the case for the applicant with admirable lucidity. Unfortunately, it is that case that we have to demolish if we can do so by fair means and consistently with what we believe to be the truth. Wherefore I now call upon my learned friend to bring his mighty intellect to bear on the opposite proposition. Come, now, Jervis, here is an opportunity to exercise your wits and utilize your experience. You have just given a masterly exposition of the reasons for presuming that Lotta Schiller is dead. Now cross over to the other side and see what reasons you can find for presuming that she is alive."

With a strong and growing suspicion that I had, as usual, overlooked some material fact, I promised to reconsider the case, and, as a first indispensable step, to refresh my memory as to the whole set of circumstances; to which end I repaired to Polton's lair, and, having conveyed to him the tidings of the proposed application, had no difficulty in obtaining the loan of his voluminous collection of newspaper cuttings, which I bore off to study at my leisure.

CHAPTER TWELVE

Tom Pedley Receives Visitors

The question with which Thorndyke had closed his narration had rather taken me aback; but what had really surprised me was his clear and complete recollection of the case in all its details. Yet it ought not to have surprised me, for the thing had often happened before, but I always failed to allow for a fundamental difference between us; Thorndyke was a genuine criminologist and I was not. By me, the report of a criminal case was read with mild interest, and then, if it did not concern us, was straightway dismissed and forgotten.

Not so Thorndyke. To him, every case was a problem; and if there was any element of mystery or obscurity, he would study it, evolve one or more possible solutions, and retain the case in his memory until it was cleared up – if ever it was – and the actual solution was disclosed. It was a useful habit, for, apart from the mental exercise amounting in effect to experience, there was the practical advantage that if an obscure case was ultimately referred to us – as often happened – it found Thorndyke fully informed as to the facts and perhaps with a solution already arrived at.

This, I suspected, was the present position. Reading attentively through Polton's collection of reports, I realized that the whole case, including the murder of Emma Robey, was profoundly mysterious. But I also realized the significance of Thorndyke's question. Lotta Schiller was definitely implicated in the murder. This, Penfield would have said, was not material to the question whether she was dead or alive. But it was material. The disappearance of a person who is under suspicion in regard to a murder calls for a much more critical consideration than that of a person who has no known motive for disappearing.

In due course the notice of motion was served on Mr Penfield, and copies of the affidavits were sent on to us; and as I read them through, I saw that Thorndyke had been right. The facts sworn to were concerned exclusively with evidence of Lotta Schiller's death. The murder of Emma Robey was referred to only incidentally (in an affidavit by a Mrs Bigham) in connection with the mysterious man who, accompanied by a woman, had let himself into the premises of 39 Jacob Street with a latchkey. Evidently, the inference advanced by the applicant would be that this man had already murdered Lotta Schiller and possessed himself of her keys.

Thus the case for the application was fairly clear. We could see what "the other side" proposed to prove; and, taking the facts at their face value, it was a reasonably good case. But the next question was, What did Thorndyke propose to prove, and what was he going to do about it? Assuming – as I did – that he had already considered the case and probably arrived at some provisional conclusions, my expectation was that he would follow his usual practice and begin by seeking to enlarge his knowledge; by searching for some new facts to supplement those already known; and mighty curious I was as to what line his investigations would take, and not a little surprised when his intentions were disclosed.

"So," he remarked on the following day, "my learned friend has studied the affidavits and the Polt —— dossier and now knows all the available facts? Probably he has found them a little sketchy?"

"On the contrary," I replied, "I thought that we had a pretty full account of the case. What more do you want to know?"

"I want to know all that I can learn. For instance, there is Lotta Schiller, the central figure in the case. What do we know about her? She is little more than a name; a sort of algebraical symbol. I want to turn her into a real person; to know what she was like, physically, mentally, and morally."

I was about to object that such knowledge was not likely to help us much in opposing the application, but fortunately I saw the red light in time.

"And how do you propose to get that knowledge?" I asked.

"The most likely source is Mr Thomas Pedley. He, apparently, knew her quite intimately and should be able to tell us quite a lot about her. So I wrote to him a day or two ago, and he has kindly given me an appointment for tomorrow afternoon. May I take it that I shall have your support at the interview?"

As it happened, fortunately, that I had the afternoon free, I accepted gladly – indeed, I may say eagerly. For my curiosity about this visit was intense. That its object was simply to get a description of Lotta Schiller's appearance and personality seemed incredible; and I hoped that by listening attentively to Thorndyke's questions I might get some inkling of what was really in his mind.

Jacob Street we found to be a shabby, old-fashioned street turning out of the Hampstead Road, in which Mr Thomas Pedley's studio was distinguishable by a green-painted wooden gate bearing the number 38A in polished brass characters, and by a small brass plate at the side inscribed "T Pedley" surmounted by a shining brass bell-knob. A tug at this resulted in the distant jangling of a large bell, followed by the opening of the gate and the appearance thereat of a big, hearty, pleasant-faced man who surveyed us for a moment with a friendly blue eye and then, apparently recognizing us or taking our identities for granted, bade us "come along in"; whereupon we followed him along a stone passage and across a small yard to the studio, the size of which, and especially of the great north window, I found quite impressive.

"It is very good of you, Mr Pedley," said Thorndyke, "to let us come here occupying your time with matters in which I don't suppose you are much interested."

"Oh, I am interested enough," replied Pedley, "but I am afraid you will find me rather disappointing, for I really know nothing about Lotta Schiller or her affairs."

"Well," Thorndyke rejoined with a smile, "that is a fact, to begin with, and not entirely without significance. But at any rate, you know more about her than I do. So I stand to learn something."

"I am afraid it will be mighty little," said Pedley. "But perhaps a cup of tea may brighten my wits. Yours probably don't need any brightening."

He led us across to the tea table which had been placed, with three armchairs, in front of the fire, and, having installed us, proceeded to make the tea at a gas ring by the large sink; and while he was thus occupied I cast inquisitive glances around, and was not a little impressed by the fine china and elegant table appointments and the various signs of a refined and fastidious taste in the furnishing of the place, which contrasted rather oddly with the sink, the cooking stove, and the working appliances.

"I think," said Pedley when he had poured out the tea and taken his seat, "that, as you know what information you want and I don't, you had better treat me as a witness. You ask your questions, and I will answer as well as I can."

"Very well," said Thorndyke, producing a notebook and opening it, "then, as I have never seen Mrs Schiller and have no idea what she was like, we will begin with her personal appearance. Can you give me a description of her?"

Pedley was obviously astonished – as well he might have been – but he replied readily enough:

"Yes, I can do that all right, for it happens that Inspector Blandy made the same request, and I drafted out an exhaustive description and gave him a copy. I can show you the original draft."

He went to a shelf on which was a long row of linen-bound books, each having on its back a paper label bearing a date.

"Let me see," said he, running his eye along the row, "it would be about 1930. Yes, here we are."

He picked out the little volume and brought it to the table, explaining, as he turned over the leaves: "This is the notebook that I was using at the time. It contains all sorts of notes; sketches, drawings, and written memoranda, and, as I date every entry, it serves well enough as a diary. This is the draft that I made for Blandy."

He handed the open book to Thorndyke, who glanced through it rapidly though with close attention and, I thought, some signs of surprise.

"But, Mr Pedley," he exclaimed, "this is an extraordinarily complete description. You seem to have observed everything and forgotten nothing."

"Well, you see," Pedley replied, "that is an artist's job; to look at things attentively and remember what he has seen. But I am glad you approve. Blandy was quite pleased, though he wanted one or two points elucidated."

"For instance?"

"Well, there were the ears. He asked me if I could draw them from memory, which, of course, I could and did."

"He was quite right," said Thorndyke. "A drawing is better than the best verbal description. I wonder if you would kindly do the same for me?"

Though still looking a little puzzled, Pedley complied readily. On a small cartridge paper block he drew, very deliberately and yet quickly, a pair of ears, facing each other.

"There," he said, taking off the sheet and handing it to Thorndyke, "you see they are just normal, well-shaped ears with a small Darwinian tubercle on the right one. I have marked in the line of the jaw to show how they were set."

Thorndyke thanked him for the drawing, and, having examined it, put it away carefully in his wallet. Then, glancing once more at the description, he said:

"There is one point here that seems to require some amplification. You say that the hair had some peculiarity of texture that made it seem variable in colour. I don't quite understand that."

Pedley grinned. "Blandy again," said he. "He didn't understand it and neither do I. So I couldn't tell him anything beyond the bare fact that it certainly did seem to change colour in different lights. The change was very slight and I don't suppose the majority of people would have noticed it at all. But there it was; and I've never seen any other hair like it before or since."

"Do you think," I suggested, "that it might have been dyed or faked in some way? Women do all sorts of queer things to their hair in these days."

"I thought of that," replied Pedley, "but there was one circumstance that seemed to exclude it. Dyed or faked hair, as you know, won't bear close inspection especially at the roots. But Mrs Schiller had no objection at all to a close inspection. When Polton wanted a sample of her hair, she made no difficulty but let him cut it off himself. He separated out a little tress and cut it off close to the roots, exposing the skin of the scalp, and, apparently, he noticed nothing unusual there."

"Did you ever mention the peculiarity to her?" asked Thorndyke.

"No; and I don't think she was aware of it herself."

"By the way," said I, "what did Polton want a lock of her hair for?"

"He was making a locket for Mr Vanderpuye, and it was arranged that there should be a specimen of her hair set in one side to face the portrait in the other."

"Oh, yes, I remember the locket – the two lockets, in fact – but they were empty when I saw them. I never heard what was to be put in them."

"As to the portrait in Vanderpuye's locket," said Thorndyke; "was it a miniature or a photograph?"

"It was a photograph; but not from life. She painted a self-portrait in watercolour and Polton did a reduced photograph of it."

"Was it a fairly good likeness?"

Pedley grinned. "It wasn't a likeness at all. There was no resemblance whatever to Lotta, and hardly any to a human being."

"But I wonder Vanderpuye didn't object," said I, "seeing that a likeness was what he wanted."

"He did; in fact he was really angry. He wanted me to paint or draw a portrait of Lotta of which Polton could make a reduced photograph to fit the locket. But she would not have it, nor would she allow Polton to do a photograph of her. She insisted that the portrait should be her own work, and from that she wouldn't budge. So poor Vanderpuye had to accept her drawing; but I shall never forget Polton's face when he first set eyes on it. He thought that it was a practical joke, but he realized his mistake in time."

"But what was it like?" I asked, a little bewildered by his account of the incident.

"It was a drawing of a woman's head such as might be done by a child of nine or ten – not a clever child, mind you, but just an ordinary child with no natural aptitude for drawing."

"But," I exclaimed, "I don't understand this. Wasn't she a professional artist?"

"She claimed to be one, but, of course, anyone can call himself an artist. The fact is that she couldn't draw and she couldn't paint."

"Do you mean that she drew badly," Thorndyke asked, "or that she, literally, couldn't draw at all?"

"Her drawing," replied Pedley, "was like that of an ordinary child; and I am quite sure that she couldn't do anything different."

"This is rather remarkable," said Thorndyke, "and it suggests one or two questions. The first is as to her state of mind. Was she cranky enough to believe that she really could paint?"

Pedley chuckled. "Blandy again," said he. "That is what he wanted to know and I rather dodged his questions. But I won't hedge with you because I have thought the matter over since, and I have come to the conclusion that she was a rank impostor. There was nothing cranky about her. She was a pretty shrewd, level-headed young woman, and I am sure that she had no delusions about her painting. It was a deliberate fraud. What her object was in posing as an artist, I have no idea; but what I am quite clear about is that she just took advantage of the present fashion for freak pictures and started producing freaks. Anybody can do it. All you have to do is to paint something quite unlike a normal picture and leave it to the highbrows to explain it to the multitude. But she knew all about it, and she had got all the highbrow jargon at her finger-ends."

"That," said Thorndyke, "partly disposes of the next question, which is how she maintained the pose. Did she ever offer her work for sale?"

"No. She spoke of an intention to send some of her stuff to an exhibition, but she never did send any."

"I suppose she signed her pictures with her own name?"

"She didn't sign them at all, properly speaking. She used a cipher – a sort of conventionalized flower with a little circle on each side of the stalk."

"It all sounds rather tortuous and secretive," I remarked.

"Yes," Pedley agreed, "but she was secretive in everything. Polton first drew my attention to her capacity for keeping her own counsel. But the secrecy about her paintings I don't understand. It looks rather as if the artist pose was a temporary stunt which she meant to drop when it had served her purpose, whatever that may have been."

"It does," said Thorndyke, "and yet the brass plate by her door seems to exclude the idea of secrecy. It was a public announcement."

"It wasn't very public," replied Pedley. "It was only a small plate, about six inches by four, with just the bare name in small copperplate script. It wasn't very easy to read from the pavement even when it was new, and, by the time she had kept it polished for a few weeks and rubbed most of the black out of the engraving, it was nearly illegible. No passing stranger could have read it."

"That seems to answer my objection," said Thorndyke. "And now, to come back to the description. I suppose you don't possess a photograph of her?"

"No," replied Pedley, "and I never saw one."

"Did you ever draw a portrait of her?"

"Not from life. I had thought of suggesting that I should paint her portrait and then I decided that I had better not. But I made one or two trial sketches from memory to see how a profile portrait would look. They are in that notebook that you have. Would you like to see them?"

"I should, very much," replied Thorndyke, handing him the book and watching him, expectantly, as he turned over the leaves.

"This is the best one," said Pedley, passing the book back, "and as the others were preliminary trials, we can disregard them."

Thorndyke examined the drawing with deep interest, as also did I, though what chiefly interested me was the liveliness of the representation and its finished character. It might have been a careful drawing done direct from the model.

"This is rather more than a sketch, Mr Pedley," said Thorndyke. "It gives the impression of an actual portrait, but, of course, I can't judge as to the likeness. What do you say about it? Is it really like her?"

"Yes," replied Pedley. "I should say it is quite a good likeness."

"Do you think it would be recognized by anyone who had known her?"

"Oh, certainly. Looking at it now, after all this time, it recalls her to me perfectly. You see, in drawing from memory one instinctively chooses the most characteristic and easily remembered aspect."

"Yes, I see that," said Thorndyke. "But you seem to have a rather remarkable memory."

"Not remarkable," replied Pedley. "I have a good memory, and I have made a point of training it. But, in effect, all drawing is memory drawing. You can't look at the model and draw at the same time. You have, first, to look at the model with concentrated attention and try to memorize the part you are working on. Then, as a separate act, you draw it; and then you compare what you have drawn with the actual facts and correct your drawing if necessary. Memory drawing is only the same thing with a longer interval between seeing and drawing."

Thorndyke pondered this explanation with his eyes fixed on the portrait. At length he said:

"If this is a perfectly recognizable likeness of Lotta Schiller it may be of some importance as the only existing record of her personal appearance. I wonder if you would allow Polton to bring a camera here and take a photograph of it."

"Of course I would, with the greatest pleasure. But why take all that trouble? Better just slip the book in your pocket and let me have it back when you have done with it."

"That is very gracious of you, Mr Pedley," said Thorndyke, "and it will certainly be much more convenient. I didn't like to ask you for the loan as I understood that the book contained some private memoranda."

"You needn't have been so punctilious," Pedley replied with a smile. "I have no secrets, and, if I had, I shouldn't write them in my notebook. No, Doctor, I give you the free run of the book if the sketches and notes are of any interest to you. Perhaps you might like to see the fingerprints that Polton took from that poor murdered woman. They are in the book somewhere. Shall I see if I can find them?"

"I don't know that they are of much interest now," said Thorndyke, handing him the book nevertheless, "excepting as to Polton's improvised method of taking them."

"And his motive for doing it," I added. "It wasn't a very correct proceeding, and I never understood why he wanted to meddle."

"I think that is pretty clear," said Pedley. "He wanted to know, then and there, whether it was a case of suicide or murder. Ah, here are the prints."

He returned the book to Thorndyke, who, notwithstanding what he had said, looked at the rather feeble impressions with some interest; which seemed to deepen as he looked, for, presently he produced his lens from his pocket and made a closer examination, finishing up by viewing the prints with the book held at arm's length.

"Quite a creditable performance," he remarked, "considering the very inadequate means. What do you think of them, Jervis?"

He handed me the book with his lens, and I examined the prints with some curiosity.

"Yes," I agreed, "they are not bad; rather weak and faint, but you can make out the pattern quite clearly, even in the last three fingers, where the impression seems to have partly failed. I shall make a note of the method for use in a similar emergency. And, by the way, the method is not new to us. The original Thumbograph was provided with an inking-pad."

I returned the book to him, and, when he had closed it and slipped it into his pocket, I waited expectantly for the next question. But there was none. Apparently the "examination in chief" was finished. I say "apparently", for with Thorndyke you never knew when the examination had really ended. He had a way of directing a conversation without appearing to and thus allowing the information that he was seeking to transpire, as it seemed, spontaneously; and I had a faint suspicion that, on the present occasion, Pedley was being gently guided along the paths of reminiscence in the desired direction.

And yet it seemed incredible; for though Pedley's account of his relations with Lotta Schiller was amusing enough, described in his quaintly humorous way, it was utterly trivial and seemed to have no bearing whatever on our problem. The way in which she had opened the acquaintance by a transparent pretext and thereafter adopted him as her dearest friend, in spite of his struggles to escape, was rather funny, but relevant to nothing that concerned us. At least, so I judged; though even then my judgment was confounded by Thorndyke's concentrated attention to these trifling reminiscences and by the little aids to amplification that he applied.

"It is a quaint picture," he remarked with an appreciative chuckle; "the masterful lady and the lover *malgré lui*."

"Not lover," protested Pedley. "There was not even a pretence of that."

"But you seem to have been on quite affectionate terms," Thorndyke maintained.

"On her side only," said Pedley, "and that was all bunkum. It was just a pose, like her painting. But it was very queer. I never understood what her game was. She called me 'Tom' from the very beginning, and soon it came to Tom, dear, or darling or duck. But it was all verbal; there was no demonstration of affection. Anyone listening in an adjoining room might have taken us for an engaged couple; but our actual behaviour was perfectly matter-of-fact."

"Do you mean that there were no physical endearments? Did she, for instance, never kiss you?"

"Lord, no! I shouldn't have let her. But she never made any approach to that sort of thing. As I say, it was purely verbal. I took it to be just a silly habit of speech, especially as she used the same terms to others. Why, she even called Polton a duck, and as to poor Vanderpuye – but his case was different. He took the endearments quite seriously. Still, even he was not on kissing terms. He swore, at the inquest, that he had never kissed her, and I suspected that he had made an attempt and not brought it off."

"Very odd," Thorndyke commented, "particularly as the modern woman seems to be so far from squeamish in such matters. Did the verbal endearments extend to written communications? How did she address you in writing?"

"She never did, and I am glad she didn't; for if her handwriting was at all like her drawing, it would have taken some deciphering. But she never wrote to me, and I gather that she never wrote to Vanderpuye. It almost looks as if she avoided putting any of her nonsense down in black and white, though there was nothing very incriminating in it."

"Not incriminating," said Thorndyke, "but, after all, she was a married woman, and compromising letters are apt to be dangerous things if there happens to be an unfriendly husband in the background."

"I don't think her husband was unfriendly. The position seemed to be that they had separated by mutual agreement and gone their respective ways, simply ignoring the marriage. On the few occasions when she referred to him, she did so without the slightest trace of animosity."

"Apparently she was not very communicative about him."

"No; he was rather a shadowy figure. All I learned from her was that his name was Carl, that by profession he was a sort of travelling wine merchant, that he was, in a sense, domiciled somewhere in Germany, but spent most of his time rambling about the Continent with occasional visits to this country and the United States. That is all that she let drop. Of course, I never asked any questions."

This apparently exhausted Pedley's store of reminiscences, for the conversation now drifted in the direction of his work and mode of life; and when he had shown us some of his paintings and taken us on a personally conducted tour of his premises, including the very pleasant little cubicle bedroom that he had built in a corner of the studio, we felt that we had stayed long enough.

"It is most kind of you, Mr Pedley," said Thorndyke, "to have let us take up so much of your time and to give us so much help in our inquiry."

"I am glad to hear that I have been helpful," replied Pedley, as he escorted us along the paved passage. "It seemed to me that I was ladling out some rather small beer. But I enjoyed doing it. To a solitary man a real good chinwag comes as a refreshing novelty."

With this exchange of courtesies and a hearty handshake we took our departure, and, crossing the Hampstead Road, set a course for the Temple by way of the less-frequented back streets. For some time we walked on in silence; but presently, according to custom, I ventured to put out a cautious feeler.

"Pedley's estimate of the conversation was rather like my own, and we are probably both wrong; but, apart from the description and the portrait (the value of which is not obvious to me), I don't see that we have learned anything very significant."

"That," replied Thorndyke, "must be because you have not got the issues in this case clear in your mind."

"But I think I have. The simple issue is whether or not Lotta Schiller is presumably dead."

"Yes, but put it another way. Either the woman is dead and her body concealed in some unknown place, or she is alive and keeping out of sight. The issue is between the alternatives of a concealed dead body or a concealed living person."

"She would be mightily well concealed to keep out of sight for two years with the police on the lookout for her all the time. I should have thought it practically impossible considering all the modern means and facilities at their disposal."

"Still," said he, "the possibility of her being alive is the one that concerns us, and the value of the information that we have got from Pedley is in its bearing on that question. What I recommend you to do is this: when you get home, while the matter is fresh in your memory, take a sheet of paper and write down a full report of our conversation with Pedley. Then read it over and extract from it any facts, explicitly stated or implied, without regard to their significance, and write them down on another sheet. Finally, consider those facts, separately and together, in relation to the two alternatives that I mentioned. I think you will find Pedley's small beer more nourishing than it appeared at the time."

CHAPTER THIRTEEN

Thorndyke Becomes Secretive

Thorndyke's suggested procedure for extracting the nourishment from Mr Pedley's "small beer" – which I duly put into practice – proved highly effective. But yet it was not effective enough. For while it brought into view several facts which might be important in certain circumstances, it threw no light on their application to our present problem; wherefore, and because the reader, quicker in the uptake than I, has no doubt already noted them, I shall make no further reference to them.

But if not very enlightening, my study had the effect of stimulating my curiosity as to what was in Thorndyke's mind. That he had a definite theory concerning Lotta Schiller's disappearance, and that his theory was strictly relevant to the main problem, I had no doubt, and since I could make no guess as to the nature of that theory, I could only seek enlightenment by observing his proceedings and trying to deduce their object. This, however, turned out a complete failure, for the more I saw of his methods, the more bewildered I became, and the less able to connect them in any way with Mr Penfield's case. I shall therefore put my observations briefly and baldly on record without unnecessary comments.

A few days after our visit to Pedley, Thorndyke, when he came in to lunch, took from an inner pocket a couple of documents and deposited them in the cabinet in which such things were usually kept;

and I noticed that they went into the drawer which contained Mr Penfield's papers.

"You have been to Somerset House," said I, having recognized the official copies.

"Yes," he replied. "An unnecessary visit, perhaps, but one never knows what unexpected questions may arise during the hearing; so I have provided myself with certified copies of two of the wills concerned in Penfield's case. We have a copy of the third, Lotta Schiller's."

"Whose are the other two?" I asked.

"One is that of Barbara Dalton who left the twenty thousand pounds to Lotta. The other is that of a Mr Charles Montagu, which contains, among many other legacies, the bequest of twenty thousand pounds to Barbara. Would you like to look over them?"

"No, thanks," I replied. "They don't interest me, unless they contain something unexpected or curious. Do they?"

"No, they are quite simple and straightforward, and, of course, they are not disputed."

"Then I think we can leave them to Penfield, if they come into the case at all."

Thus the matter was dismissed, leaving me with a faint feeling of surprise that even Thorndyke should have concerned himself with such remote antecedents. But apparently it was only another instance of his almost fanatical insistence on knowing all the facts.

The next proceeding of his that attracted my attention had, at least, some connection with Penfield's case, though I failed utterly to discover any relevancy. It took the form of an exhaustive interrogation of Vanderpuye, of whom we now saw a good deal as the Long Vacation had brought him back from his travels on the South-eastern Circuit. It was not, of course, a formal interrogation, which would have been quite alien to Thorndyke's usual methods. But Vanderpuye was perfectly willing to talk about his liaison with Lotta Schiller — it had been the great adventure of his life — and a little skilful guidance of the conversation brought out all the details. But of these conversations, which seemed to elicit nothing that was new even to me, I shall record only one; and that one chiefly because it led to further activities on Thorndyke's part. We had been discussing Pedley's portrait of Vanderpuye and the incidents connected with the painting of it, when my colleague led off in a new direction with the remark:

"It was a very successful portrait; a faithful likeness and an extremely becoming one, too. I am rather surprised that you did not get Pedley to paint one of Lotta. I should have thought that you would have liked to have a portrait of her."

"I should," Vanderpuye replied emphatically, "and I begged her to let him paint one of her, but she refused flatly. It was at the time when the lockets were being made, and I wanted him to paint her portrait so that I could have the original to hang beside my own and a little photograph of it to carry about with me in my locket. But she was most obstinate and perverse. She insisted on painting the portrait herself, and she wouldn't even agree to letting Polton take a photograph of her for the locket. It was really very awkward. I had seen her work and I knew that she couldn't paint a portrait. But she stuck to her decision and I had to accept her self-portrait. But I was very annoyed."

"Then I infer that it was not a very good likeness?" Thorndyke suggested.

"Bah!" exclaimed Vanderpuye. "It was not a likeness at all. But you can see for yourself"; and, as he spoke, he unshackled the locket from his watch-guard and handed it to Thorndyke, who carefully prised it open and looked curiously at the little portrait.

"I was going to remark," said he, "that as I have never seen the lady, I could hardly judge the likeness. But I see that I was wrong. This drawing only faintly resembles a human being and certainly could not be a recognizable likeness of any particular person. By the way, did she give you the original drawing?"

"No, she never offered it to me, and I should not have accepted it if she had."

"I ask," said Thorndyke, "because her work as an artist may have some bearing on the case that is pending and I should have liked to produce a specimen. But this is rather small, particularly if the judge's eyesight should happen to be at all defective. What do you think, Jervis?"

I took the locket from him and gazed in astonishment at the incredibly crude and childish drawing – though Pedley's description had prepared me for something abnormal – which, small as it was (about the size of a shilling), offered evidence enough of the artist's incompetence. But I couldn't understand Thorndyke's difficulty, and said so.

"I don't see that the size matters. It would be quite simple to make an enlarged photograph; that is, if Vanderpuye would give his permission."

"But of course," protested Vanderpuye. "I should be delighted to help in any way. By all means take the locket and let me have it back when you have done with it."

Thereupon, having thanked the owner warmly, Thorndyke slipped the little bauble into an envelope and folded it up securely; but I noticed that instead of locking it up in the cabinet according to his usual custom, he stowed it carefully in an inner pocket. It was a small matter but it attracted my attention; and when, on reflection, I realized how adroitly Thorndyke had managed to obtain possession of the trinket without asking for the loan, I began to suspect that there was more in the transaction than met the eye. Accordingly, I followed the fortunes of the locket closely to see whether any ulterior purpose should come into view. But apparently there was none. On the following day Thorndyke handed the locket to Polton, who gazed at it fondly and then returned it.

"I don't want the locket, sir," said he. "You are forgetting that I did the miniature. I have the original negative that I made from the drawing, which will be much better for doing the enlargement as it is a good size already."

"Of course," said Thorndyke. "My wits must have been wool-gathering. Why didn't you remind me, Jervis?"

I replied that my wits were probably on the same quest as I had suggested the borrowing of the locket, but protested that no harm had been done.

"No," he agreed, turning the locket over in his hand; "and I am glad to have seen the little bauble again. It is a charming specimen of goldsmith's work and it does Mr Pedley and his executant very great credit. How on earth did you manage, Polton, to work the hair into that beautifully regular spiral? Hair isn't a very kindly material, is it?"

"It's all right, sir, if you know how to manage it. I just soaked two of the hairs from the little tress that I had cut off and wound each of them tightly on a thin steel spindle. Then I carefully heated the spindle, and, when it was cool, the hair slipped off in a little close cylinder like a cylindrical spring. After that, it was quite easy to work it into a flat spiral on the card."

"So you used only two of the hairs. What did you do with the remainder of the tress? Did you throw it away?"

Polton crinkled slyly. "No, sir," said he, "I've got the regular craftsman's vice. I never throw anything away. You see, even a hair comes in handy, if it's long enough, to string a small bow for use on the turns. Would you like to see what's left of it?"

Without waiting for an answer he went to one of his innumerable cabinets, and, from a labelled drawer produced a seed envelope inscribed in pencil "Mrs Schiller's hair", which he handed to Thorndyke; who drew out of it a little tress of pale brown or dull flaxen hair neatly tied up with bands of thread.

"I don't see anything unusual in it," said I, as Thorndyke held it at arm's length in the light of the window.

"No," he agreed, "but we haven't Pedley's trained colour sense; and probably the peculiarity that he described would be noticeable only in large masses. But it couldn't have been very conspicuous even then as nobody else seems to have observed it."

He pulled the tress out taut, and, having measured it against a two-foot rule on the bench, wrote the length (nine and a half inches) on the envelope. Then he recoiled the tress and slipped it back into its receptacle.

"I am going to rob you, Polton," said he. "This specimen had better go with the rest of the possible exhibits; and on the remote chance of its having to be produced in court, you may as well sign your name on the envelope under the description."

This ceremony was duly performed, and, when Thorndyke had declined my derisive offer to witness the signature, he put the envelope in his wallet and we then reverted to the enlargement of the portrait.

I make no comment on these proceedings, having already said that I found myself utterly unable to connect any of them with Mr Penfield's problem. Nor shall I, for obvious reasons, say anything about certain other activities which Thorndyke carried on in his private laboratory with the door locked; which from experience I judged to be experiments connected with his inferences from the facts known to me. No doubt they would have been highly revealing if I had known what they were; but, in accordance with the queer convention that existed between us, by which Thorndyke gave me every opportunity to observe the facts but refused to disclose his inferences or hypotheses until the case was concluded, I was left in the dark; and even Polton, bursting with curiosity, could only gaze wistfully at the locked door.

Of what went on, then, in the private laboratory, I had no knowledge at all; but in two other instances I was permitted, so to speak, to inspect the backs of the cards. Thus, on a certain day, returning at lunchtime I perceived my colleague pacing up and down the lower end of King's Bench Walk in earnest conversation with one Mr Snuper. Now, Mr Snuper was a very remarkable man. Originally a private inquiry agent, he had been employed by Thorndyke on one or two occasions to collect information or to keep certain persons under observation; but he had proved so ingenious, resourceful, and dependable, that Thorndyke had engaged him permanently; and a very valuable member of our staff he had proved in making inquiries and observations where it was undesirable for us to appear.

But what could this meeting portend? Usually, Mr Snuper's appearance foreshadowed some more or less sensational developments. But at present the Schiller case was the only one that we had on hand in which sensational developments were possible; but of that case we seemed to be in possession of all the relevant facts. Our problem was concerned with the application of those facts and seemed to offer no opening for Mr Snuper's activities.

But my bewilderment reached a climax that very evening when, entering our sitting room, I found Polton placing an easy chair before the fireplace and setting beside it a little table on which were a whisky decanter and a box of cigars. I watched him with growing suspicion, and when he added an awl, borrowed from the workshop, suspicion grew into certainty.

"Expecting the superintendent?" I asked.

"Yes, sir," he replied. "Mr Miller is coming by appointment at half past eight."

"You don't know what about, I suppose?

"No, sir, I do *not*. I suspect it is that Schiller case, but that is only a guess; and I don't mind telling you, sir, that I am fairly eaten up with curiosity. I can see that there is something in the wind, and that somebody is going to get a surprise."

"What makes you say that?"

"Oh, I know the symptoms of old, sir. The Doctor is in one of his exasperating moods; as secret as an oyster and as busy as a bee. He has been locked in his laboratory doing all sorts of things that are really my job; developing photographs, mounting specimens for the microscope, making microphotographs, and the Lord knows what else. I know that much, because I've done the clearing up after him."

I laughed at his undisguised inquisitiveness, but not without sympathy.

"It seems to me," I remarked, "that you have been doing Snuper's job; keeping what the plain-clothes men call 'obbo' on the Doctor."

"Well, sir, there's no harm in keeping him under observation when his actions seem to invite it; and I believe he likes to be watched. It's part of the game. Why, only this morning I saw him colloguing with Mr Snuper on the Walk. He knew I could see him from the window. And now there's Mr Miller coming, and he isn't giving much away. And what do you make of that?"

He produced from his pocket a little slip of mahogany about four inches by two in which was a shallow, elongated cavity about two and a half inches by one, with straight sides and rounded ends, and a little round hole about a sixteenth of an inch wide, just outside the middle of the cavity.

"I made it from the Doctor's own full-scale drawing," Polton continued, "and, as he said nothing about its purpose, I suspect it is part of the surprise packet."

"It looks rather like some sort of a microscope slide," I suggested; but at this moment, as a quick footstep became audible ascending the stair, Polton picked up the slide and returned it to his pocket, smiling guiltily as the door opened and Thorndyke entered.

"I see we are to have the pleasure of a visit from Miller," I remarked.

He glanced at the little table and then asked with a smile:

"Is that information received or observation and inference?"

"Both," I replied, "but the inference first. It was the awl that clinched the diagnosis."

"Yes," Thorndyke chuckled, "it is wonderful how Polton remembers all the likes and dislikes of our visitors. He would have made a perfect innkeeper. How do you do it, Polton?"

"Well, sir," he replied with a gratified crinkle, "the proper study of mankind is man, and that includes Mr Miller – and by the same token, here he is."

The crescendo of approaching footsteps culminated in the characteristic knock, and, as Polton threw the door open, the superintendent entered and saluted us with a comprehensive smile, which took in the three easy chairs and the small table.

"It's nice to see you all again," said he, when the preliminary greetings and handshakings – which included Polton – had been disposed of. "Quite a long time since I was here. Don't get many excuses to come now that I am kept bottled up in the office."

We chatted inconsequently for a minute or two and then adjourned to the chairs, when Thorndyke and I lit our pipes while Miller carefully selected a cigar and Polton poured out the whisky.

"Well, Doctor," said the superintendent, thoughtfully operating with the awl on the proximal end of the cigar, "I've managed your little business. Rare job it was, too. Had to get the Assistant Commissioner's permission, of course, and he wasn't at all ready to give it. But I showed him your letter and coaxed him a bit and at last he gave way. But he wouldn't have done it for anyone else, and no more would I for that matter; and he stipulated that the information was to be considered strictly confidential and personal to you."

"You know that you can depend on my discretion, Miller. But supposing it were required to be used in evidence? May I take it that he would consent?"

"That you would have to settle with him. You weren't proposing to challenge the conviction, I suppose?"

"No. The conviction, whether good or bad, is no affair of mine."

"I wonder what is your affair – and so did the AC, especially what you wanted the fingerprints for. However, I suppose we shall know in due course, as you seem to hint that you may need our collaboration later. At any rate," he concluded, producing a bulky, sealed envelope from his pocket, "here is the dossier of the worthy Louisa Saunders, if that was her name – apparently it was, as it agreed with the initials on her clothing – all complete; personal particulars, fingerprints, prison portraits, summary of the police-court proceedings, everything that you asked for; and you notice that the envelope is sealed with wax and marked 'Secret documents'."

He delivered the package to Thorndyke, with a malicious leer in my direction, and, when my colleague had thanked him very warmly for his friendly offices, the transaction was concluded and the conversation drifted into other channels, mostly connected with the work of the Criminal Investigation Department. But though the superintendent's "shop" talk was highly interesting to listen to, it does not belong to this history. Nor was I very attentive to it; for my mind was occupied with the questions, Who the deuce was Louisa Saunders, what concern was she of ours, and what could Thorndyke possibly want with her fingerprints?

These questions, and the mystery surrounding the dossier, gave me abundant material for thought during the next few days; as, apparently, in a different way, they did to Thorndyke. For, once more, to Polton's exasperation, he locked himself in his laboratory and resumed his mysterious doings; and as these appeared, from Polton's reports, to be mainly of a photographic nature, I surmised that he was making reproductions of the "secret documents", but for what purpose I could not even guess.

Thus the time ran on, the Long Vacation ran out, and the day fixed for the hearing drew nearer. Once or twice we had communications from Mr Penfield, chiefly relating to Thorndyke's request that certain witnesses should be summoned to appear in court for cross-examination on their affidavits; and once I observed among the letters delivered by the first post a large, well-filled envelope addressed to Thorndyke which looked to me like a report from Mr Snuper. But that was only a guess, though Snuper's handwriting was a good deal more distinctive than his person.

Otherwise Thorndyke's preparations seemed to be complete, so far as I could judge with no knowledge whatever as to their nature; and I looked forward eagerly to the approaching date of the hearing, when, as I hoped, the obscurities in which I groped vainly should be made clear.

CHAPTER FOURTEEN
The Probate Court

The morning of the day appointed for the hearing found us with all preparations completed and – speaking for myself and Polton – all agog for the opening of the play. As the Law Courts were close at hand Thorndyke and I put on our wigs and gowns before starting, and, thus figged out and accompanied by Polton carrying a small suitcase, we set forth betimes, crossing the Temple by way of Crown Office Row and Fountain Court and finally emerging from Devereux Court into the Strand opposite to the main entrance of the Royal Courts of Justice, and, crossing the road, entered those august premises and made our way to the court in which the hearing was to take place.

With the exception of the usher and Mr Turner, Penfield's managing clerk, we were the first arrivals; but shortly after us came Mr Longford, the applicant's solicitor, escorting his client, Miss Dalton, and a gentleman whom I correctly diagnosed as Mr Carl Schiller. As we knew Mr Longford slightly, we exchanged a few words of greeting, and he then introduced us to his two companions; and as we were making polite, but not too topical, conversation, we accompanied it by a mutual inspection.

Miss Dalton, "the applicant", was a decidedly good-looking woman of about thirty-five; but I was not much interested in her, my attention being more attracted by Mr Schiller, whom I took the opportunity to examine as closely as good manners permitted. Not that he was a particularly striking personality, but he was (or had been) the husband of the mysterious Lotta, and he had the added interest of being present to learn whether he was a presumptive widower or only a mere husband. So I looked him over as we talked (as also, I noticed, did Thorndyke) and listened critically to his speech, in which I detected a faint German accent which seemed to agree with his rather Teutonic appearance. He was a smallish man, about five feet seven, spare and slight in figure, long-necked and bottle-shouldered, blond in complexion, with a rather scanty moustache and beard of a delicate ginger tint and eyes of a peculiar greenish hazel. His eyebrows were considerably darker than his beard, rather broad, and set in an almost straight horizontal line. As to his hair, it was probably of a similar colour to his beard or perhaps lighter, but as he had greased it with grease in order to comb it smoothly back over the crown of his head, I was unable to judge. On the whole, I considered him a fairly good-looking man, and our brief contact left me with a rather favourable impression.

During our short talk there had been other arrivals. Mr Lorimer, the applicant's counsel, had entered in wig and gown and was now in close conference with Mr Longford at the solicitor's table. Mr Pedley had slipped in and quietly seated himself on a back bench where, presently, he was joined by Inspector Blandy and by two middle-aged women who arrived together and who, having espied Pedley, at once seated themselves beside him. But the most interesting arrival to me was a rustic-looking gentleman who drifted in by the swing door, and, having gazed about him vaguely, wandered slowly up the court towards the solicitor's table; for in him, with my usual start of surprise, I suddenly recognized the inscrutable Mr Snuper.

He certainly enacted the part of a country cousin to a finish. The mixture of curiosity and boredom with which he stared about him was absolutely convincing, and the dropsical watch which he drew from his pocket and solemnly compared with the clock might have been an heirloom from some ancestral yeoman. But what was he doing here, masquerading under our very noses? Unable to imagine what his function could possibly be, I determined to keep an eye on him and try to solve this mystery for myself. But now the clock on the gallery announced the near approach to the hour and bade us take our seats, which we accordingly did; Miss Dalton was given a chair at the solicitor's table; Mr Schiller selected a front bench with a restfully high back; Snuper shuffled into a seat behind him, and Mr Lorimer joined us at the counsels' bench; and hardly had we taken our places when the usher threw open the door beside the bench and the judge bustled in and took his seat.

I looked at him with a good deal of interest since, as there was no jury, the decision of the case lay with him. But apart from this, I was attracted and interested by his personality; which was in several respects of an unusual type. He had none of that monumental repose that one associates with the occupants of the judicial bench. In fact he was the liveliest judge that I have ever met. He bobbed up and down in his chair, he turned to confront each speaker whether witness or counsel and leaned out sideways to address them with a curiously friendly and confidential air in keeping with his general conduct of the proceedings, which was that of carrying on a sort of family consultation.

Nor was his vivacity only bodily. He was very much alive mentally and seemed to follow every stage of the proceedings with intense, almost eager interest, watching the speaker and dropping in occasional comments in a quick emphatic manner entirely free from judicial solemnity. But he was an excellent judge, attentive, helpful and friendly, and as informal as was permissible in the circumstances.

When his Lordship had settled himself in his chair and had taken a rapid survey of the court, he turned expectantly towards Mr Lorimer, the applicant's counsel, who thereupon rose to open his case.

"Is the application opposed?" the judge asked, when Mr Lorimer had set forth the nature of the case.

"I am not quite clear, my Lord, as to the extent of the opposition. No affidavits have been filed in answer, and there have been no pleadings."

The judge glanced inquiringly at Thorndyke, who thereupon rose to explain: "The position, my Lord, is this: the executor of Lotta Schiller's will is also her solicitor and man of affairs, and, as the legal presumption at present is that she is alive, he has thought it necessary to safeguard her interests by ensuring that all facts adverse to the presumption of death are brought to the notice of the court."

"But you have filed no affidavits?"

"No, my Lord; but, if, in the course of the hearing, it should seem to be necessary, I shall ask for an adjournment to enable me to file affidavits in answer or to call witnesses."

The judge smiled pleasantly. "I see. The good old principle of not leaping before you come to the stile. Very well."

He nodded to Mr Lorimer, who continued: "As this is an application to presume death, the facts in issue are those relating to the probability of death; but it seems to me desirable that I should, very briefly, explain the circumstances which have made this application necessary.

"About five years ago – on the 16th August 1928, to be exact – Lotta Schiller executed a will leaving the whole of her very small property, about £300 in all, to her friend, Barbara Dalton; or, if Barbara should die before her, to Barbara's younger sister Linda. At about the same time, Barbara made a will in similar terms with the difference that she gave her chattels, excepting her violin, to Linda. The violin, with the residue of her estate, about £250, was left to Lotta. Thus, at the time, these two wills were quite unimportant. But on the 28th of May 1930, a certain Mr Charles Montagu died, and it then appeared that by his will a sum of £20,000 was left to Barbara Dalton and a similar sum to Linda. These bequests seem to have been quite unexpected by the beneficiaries, and it may have been that Barbara might have made some modification of her will if there had been time. But there was not. For some reason, a considerable delay occurred in the probate of Mr Montagu's will, and in the meantime Barbara died. Then, since Lotta Schiller was the residuary legatee under Barbara's will, the further sum of £20,000 accrued to her.

"But now a new difficulty arose. When it came to distributing Mr Montagu's estate, the whereabouts of Lotta could not be discovered. The usual advertisements were issued but there was no response. So, for a time, the matter remained in abeyance; it was not certain that she was alive and there was the added difficulty that, not only could the money not be paid to her, but no evidence existed that she was entitled to it, since it could not even be proved that she had been alive at the time of Barbara's death.

"Then came an announcement in the papers of Lotta's sensational disappearance and the suspicion that she had been murdered; and the astonishing fact transpired that, all this time, she had been living in lodgings at 39 Jacob Street, Hampstead Road. Either she had never seen the advertisements or – which seems incredible – had ignored them. But, however that may have been, as soon as Barbara's executor became aware that Lotta either was, or had recently been, alive, he endeavoured to get into touch with her, but without success. Nor have his efforts, repeated from time to time, had any better results; and now, after the lapse of two years, since it appears nearly certain that Lotta Schiller is dead, Miss Linda Dalton, the surviving beneficiary under Lotta's will, acting on the advice of her solicitor, is applying to the court for permission to presume the death of the testatrix in order that the will may be proved. As the facts on which we rely in support of the application are principally those connected with the disappearance of the testatrix, I shall now proceed to a more detailed account of that incident.

"On the 16th of July 1930, Lotta Schiller engaged furnished rooms at 39 Jacob Street, Hampstead Road. She gave no references but paid a month's rent in advance; and that payment and all subsequent payments were made in cash although she had a banking account, which suggests that, for some reason unknown to us, she did not wish to disclose her whereabouts to any of her friends. This suggestion is supported by the fact that during the whole of her residence in Jacob Street she made no local acquaintances excepting Mr Pedley, an artist who lived next door, and Mr Polton and Mr Vanderpuye, both of whom were introduced to her by Mr Pedley.

"During this time she seems to have made a pretence of practising as an artist. But this must have been a mere pose, as we have evidence that her work was quite incompetent, which is not surprising, seeing that she had never previously been known to paint or even to draw. However, it enabled her to strike up an acquaintanceship with Mr Pedley which soon grew into definite friendship, and thereafter she used frequently to visit his studio. In this way she presently made the acquaintance of Mr William Vanderpuye, a barrister of the Inner Temple, who came to the studio to have his portrait painted by Mr Pedley. This new acquaintance soon ripened into a quite intimate friendship, accompanied on her side by unabashed flirtation and on his, perhaps, by real affection."

I need not report the rest of Mr Lorimer's opening, since it dealt with matters with which we are familiar and which have already been recorded. In close and conscientious detail he described all the circumstances connected with Lotta Schiller's disappearance, including the murder of the ill-fated Emma Robey and the search by the police for Lotta, the discovery of the relics, and, finally and at considerable length, the exploration of the ancient British camp and the various efforts which had been made during the last two years to get into communication with Lotta.

Meanwhile, since I was not much concerned with the speech, I entertained myself by observing what was going on in the court; watching the judge, who was listening with an air of intense concentration to the counsel's recital, the one or two strangers who drifted in by the swing door and soon drifted out again, and especially Mr Snuper. Not that he offered much entertainment. At first he had seated himself directly behind Mr Schiller, but had gradually worked his way along the bench, apparently to get nearer to the speaker, and there he sat listening open-mouthed, seeming to be as much engrossed with Lorimer's recital as the judge himself. As to Mr Schiller, after the opening statement, he appeared to take little interest in the proceedings, having, no doubt, heard it all before. Most of the time he sat with his eyes closed, his head reposing restfully against the high back of the seat as if he were asleep; though, from time to time, he opened his eyes and even raised his head to look about him, but subsided almost immediately into his former semi-somnolent state.

It was during one of these temporary awakenings that a very odd thing happened. Mr Lorimer had come to the end of his narrative and was just beginning his argument, when Mr Schiller opened his eyes and looked drowsily at the counsel. Then, suddenly, his eyes opened wide and a most strange expression of dismay appeared on his face. I looked at him in astonishment. He seemed to be making an effort to move, but his head remained fixed as if it were attached to the back of the seat. Almost immediately his predicament was observed by Mr Snuper, who hastily slid along the seat towards him, at the same time fumbling in his pocket. I heard him murmur, "Don't move, sir," and some other words which I could not make out, and, as he spoke, I saw him quickly open a pair of folding pocket scissors. Then, with these in his hand, he leaned over the back of the seat, and the next moment the prisoner was free, smiling a little wrily, tenderly feeling the back of his head, and looking round curiously at the spot on the bench-back which Snuper was now carefully scraping with a pocket knife.

What he was scraping I could not see, but there must have been some foreign matter on the bench-back, for I saw him hold up the knife for Mr Schiller's inspection and then wipe it on an envelope which he produced from his pocket and returned there after having folded it. But even then he was not satisfied, for he continued his scraping, wiping the knife on another piece of paper, and finally, having felt the surface with his hand, gave it a vigorous rub with his handkerchief. Meanwhile, Mr Schiller, having acknowledged Snuper's services with a smile, moved along the bench, and, taking the precaution to examine the surface by sweeping his hand over it, leaned back and once more closed his eyes.

It was a queer episode, trivial enough to a casual observer and over in less than a minute; apparently unobserved, too, excepting that the judge cast one quick, inquisitive glance during the scraping operation. But its triviality was not quite convincing to me, and I continued to keep an eye on Mr Snuper notwithstanding that he was now once more the open-mouthed listener, and I noticed that he seemed to be imperceptibly creeping along the bench towards its farther end. He had just reached his goal when Mr Lorimer's speech came to an end, and, as the counsel sat down and preparations were being made for the reading of the affidavits, I saw him rise, and, having anxiously consulted the ancestral turnip, steal away quietly towards the swing door and vanish without a sound. So whatever his purpose might have been in attending at the hearing, it had apparently been achieved.

The first of the affidavits to be read was that of Thomas Pedley, and, as it set forth all the material facts, I did not quite see why Thorndyke had asked for his attendance for cross-examination. Nor did my colleague elicit any new facts of importance. His purpose was evidently to stress the significance of those facts that had been stated, and this he did most effectually.

"You have said, Mr Pedley," he began, "that you were somewhat intimately acquainted with Mrs Schiller for about five months. During that time, did you learn much about her as to her past history, her former places of abode, her friends and her relatives?"

"No," replied Pedley. "She never referred to her past at all, and she never mentioned any friends or relatives except her husband, and she only referred to him on one or two occasions, and then very slightly."

"Would you be able to recognize her handwriting?"

"No. I have never seen any writing of hers."

"But the signature on her pictures?"

"She did not sign her pictures. She used a conventional mark somewhat like a flower."

"Did you ever see a portrait of her husband or of herself?"

"I never saw a portrait of her husband, and the only portrait of herself that I ever saw was one that she drew for reduction to put into a locket that she was to give to Mr Vanderpuye."

"Was Mr Vanderpuye satisfied with her portrait?"

"No. He begged her either to let me paint her portrait or to ask Mr Polton to take her photograph. But she refused absolutely. She insisted on painting the portrait herself, and did so."

"Was her portrait a good likeness?"

"It was not a likeness at all. It bore no resemblance to her."

"Do you recognize this?" Thorndyke asked, handing a mounted photograph to the usher, who passed it to the witness.

"Yes," Pedley replied with a faint grin. "It is a photograph of Mrs Schiller's portrait of herself."

"And do you recognize this locket?"

As he spoke, Thorndyke produced from the suitcase Polton's mysterious wooden slide, on which Vanderpuye's locket had been fixed by a clip, opened to show the miniature and the hair, and provided with a pair of lenses, one over the portrait and the other (a Coddington) over the hair.

"Yes," replied Pedley as the usher handed it to him, "it is Mr Vanderpuye's locket, and it contains Mrs Schiller's portrait of herself and a specimen of her hair."

Here the locket and the photograph were passed up to the judge, who looked first at the photograph and smiled broadly and then peered through the lens at the miniature and compared it with the photograph.

"Yes," he remarked, "one can readily believe that this is not a good likeness, unless the testatrix was a very unusual-looking woman." Before returning the "exhibit" he applied his eye to the other lens and examined the hair. Then he turned sharply towards Pedley and asked:

"Was there anything at all peculiar about Mrs Schiller's hair?"

"Yes, my Lord," was the reply, "but I can't say exactly what it was. There seemed to be something unusual in its texture."

"Ha," said the judge, "so it appeared to me. However – "

Here he handed the locket to the usher, and, as the latter conveyed it to Mr Lorimer, he seemed to reflect on the circumstance as if it had suggested some idea to him. Lorimer, on the other hand, was not interested at all, bestowing only an impatient glance at the two exhibits and pushing them along the desk to Thorndyke, who passed them on to me. Naturally, remembering Pedley's description of Lotta's hair, I examined it with keen interest, but the light was not good enough, and the magnification not sufficient to show much detail. All that I could make out was a faintly speckled appearance quite unlike that of normal human hair. Reluctantly I returned the exhibits to Thorndyke, who, when he had put them back into the suitcase, resumed his cross-examination.

"Apart from this drawing of Mrs Schiller's, have you ever seen any portrait of her?"

"No portrait drawn from life. I once drew a portrait of her from memory."

"Is this the portrait that you drew?" asked Thorndyke, handing to the usher Pedley's own notebook, fixed open with a rubber band, and a photograph.

Pedley looked at them with a shy grin and replied:

"Yes. The original drawing is in the book, and this is a photograph of it."

"Is the portrait a good likeness?"

"I should say that it is a fairly good likeness. I think it would be recognizable by anyone who knew her."

The book and the photograph were passed up to the judge, who inspected them with apparent interest, and from him they were conveyed to Lorimer, who glanced at them almost contemptuously and pushed them along to Thorndyke. Evidently the learned counsel regarded my colleague's proceedings as a regrettable waste of time, and he made no secret of his relief when Thorndyke sat down, indicating that his cross-examination was finished.

As Lorimer made no sign of re-examining the witness, and it was now within a few minutes of the luncheon hour, the judge announced the adjournment; whereupon we all stood up; his Lordship whisked out by the private door, Polton hurried forward to seize the suitcase, and the occupants of the court trooped out by the swing door. We followed almost immediately, and, issuing into the Strand, set a course for our chambers by way of Devereux Court.

CHAPTER FIFTEEN

Mr Lorimer Objects

As we approached the end of Crown Office Row I observed with interest, but no surprise, a rustic-looking person who appeared to be making a leisurely survey of the old houses in King's Bench Walk. Needless to say it was Mr Snuper, apparently unconscious of our existence until Thorndyke, with the nearest approach to eagerness of which he was capable, accosted him. Then he turned with a start of surprise and he and my colleague drifted down the Walk together, apparently in earnest conversation. I slowed down my own progress to keep an eye on them, for I was devoured by curiosity as to Snuper's proceedings in court. But there was little to see and less to hear, for neither of them was addicted to shouting, and they were near the garden end of the Walk before any visible action took place. Then I thought I saw Snuper hand something to Thorndyke, but I could not see what it was, and, as it disappeared instantly into my friend's pocket, I judged that it was lost to me, at least for the time being; whereupon I abandoned my spying and hurried indoors in quest of lunch.

As the table had been laid by Polton's deputy, who was in the act of bringing in the food, I sat down to wait for Thorndyke's arrival; but when he looked in a few minutes later, it was only to beg me to proceed with the meal in his absence.

"I have a little job to do in the laboratory," he explained. "It will only take me a minute or two, but there is no need for you to wait."

Accordingly, as we had to be back in court punctually, I lifted the cover and fell to; but in less than five minutes Thorndyke joined me; and, looking at him critically, I seemed to detect, under his habitual impassiveness, an expression of satisfaction and even of elation, suggesting that the "little job" had turned out a success. Which led to speculations on my part as to the nature of that little job, and in particular, whether it had any connection with Mr Snuper's activities. But, of course, I asked no questions, and, equally of course, Thorndyke volunteered no information.

When the hearing was resumed after lunch, Mr Lorimer rose to request that Miss Linda Dalton's evidence might be taken next, to enable her to catch a train; and, as the judge raised no objection, she took her place in the witness box and her affidavit was read. Most of it was concerned with her claim under the will, but it finished up with the statement that she had last seen Lotta Schiller early in June 1930, and that since then she had received no communication from her nor had any knowledge of her until she heard of the disappearance.

When the reading was finished, Thorndyke rose to cross-examine.

"Do you happen to remember what kind of dress the testatrix was wearing when you last saw her?"

Miss Dalton smiled. "I do, indeed," she replied. "It was a very ugly dress and I thought it rather eccentric. The bodice and skirt were a sort of dull violet and there was a broad turndown collar of a deep orange and sleeves of the same colour. It was a dress that one could not forget."

"Did the testatrix play any musical instrument?"

"Yes. She played the violin."

"Did she spend much time practising?"

"Latterly, she did. My sister Barbara used to make a little income by playing in a small orchestra – at a cinema, I think – and she got Lotta an engagement at the same place, and they used to practise together; and, of course, she was playing for some hours every day in the orchestra."

"You will, of course, remember her appearance quite well. Will you look at this portrait and tell me whether you consider it a good likeness?" As he spoke he handed to the usher a photograph which I saw was the reproduction of Pedley's drawing.

Miss Dalton looked at it rather blankly.

"Is this supposed to be a portrait of Lotta?" she asked; "because I don't think it can be. I can't discover the faintest resemblance to her."

Glancing at Lorimer, I thought I detected a faint smile on his face. The judge, on the other hand, looked surprised and keenly interested; and, when the photograph was passed up to him, he examined it closely, turned it over to examine the back, on which a number had been pencilled, and made a note.

Meanwhile, Thorndyke had produced a small portfolio which was handed to the witness.

"In that portfolio," said Thorndyke, "are half a dozen photographs. Will you look through them and see whether any of them resemble Lotta Schiller?"

Miss Dalton glanced quickly at the first two which came to hand but at the third she paused. Then she took it out and said:

"This is a portrait of Lotta Schiller; a very odd one, but an excellent likeness. And so is this other one," she added, taking it out and holding it up.

"You feel no doubt that those two photographs are portraits of Lotta Schiller?"

"None whatever. They are both unmistakable."

The two portraits were now passed up to the judge, who examined them with intense interest and compared them minutely with Pedley's drawing. When he had looked at the backs and made his notes, he passed them down but still seemed to reflect with a rather puzzled air, and when they reached me I could understand his surprise, for the discrepancy between the drawing and the photograph seemed incredible in the case of a competent artist like Pedley. However, there was no time to consider the point, for Thorndyke had finished his cross-examination, and, a minute later Miss Dalton left the box, and, with a wave of the hand to Mr Schiller, tripped out of the court.

The next witness was Mrs Mitchens, whose affidavit set forth concisely the facts known to her relating to the case from the 16th of July 1930, when Lotta engaged the rooms, to the time of her disappearance, including the finding of Emma Robey's body. When the reading was finished, Thorndyke rose and led off with the question:

"Would you recognize Mrs Schiller's handwriting if you saw it?"

"No," was the reply. "I have never seen her handwriting; she had no occasion to write to me – at least she never did write, and, as she always paid her rent in cash, there were no cheques."

"Did she ever play any musical instrument?"

"No, never; but she had a violin. I didn't know it until after she had left, but then, as I was going through her things to store them, I found it under the bed."

"When you were going through her things, did you come across a dress with a violet bodice and skirt and orange-coloured sleeves and a broad collar of the same colour?"

"No indeed, sir; and I don't think Mrs Schiller would have worn such a dress. Her costumes were usually rather quiet and tasteful. But I only found one or two dresses and I am sure there was nothing of that kind among them."

"When Mrs Schiller engaged your rooms, did she give you any references?"

"No. She paid a month's rent in advance – in cash."

Here Thorndyke again produced the portfolio, and, when it had been handed to the witness, said:

"I want you to look through those portraits and see if you can find any that you think is like Mrs Schiller."

Mrs Mitchens turned over the first two portraits and then, as she came to the third, she picked it out, and, holding it up triumphantly, announced:

"That is Mrs Schiller."

The judge, who had been watching eagerly, now held out his hand for the identified portrait; and when it was passed up to him, he looked at it with intense interest, and, leaning out towards the witness, said:

"Now, Mrs Mitchens, are you perfectly sure that this portrait is really like Mrs Schiller?"

"I am perfectly sure, my Lord," she replied. "It's a speaking likeness."

On this his Lordship scribbled a note and then asked to have the portfolio handed up to him. When this had been done, he picked out two photographs and passed them down to the witness.

"Did you look at these two portraits?" he asked.

"Yes, my Lord," she replied, "but they are not Mrs Schiller. They are not the least bit like her."

The judge noted down the answer and having passed the portfolio back, nodded to Thorndyke, who now put his final question.

"Did Mrs Schiller ever receive visitors?"

"Only Mr Pedley and Mr Vanderpuye. I never saw anybody else."

On this, Thorndyke sat down, and when Mrs Mitchens had been released from the box, the name of the next witness – Mrs Bigham – was called, and a very unprepossessing woman advanced with something of a swagger. The evidence contained in her affidavit was of some importance in regard to the disappearance, but when it came to cross-examination, Thorndyke confined himself to the question of identification. Producing the inevitable portfolio, and passing it to her, he asked: "You say that you knew Mrs Schiller well by sight; do you think you would be able to recognize a portrait of her?"

"I am quite sure I should. I've got a rare memory for faces."

"Then will you look at the portraits in that portfolio and tell me whether any of them appears to be a portrait of Mrs Schiller?"

Mrs Bigham opened the portfolio with a judicial air, and, pursing up her lips, glared critically at the top photograph and thrust it over with the remark, "That ain't her," and passed on to the next, which she dealt with in the same fashion, and so on with the others until she came to the fifth; at which she gazed intently for an instant and then, picking it out and holding it aloft with the face towards us, exclaimed, "That's her."

I recognized it as the reproduction of Pedley's drawing, and so did the judge, who listened with rapt attention for the next question.

"You are quite sure that that portrait is really like Mrs Schiller?"

"Lord, yes," was the reply. "It's her spit image. I reckernized it at the first glance."

"There are two others that I want you to look at very carefully. They are numbered three and four."

The witness turned over the photographs and, selecting two, held them up for our and the judge's inspection. They were the portraits that had been identified by Miss Dalton.

"If you mean them," said Mrs Bigham, "I can tell you that they ain't Mrs Schiller. Nothink like her."

"You are quite sure of that?"

"Positive. They ain't no more like her than what I am."

With this answer Thorndyke appeared to be satisfied, for he asked no further questions; and, when he had sat down and Mrs Bigham had – somewhat reluctantly, I thought – vacated the box, I waited with some interest for the next item; and when it came, it was not altogether unexpected. For some time past I had noticed signs of restiveness on the part of the learned counsel for the applicant; and I was not surprised. For I had an uneasy feeling that Thorndyke had been taking some slight liberties with the legal proprieties. That was evidently Mr Lorimer's view, and he now gave expression to it.

"I am unwilling, my Lord," he began, "to occasion delay in the hearing, but there seems to have been a departure from customary procedure on the part of the opposition to which I feel bound to object. My learned friend appears to be raising an entirely new issue, of which we have had no notice, and supporting it by the production of documents – to wit, photographs – the existence of which has not been disclosed to us."

"Yes," the judge agreed with a smile; "the learned counsel does certainly seem to have sprung a little surprise on us."

Here he cast a somewhat quizzical glance at Thorndyke, who thereupon rose to reply.

"I shall not deny, my Lord, that some apology seems to be due to my learned friend, but I would submit that the raising of a new issue is only apparent. There are really two issues in this case; one is whether the person known as Lotta Schiller, who disappeared in Epping Forest, is, or is not, presumably dead; the other is whether that person was the testatrix. We have all assumed that Lotta Schiller of Jacob Street and Lotta Schiller, the testatrix, were one and the same person. There seemed to be no reason to question the identity. Nevertheless, I considered it desirable, *ex abundantia cautelae*, to test the correctness of our assumption; with the surprising result that there now seems to be some doubt whether we are not dealing with two different persons."

Lorimer and the judge both smiled appreciatively at Thorndyke's ingenious evasion, and his Lordship replied:

"That is quite true, though it does not answer the learned counsel's objection. But the question of identity has been raised, and it has evidently got to be settled before the other issue can be considered. So the problem now is, what is to be done about it? You mentioned at the opening that you might ask for an adjournment to enable you to file affidavits in answer or to call witnesses. Are you going to apply for an adjournment now?"

"I think, my Lord," replied Thorndyke, "that, in view of the conflict of testimony, some new evidence is required, and I should wish to call witnesses; but, as those witnesses would have to attend for cross-examination, there seems to be no object in filing affidavits, and time would be saved by not doing so. We are now at the weekend, and I submit that if your Lordship would consent and my learned friend would agree, he and I might confer in the interval and thereby avoid the necessity for an adjournment."

The judge looked a little dubious at this suggestion, but, as Lorimer signified his agreement and was evidently anxious to get on with the case, his Lordship consented to the arrangement and adjourned the hearing for the weekend.

As the court rose, Lorimer turned to Thorndyke, and spoke to him in a low tone. Then they walked together to the solicitors' table and apparently held a short discussion with Turner and Longford; at the end of which they came back and we set forth in company towards the Temple.

"We have arranged about the conference," said Thorndyke. "The solicitors prefer to leave the matter for counsel to settle, so Lorimer and I are going to dine together and then adjourn to his chambers for the powwow. That will leave us a free weekend."

Accordingly, when he had shed his wig and gown, he went off with his learned opponent and I saw him no more until about eleven o'clock, when he turned up at our chambers in obviously good spirits.

"Well," I asked, "how did you get on with Lorimer?"

"Admirably," he replied. "He is quite a reasonable fellow and I had no difficulty in getting him to see my point of view. I had to tell him more than I wanted to, but as we were alone it didn't matter."

"And what did you arrive at?"

"We agreed to treat the question of identity as a separate issue to be settled definitely before going on to the main issue. I made him understand that whichever way it went the result would not affect his case."

"The devil you did!" I exclaimed. "I should like you to make me understand that. It seems to me that if you make out your contention of two different persons, his case collapses at once."

He regarded me with an exasperating smile.

"That, you know, Jervis, is because you have not been following the evidence in this case, or have not reflected sufficiently on its significance. Turn it over in your mind between this and next Monday and see if you cannot anticipate the revelation that I hope to make at the next hearing."

With that tantalizing hint I had to be content. Of course, I did not trouble to "turn it over in my mind". I realized that Polton had been right as usual. Thorndyke's devilish machinations in his laboratory had been the prelude to "a little surprise for somebody"; and I was going to be one of the surprised.

CHAPTER SIXTEEN

Superintendent Miller Intervenes

Of what took place during the weekend I am not very clear. On the Saturday Thorndyke was out and about most of the day, making, as I assumed, his final arrangements; which assumption was confirmed by a late telephone message from Superintendent Miller asking me to "let the Doctor know that Miss Rendell had been warned and would attend in court on Monday". Who Miss Rendell might be I had no idea and I did not inquire. For the time being my curiosity was in abeyance.

One small piece of enlightenment I did indeed acquire. Finding Polton at a loose end in the laboratory, I attacked him facetiously on the subject of Mr Snuper's watch, which I suggested was a disgrace to an establishment that included on its staff a first-class artificer. "Really," I concluded, "I think you ought to provide him with something less prehistoric for the credit of the house. Just get him to show it to you."

Polton regarded me with a cunning and crinkly smile.

"I've seen it, sir; in fact I made it. But it isn't a watch, though it has hands that you can set to time for the sake of appearances. It is really a camera; but Mr Snuper carries his watch in another compartment of the same pocket."

"A camera!" I exclaimed. "But it can only be a mere toy."

"Well," Polton admitted, "it isn't much of a camera; just a makeshift. But it answers Mr Snuper's purpose, as you can use it anywhere without being noticed, and a poor photograph is, for him, better than no photograph. It is a record, you know, sir."

"And what sort of picture does it give?"

"Better than you would think, sir. The negative is half an inch by five-eighths, and it will bear enlarging up to four inches by five. It has a beautiful little lens and the definition is perfect. Perhaps you would like to see it. I've got it in for recharging."

He produced the illusive turnip from a drawer and exhibited it with excusable pride; for it was a miracle of ingenuity, with its arrangement for changing the film, which also set the shutter, and that for setting the hands. But almost more surprising were the tiny negatives, microscopically sharp, which Polton also showed me, and the clear and admirable enlargements; which caused me to view the turnip and its creator with a new respect.

The following day Thorndyke spent mostly in his private laboratory, making, as I supposed, some final preparations for the resumed hearing. But I had no idea what they might be, nor did I speculate on the subject. I had given the problem up, and reserved my curiosity for the promised revelation on the morrow.

Apparently I was not alone in this attitude, for, when we took our places in court on the Monday morning, I detected in Mr Lorimer an air of lively expectancy; and the judge, as soon as he had nipped into his seat, glanced at the counsel for the applicant with evident curiosity; whereupon Lorimer rose to make his announcement.

"During the weekend, my Lord, I have conferred with my learned friend, and we have agreed, with your Lordship's consent, to treat the question of identity as a separate issue, to be disposed of before taking any further evidence on the main issue."

"That seems a reasonable proceeding," said the judge. "Evidently it would be futile to consider the presumption of death until we know whose death it is sought to presume. Are there any new witnesses?"

"Yes, my Lord. I am calling Mr Carl Schiller, the testatrix's husband, whose affidavit has been filed. When he has given his evidence, as I have no other witnesses to identity, I have agreed that my learned friend should, with your Lordship's consent, produce his evidence forthwith."

The judge nodded, and thereupon Mr Schiller stepped into the witness box and stood there, listening attentively while his affidavit was read. It was quite short, setting forth merely that he had not seen or heard of, or from, his wife for more than three years, and that he had no knowledge whether she was alive or dead. When the reading was finished, Lorimer took the portfolio, which was handed to him by Thorndyke, and passed it across to the witness.

"There is some conflict of testimony, Mr Schiller," said he, "as to which of the portraits in this portfolio is a true portrait of your wife. Will you kindly look through them and see whether you can settle the question for us?"

Mr Schiller opened the portfolio and went systematically through the whole of its contents – some seven or eight photographs. Having looked at them all, he selected one and held it up for inspection; and I saw that it was Pedley's drawing, or rather the reproduction of it.

"This," said he, speaking with a perceptible German accent, "is the only one that seems to me to resemble my wife, and it is quite a fair likeness. The others I do not recognize at all."

I was a good deal surprised, and so, I think, was the judge; for Schiller's evidence directly contradicted that of Miss Dalton (who was not present on this occasion). However, there was nothing to be said as the witness had looked carefully through the whole set of photographs, and, as neither the judge nor Thorndyke questioned the evidence, the witness was released and returned to his seat, or rather to a seat at the extreme end of the bench, and Thorndyke called his first witness, a Mrs Matilda Wharton; whereupon a pleasant-looking elderly woman stepped into the box.

"What is your full address, Mrs Wharton?" Thorndyke asked.

"I live at 16 Corby Street, which is a turning out of the Linton Green Road."

"Have you ever been acquainted with Mrs Lotta Schiller?"

"Yes. She lodged with me for about three years."

"Did her husband live with her?"

"No. He travelled about a good deal, but when he was in London he used to call on her and they used to go out together. But he never lived in the house. I think he used to stay at hotels."

"On what kind of terms were they?"

"They seemed quite friendly though not affectionate; but shortly before she left there seemed to have been some sort of disagreement, for she became rather strange in her manner and appeared to avoid him."

"When, and in what circumstances, did she leave you?"

"She left me on the 13th of June 1930. She went out one morning and never came back; but she sent me a telegram saying that she had gone away and would write. She never did write, but a couple of days later her husband came to the house and told me that she had been suddenly called abroad and that she would not be coming back for some months. He paid what was owing and took away her belongings, including her violin. I have never seen or heard of her since."

"Was there anything remarkable about the manner of her departure?"

"Well, it was rather strange. She said nothing about going away before she went out, and she had nothing with her but the things that she stood up in."

"During the time that she lodged with you, did she receive many visitors?"

"No. The two Miss Daltons used sometimes to call to see her or to take her out; and once or twice Mr Montagu – the poor gentleman who was murdered – came to see her or to fetch her out."

Here Thorndyke gave me – and not me alone – the first of the surprises by producing from the suitcase a small oil painting, which I recognized as a sketch of Pedley's that I had seen hanging on the wall of Polton's private room.

"I want you, Mrs Wharton," said he, passing it across to her, "to look at this painting and tell me whether the figures in it suggest any particular persons to you."

The witness examined the painting closely and then at arm's length.

"Of course," she said cautiously, "I can't recognize any of these people, but the woman looks to me very much like Mrs Schiller."

"In what respect is she like Mrs Schiller?"

"I think it is chiefly the dress. It's rather a peculiar dress and Mrs Schiller had one just like it; in fact she was wearing that very dress on the morning that she went away. But the figure is like her, too, and the colour of her hair. Still, it is only a resemblance. I don't say it actually is her. You see, there are no features to recognize it by."

"And as to the other figures; do they seem to suggest anybody that you have known?"

Mrs Wharton again looked at the picture critically. At length she replied, in a rather doubtful tone:

"It's only a mere guess as they have their backs to us, but I think the taller of the two men rather reminds me of Mr Montagu. I often used to see him in the street and he was always dressed in this way, and he had a habit of gesticulating with his umbrella as he talked, as this man seems to be doing; and the umbrella in the picture seems to have an ivory handle as his had. And he seems to be about the right height, comparing him with the other man. Still, I don't profess to be able to recognize him."

"Of course you can't," said Thorndyke; "but I must compliment you on your memory and powers of observation. And now I will try you with something that it is more possible to be certain about."

Here he produced the inevitable portfolio and passed it across to her. Meanwhile the picture was handed up to the judge, who looked at it curiously and returned it; and I noticed that Lorimer examined it with more than his usual faint interest in exhibits. But attention was now focused on Mrs Wharton, who, at Thorndyke's request, was looking very carefully through the collection of portraits. When she had examined them all, she very deliberately selected two, which she held up with their faces towards us, and which I could see were the two that Miss Dalton had recognized.

"These," said she, "are portraits of Mrs Schiller. They aren't very flattering, but they are quite good likenesses."

The judge inspected them with a surprised and rather puzzled expression and then glanced at Thorndyke; who, as he received the portfolio, took from it Pedley's drawing and passed it across to the witness.

"What do you say to this? It is supposed to be a portrait of Mrs Schiller. Is it a good likeness?"

The witness looked at it with evident surprise. After a prolonged inspection she handed it back, shaking her head.

"I don't think it can have been meant for Mrs Schiller," said she. "It doesn't seem to me to be like her at all. It looks like quite a different person."

This evidently completed his Lordship's perplexity, for he asked that the portfolio should be passed up to him, and, when he had it, he laid the three portraits in a row on his desk and made a prolonged and careful comparison. But clearly he could make nothing of them, for he finally gathered them up, and, glancing at Thorndyke with raised eyebrows, handed back the portfolio.

Among the new arrivals in court I had noticed a rather prim-looking lady dressed in a neat and becoming uniform which associated itself in my mind with the idea of "chokee" – formerly known familiarly as "the jug". And so it turned out to be; for, when Mrs Wharton had vacated the box – there being no cross-examination – the lady in question took her place, and, facing Thorndyke with professional composure, introduced herself as Miss Julia Rendell, a Female Officer at Holloway Prison. Thereupon, Thorndyke produced the everlasting portfolio; but he did not on this occasion pass it across to the witness. Instead, he opened it, and, selecting from the collection the two photographs which Mrs Wharton had identified, sent them across for the lady's inspection.

"Do you recognize those two photographs, Miss Rendell?" he asked.

"Yes," she replied promptly. "They are incomplete copies of two prison portraits of a prisoner named, or known as, Louisa Saunders."

"Do you recognize these two?" he asked, handing over two other photographs which he had just fished out of the suitcase.

"Yes. They are the original portraits, or facsimile copies of them."

"Are they good likenesses of Louisa Saunders?"

"Yes, quite good. I recognized them at once."

"When did you first see Louisa Saunders?"

"On the 13th of June 1930 at the evening receptions. She had been arrested that morning and remanded in custody."

"Do you know any particulars of the charge on which she was arrested?"

"Yes. I accompanied her, with some other remands, to the police court and was present at the hearing. She was charged with having uttered a forged one-pound note and with having in her possession four other forged notes."

"Did she plead 'Guilty' or 'Not guilty'?"

" 'Not guilty'. She said that the notes had been given to her in a bundle and that she had no suspicion of their being bad notes."

"Was any evidence given to show that she knew the notes to be bad notes?"

"No. The only evidence against her was that she had offered the bad note in payment for some goods that she had bought, and that she had the other notes in her possession. But, as she would not give any account of herself or say where she had obtained the notes or who had given them to her, she was convicted and sentenced to six months' imprisonment."

"Is that, in your experience, a usual sentence for this offence?"

"No. I should say that it was an unusually lenient one."

"Did the prisoner give any address?"

"No. She would give no account of herself whatever except her name."

"Was there any evidence that Louisa Saunders was her real name?"

"None beyond the fact that her clothing was marked with the initials 'L S'."

"Was she a married woman or a spinster?"

"She refused any information about herself, but, as she was wearing a wedding ring, we entered her as a married woman."

"While she was in prison, was her hair cut?"

"No. It was rather short when she came in, and, as she was perfectly clean, there was no necessity."

"Do you remember how long it was when she was discharged?"

"So far as I remember, it was about down to her shoulders."

"On what date was she discharged?"

"On the 12th of December 1930, at noon."

"I suppose you don't know whether anybody met her when she left the prison?"

"As a matter of fact, I do. I happened to be going out of the prison at the same time, and I saw a man who seemed to be waiting for her at the corner of Hilmarton Road. At any rate, she crossed the road and joined him."

"Do you remember what he was like?"

"Not very clearly. I did not notice him particularly and should not know him if I were to see him. All that I remember about him is that he seemed to be a fairly well-dressed man and rather short."

"You saw the prisoner, Saunders, at receptions on the day of her arrest; you accompanied her to the police court; and you saw her in the street when she left the prison. Do you remember how she was dressed on those occasions?"

"I remember that she was wearing a rather conspicuous dress with sleeves a different colour from the bodice and skirt."

Here Thorndyke produced Pedley's sketch and passed it across to the witness.

"I want you," said he, "to look carefully at that picture and tell me whether it recalls anything to your memory."

The witness looked at the painting attentively for a few moments, and then replied:

"The woman in the picture reminds me strongly of Louisa Saunders. She is like her in figure and in the colour of her hair, and the dress is exactly like the one that Saunders was wearing when she came to the prison and when she left it. Of course, I can't identify her as Saunders because the face is not recognizable, but otherwise the resemblance seems to be complete."

This concluded the examination-in-chief, and, as Thorndyke sat down, Lorimer rose to cross-examine.

"Is it not rather remarkable," he asked, "that you should have so clear a recollection of this prisoner after the lapse of so long a time?"

"I don't think so," she replied. "A prison officer is expected to be able to remember and recognize persons, and Saunders was a rather unusual prisoner. Most of the women who come in at receptions are of the lowest class; and then the dress that she was wearing was a distinctly striking one. And," the witness added with a deprecating smile, "a female prison officer, like any other woman, is apt to have a good memory for an unusual dress."

"This one," his Lordship remarked, "certainly seems to have made a deep impression on the ladies who had seen it, judging by the evidence, as they all remembered it clearly. But the photographs give a very misleading rendering of it, though one can see that the sleeves and collar are of a different colour from the bodice. The painter has still some advantage over the photographer."

"In the matter of colour, my Lord," said Lorimer. "Not in respect of personal identity. I do not admit that the figure in the painting has been identified."

"No, no, no!" exclaimed the judge. "I was referring only to the colour of the dress. No one has suggested that there has been actual identification of the person."

" With this, Lorimer opened a new subject. You have said that you were present at the police court proceedings. Was any evidence produced to show that the accused had any guilty knowledge of the character of the notes?"

"None except the fact that she had the notes in her possession and had passed one of them."

"Was there any evidence that her explanation of the way she came by those notes could not be true?"

"No. But the trouble was that she refused to say where she got the notes or who gave them to her.

On receiving this answer Lorimer discreetly closed his cross-examination, having apparently made his point, which seemed to be that the accused might quite possibly have been innocent, the conviction notwithstanding.

Why he should stress this point I could not quite see, unless he was beginning to entertain the same suspicion as that which was creeping into my own mind.

I had listened to Miss Rendell's evidence with intense interest; indeed, I had been considerably startled, not only by the identification but by the curious coincidence of dates. But my interest was feeble compared to his Lordship's. The new identification had evidently astonished him, and, when the date of the prisoner's arrest was mentioned he hurriedly turned over his notes and made some comparisons; and when the photographs were handed up to him, he spread them out in a row and rapidly compared them.

There was no need for a prolonged examination, as I realized when they reached me, for the two pairs appeared to be from the same negatives. The only difference was that the "originals" showed a black batten with the prisoner's name chalked on it fixed across the chair and occupying the foot of the portrait, whereas, in the "incomplete copies" the batten had been masked out.

But there were other interested listeners besides the judge and me. Mr Schiller, although he still made a show of keeping his eyes closed, was evidently wide awake. Inspector Blandy followed the evidence with close attention; and Superintendent Miller, who had slipped quietly into the court some time previously with my friend, Dr Oldfield, was listening and watching attentively, though he must have known all about Miss Rendell's evidence.

As the latter lady made her dignified exit from the box, the judge cast a quick, expectant glance at Thorndyke; then the name of the next witness was called, and Dr James Oldfield came forward and presented himself to be sworn and to give evidence.

In his case, as in that of the previous witness, the examination began with the passing across of the two "incomplete copies".

"Will you look at those two photographs, Dr Oldfield," said Thorndyke, "and tell us whether they seem to be portraits of any person whom you have ever seen?"

Oldfield examined the photographs closely for nearly a minute; and as he looked at them, there stole gradually over his face an expression of surprised recognition. At length he replied cautiously:

"These photographs appear to me to be portraits of Emma Robey, the woman who was murdered about two years ago at 39 Jacob Street, Hampstead Road."

"Can you say definitely that they are portraits of Emma Robey?"

"I don't like to swear, positively, that they are. The woman had been dead about three weeks when I examined her body, and some changes had occurred. But I feel a strong conviction that these are portraits of her. Would it be permissible for me to refer to my notes?"

"When did you take the notes?" the judge asked.

"I made them in the mortuary in the presence of the body, and I compared and verified them, point by point, after I had written them."

"Then you may certainly refer to them," said the judge.

On this, Oldfield produced from his pocket a small book, and, opening it at a marked place, made a systematic comparison of the notes and the photographs. When he had finished, he announced:

"I have compared the description in the notes, detail by detail, with the photographs, and I find that they agree in every respect except one. That is that the hair in the photograph is considerably shorter than the hair of the corpse when I examined it."

"Did you note the exact length of the hair?"

"I did not measure it, but I noted it in the description as just down to the shoulders."

"With that exception, you find complete agreement between your description and the photographs?"

"Yes; the agreement is complete in every detail."

"And, apart from the written description, do you recognize the portraits as being like Emma Robey?"

"Yes. As soon as I saw the photographs I felt that they were portraits of somebody whom I had seen; and when I tried to recall who that somebody was, I suddenly realized that she was Emma

Robey. I may say that I have now no doubt that these are really portraits of her."

At this point my attention was attracted by Mr Schiller; who had suddenly awakened, and now, pulling out his watch and glancing at it with a startled air, stood up abruptly, and, with a little bow to the judge, began to make his way slowly and silently towards the door.

As he rose, so also did Inspector Blandy and Superintendent Miller, both of whom moved off unobtrusively in the same direction. I followed the three figures eagerly with my eyes as they converged on the exit, Schiller leading and slightly quickening his pace.

One by one they passed out, and as the door swung to noisily, after the last of them, the judge (who had also been observing the exodus) took the photographs in his hand and remarked:

"This is a most extraordinary affair. These portraits have now been confidently identified as three different persons."

"My submission is, my Lord," said Thorndyke, "that those three are one and the same person."

"That would seem," the judge began; but at this moment a heavy thump on the swing door sent it flying inwards, and, through the opening came a sound as of several persons scuffling, mingled with low but excited voices.

Then, in the midst of the confused noises, a pistol shot rang out.

And as the door swung to, the sounds became more muffled and distant. After a short interval, at a sign from the judge, the usher hurried towards the door, and, having peered out cautiously, disappeared, and the door swung to after him.

There was a brief silence during which we all waited expectantly. Then the usher reappeared, in company with Superintendent Miller, and announced: "This officer, my Lord, has a communication to make to your Lordship."

The judge made no comment but looked inquiringly at Miller, who stepped up to the bench and made his "communication".

"I have to inform your Lordship," said he, "that Mr Carl Schiller has just been arrested on a charge of having murdered his wife."

"Is it permissible," asked the judge, who seemed more interested than surprised, "for you to give any particulars of the charge?"

"It is quite permissible, my Lord," replied Miller, "as the prisoner will be brought before a magistrate immediately. The arrest was made on an information sworn by Dr Thorndyke, and the charge is that the accused did, on the 12th of December 1930, at Number 39 Jacob Street, Hampstead Road, murder his wife, Lotta Schiller, by forcibly administering poison to her."

"Ah," said the judge, "thirty-nine, Jacob Street. Then the Epping Forest tragedy, if there ever was one, is irrelevant to the case of this poor woman?"

"Quite irrelevant, my Lord," Miller agreed.

The judge reflected for a few moments; then, addressing the court, that is to say the counsel and solicitors, he said:

"You have heard this officer's remarkable announcement. Obviously this new information involves at least the suspension of these proceedings. If there is evidence that Lotta Schiller was murdered, there must be evidence that she is dead; and if her death can be proved, that proof excludes the idea of presuming it. The hearing will therefore be adjourned *sine die.*"

On this, we all rose. The witnesses – there were no spectators – faded out of the court, and we were preparing to depart also. But the judge made no sign of retiring. Instead, he craned out of his seat towards Thorndyke, and, in a low voice, suggested his desire for a little further enlightenment.

Accordingly Thorndyke stepped over to the bench, and Lorimer and I had no false delicacy about following him.

"Well, Doctor," said the judge, "as you seem to have been making use of the Probate Court for your own purposes, I think that the least you can do is to satisfy our legitimate curiosity. Now, what I want to know is, what has happened to the woman who personated Lotta Schiller at 39 Jacob Street, and what part did she take in the crime?"

"There was no woman, my Lord," replied Thorndyke. "The person who was known at Jacob Street as Lotta Schiller was Carl Schiller, dressed and made up as a woman."

"God bless me!" exclaimed the judge, "it sounds incredible. I suppose you have clear evidence as to the identity?"

"Yes," Thorndyke replied. "The two persons are identical in their physical characteristics; in size, eye colour, form of features, and in the exact shape of the ears."

"That won't carry you very far in support of a capital charge," the judge commented.

"No," Thorndyke agreed. "It would be of no use excepting for corroboration. But there is one piece of evidence that is quite conclusive. Providence has been kinder to us than to the criminal. It happens that Carl Schiller has a most unusual type of hair."

"Ha!" the judge exclaimed. "There is something queer about the hair, is there? I thought, when I looked at the locket, that it was odd-looking hair. Very unusual, is it?"

"It is more than that, my Lord. It presents one of the rarest of anomalies. This ringed hair, as it is called, each hair being marked by alternate light and dark bands, is of such extreme rarity that, in the whole of my professional experience, I have never before met with a case. Only a very few examples exist in museums."

"That is farly impressive," said the judge. "But the specimen in the locket, which, I suppose, is what you rely on, appertains to the lady. Do you know as a fact that Carl Schiller has hair of this character?"

"I do," replied Thorndyke.

"There, again, Providence has been kind to us. During the last hearing, a very curious accident happened in court. Mr Schiller's head became in some way stuck to the back of the bench, and it was necessary for a person who was sitting in the bench behind him to cut the hair in order to liberate him. The piece of hair which was cut off came into my possession, and, of course, as soon as it was examined with the microscope, the murder was, literally, out."

The judge's eyes twinkled. "Ha!" said he. "Now I wonder how that gentleman's head became stuck to the bench? Do you happen to know?"

"I don't actually know," Thorndyke replied, "but I have certain suspicions."

"So have I," said his Lordship.

CHAPTER SEVENTEEN

Observations on the Art of Disguise

It might perhaps be of interest, if space permitted, to describe in detail the trial of Carl Schiller for the murder of his wife, Lotta. But space does not permit, nor is there any need for such description, since all the facts brought forward in evidence against him are known to the reader of this narrative. It is, however, one thing to know the facts, but quite another to perceive their application or the inferences deducible from them. I had known all the facts that were known to Thorndyke; but it was not until I had heard him reconstruct the course of the investigation that I perceived their exact connections and understood how, by piecing them together, he had evolved his startling conclusion.

The trial had run its course to its inevitable end. The jury, without leaving the box, had brought in their verdict of "Guilty"; the judge had pronounced sentence of death; and the prisoner had descended the stairs from the dock, vanishing for ever from the sight of men; and the spectators, having thus witnessed the fall of the curtain, rose and began to surge out through the open doors. I followed them as soon as I could, and, presently, in the great hall, encountered Polton, Pedley, and Vanderpuye, whom I joined to wait for Thorndyke.

For my part, I had looked on at the unfolding of the drama, at the piling up of the deadly evidence with no single twinge of pity or compunction, even when the judge had assumed the black cap and pronounced the final words of doom. But it was otherwise with our two friends. For them it had been impossible, as they looked on the white-faced brute in the dock, facing his accusers like a caged wild beast, to forget the ties of friendship and even of affection that had once bound them to him. Looking at their pale and troubled faces, I realized that it had been a painful ordeal which had left them shocked and saddened. So, too, Thorndyke, when he came out and joined us, was instantly aware of their distressed state of mind, and, with his invariable sympathy and kindliness, sought for some means of distracting their thoughts from their late painful experience.

"I am wondering, Polton," said he, "whether the resources of 5A King's Bench Walk are equal to an impromptu dinner for five?"

"The resources of Number 5A, sir, are unlimited," was the confident reply, in a tone of persuasive eagerness.

"Then," said Thorndyke, "I am in a position to ask our two friends to give us the very great pleasure of their society this evening."

He glanced inquiringly at Pedley and Vanderpuye, both of whom accepted the invitation with almost pathetic promptitude; whereupon Polton excused himself and darted off like a lamplighter, while we, since it was still some time short of any reasonable dinner hour, meandered down the Old Bailey to Ludgate Hill in search of a much-needed cup of tea. When we had disposed of this, with as much lively conversation as Thorndyke and I could produce for the occasion, we set forth at a leisurely pace for the Temple by way of the Embankment.

Polton's estimate of the resources of 5A King's Bench Walk was justified by the result, though I suspected that the Rainbow or some other excellent Fleet Street tavern had been pressed into service. But however that may have been, the dinner to which we sat down in due course did credit to the establishment, handsomely supported as it was by the products of our own cellar, which Polton had raided to some purpose (though his own place at the table was marked ingloriously by a bottle of lemonade). The unobtrusive service was conducted by William, Polton's domestic understudy, aided by a mysterious stranger of waiter-like aspect, who lurked in the background performing curious feats of legerdemain with dishes and covers but never intruding into William's domain.

The opening stages of a good dinner "when beards wag all" are not adapted for sustained conversation. So, for a time, what talk there was concerned itself for the most part with cheerful trivialities. But at the back of all our minds was the drama which we had seen played out to its tragic end a few hours before, and inevitably it had to come to the surface sooner or later. But it was not until the manducatory pace had slowed down and the wine had circulated that the subject, hitherto taboo, was broached, and even then only indirectly.

"Before I forget," said Thorndyke, "let me make restitution." He produced from his pocket Pedley's notebook and Vanderpuye's locket, and, pushing them across the table towards their respective owners, added: "There is no need for me to tell you how much I am indebted to you both for the loan and the use of these things. You have heard the evidence and you know what invaluable light they threw on the mystery."

Pedley took up the book and pocketed it without remark; but Vanderpuye hesitated, looking at the little bauble as it lay on the table with intense disfavour. Eventually, however, he picked it up and dropped it into his pocket with something of a gesture of disgust.

"Your property, Polton," said Thorndyke, "is, as you see, on the mantelpiece, and is now at your disposal, with many thanks for the loan."

"You were very welcome, sir," replied Polton, "but I think that the loan benefited me more than it did you. It has given the picture a new interest for me, whereas I don't see that you got much help from it except for the colour of the lady's dress."

"I think," said Thorndyke, "that when you hear the whole story, as you shall some day, you will find that the picture played a more important part in the investigation than you have realized."

"If it did," said I, "there is at least one point that I have missed, for I had the same idea as Polton; in fact I rather wondered why you produced the picture in court at all."

"The principal object in producing it," he replied, "was to help the witnesses to remember the dress. The photographs gave no such help; but the dress was of vital importance in fixing the dates. A further purpose was to ascertain whether the figure of the woman was recognizably like Lotta Schiller."

"Yes; but you seem to hint at some other function that the picture served; and you hint at some future occasion when we shall hear the whole story of the investigation. But why a future occasion? We are all here, and I think we are all in the same condition as to our interest in the case. Speaking for myself, I am still mystified. I have heard all the evidence and found it perfectly conclusive; but what I cannot understand is how you came to build up the whole scheme of evidence out of nothing. Where did you get your start? What first put you on the track? It seemed to me that from the moment when Penfield proposed the case, you went straight ahead as if you had a considered theory already in your mind."

"But that, in effect," he replied, "was the actual position. When Penfield informed us of the impending application, he was not, so far as I was concerned, opening a new subject, but only introducing a new phase of a problem that I had already considered in some detail. But the story of the investigation is a rather long one, and, if you all really want to hear it, you had better draw up your armchairs round the fire and prepare yourselves to listen in comfort."

There was no doubt about the desire to hear the story. Polton was "on broken bottles" of curiosity, and our two guests, each in his own way, were eager to learn how the tangled skein had been unravelled. Accordingly we drew the armchairs up to the fire and Polton placed conveniently by them the little tables with their decanters and cigar boxes, while William and the alien waiter – who now came out into the open – swiftly cleared the table of its now irrelevant burden. Then, when the two operators had finally departed, Thorndyke began his story.

"The account of the actual investigation has a necessary prologue; necessary because it explains how suspicion first entered my mind in the absence of any positive suggestion from without. Jervis knows, because I have often told him, that in the early days when I had little or no practice, I used to occupy myself in the study of hypothetical cases. I would consider how a particular crime could be planned and executed with the greatest amount of security against detection; and, when I had established the principles I would apply them by working out in detail an imaginary crime. Then I would study this crime to discover its weak points and the signs by which it might be recognized in real life. The method was a really valuable one, for a hypothetical crime, systematically studied, yields practically as much experience as a real one.

"Now, the most important crime from a medico-legal point of view is the deliberately planned murder. Accordingly, I gave special attention to this type of crime, and, after trying over a number of different methods, I decided that by far the most secure from the chance of detection was that of creating a fictitious person. It seemed to me that if this method were skilfully planned and efficiently carried out it would be almost undetectable."

"I am not quite sure," said Vanderpuye, "that I understand what you mean by creating a fictitious person."

"Well, let us take an imaginary case. We will suppose that a man whom we will call John Doe has some reason for wishing to eliminate a certain person. That person may be an unwanted wife. John Doe may wish to marry another woman; or he may be haunted by a blackmailer. The reason, whatever it may be, is a permanent one. The person whom he desires to eliminate is an abiding hindrance to his happiness or a menace to his safety. Now, supposing him to adopt my method, let us follow his procedure.

"He begins by assuming a disguise which so far alters his appearance that he would not be easily recognized by anyone who knew him, and that gives him certain new and easily recognizable characteristics."

"That would not be particularly easy," I remarked.

"It would not," Thorndyke agreed, "but we will consider that question separately. Now, we will assume that John Doe has so disguised himself and has taken a new name. Let us say, Richard Roe.

Under that name he takes up his abode in a neighbourhood where he is not known and there assumes a character which will bring him into fairly close contact with a limited number of people. He may open a shop or an office or practise some kind of avocation whereby he will become well known by the inhabitants of the neighbourhood and more intimately known by a few; and in that way he will carry on for some months, at least, until he has become a well-established character in the locality.

"Then he proceeds to commit his crime, at his own selected time and place. He is not hurried. He can make his arrangements at his leisure. He has no occasion to take any measures for concealment of the identity of the criminal. On the contrary; the more definitely the crime is connected with Richard Roe, the more perfect will be his security. All that is necessary is to avoid any actual witnesses of the crime or any need for him to escape quickly. Probably the most perfect method would be to lure the victim to his premises, and, having committed the murder, to lock the corpse up in those premises and quietly take his departure.

"He is still, you see, not hurried or in any danger. He simply sheds his disguise and now has no connection with the murder. Some days, or perhaps weeks, will elapse before the body is discovered; in which time he can go abroad or to a distance, write to his friends describing his travels, and, in due course, after a discreet interval, return to his usual places of resort and to the circle of his old acquaintances.

"Meanwhile the body has been discovered and the police are in full cry after the murderer, Richard Roe. They have an excellent detailed description of him, vouched for by a number of reliable witnesses who knew him quite intimately and would certainly recognize him if he were produced. But he never is produced; for, in the moment when John Doe shed his disguise, Richard Roe ceased to exist. The police are, in fact, searching for a purely imaginary person."

"Yes," said I, "it certainly appears to be a very perfect scheme. But yet there seems to me to be one snag. The victim is in some way connected with John Doe, and it might be noticed that the murder is very opportune for him. For instance, the murdered person might be his unwanted wife, with whom he is known to have been on bad terms."

"I don't think that there is much in that," Thorndyke replied. "You see, the identity of the murderer is not in question. He is a known person – Richard Roe – and, consequently, no suspicion can possibly fall on any other person. Still, the matter is worth noticing. It would undoubtedly add to the murderer's safety if the corpse also could be disguised or rendered unrecognizable. We will bear that fact in mind. And now let us consider the question of disguise, remembering that a mere stage make-up would be useless; that it would have to be efficient out of doors in daylight and that it would have to be used constantly over a considerable period of time.

"To change a man's appearance so completely that his friends or acquaintances would not recognize him is not easy. But it can be done. There used to be a wig-maker in Russell Street, Covent Garden, who made a regular profession of the art of disguising, and who was able to produce the most surprising transformations. But his methods were rather elaborate, the results not at all comfortable to the subject, and, in continuing cases, the clients had to attend daily to have the make-up renewed. This would hardly do for a long-term disguise, and certainly not for an intending murderer. He would have to do his own make-up, and it would require to be reasonably comfortable.

"However, we need not dwell on the difficulties of purely male disguise, for there is another kind that is comparatively easy and extremely convincing; change of sex. When it is possible, it is completely effective; for a marked change of appearance can be produced with very little actual disguise. And the change of appearance becomes of less importance, since the change of sex creates a new personality. To his new acquaintances John Doe is a woman, and if any of them should subsequently meet him, a slight resemblance to that woman would pass unnoticed.

"Moreover, the present fashions are favourable to such personation. Women's hair is worn in all sorts of ways, from a close crop to a mop of fuzz; and it is not only waved or curled artificially but is also dyed or bleached, quite openly and without exciting remark. Again, there is the extensive make-up, which is almost universal and is a recognized fashion; the painted lips, the tinted and powdered cheeks, the false eyelashes and the pencilled eyebrows. All these materially alter the appearance, and by management could be made to alter it profoundly. A man, by simply dressing as a woman and adopting a feminine mode of wearing the hair, with some use of the lipstick and the eyebrow pencil, would at once be considerably disguised; probably enough to pass unrecognized by persons who knew him only slightly; and if he had previously worn a beard or moustache, his appearance would be totally changed. Even his friends would not recognize him.

"But it is a method that is subject to very severe limitations. To certain types of men it would be impracticable. For a tall man it would be very unsuitable. A six-foot woman would be rather remarkable; but conspicuousness is what a disguised man would need to avoid. Then a dark man would be almost impossible, for no amount of shaving would get rid of a dark beard, and no paint or powder would cover it up. A man with a bass voice would also be impossible. It is difficult to modify the voice appreciably, and anything like an assumed voice would attract attention. Other peculiarities such as a very large nose or marked hairiness of the chest or limbs would create difficulties.

"And now let us see what would be a really suitable case, remembering that the object is to produce a woman of an ordinary type whose appearance would not attract notice. He would be the opposite of the types which we have excluded; that is to say, he would be a rather small, slight, blond man with somewhat small features, a light voice, and not too much hair on his chest or limbs. Such a man, if he shaved twice a day and used the make-up judiciously, might pass as a very ordinary-looking woman, provided that, before making his appearance in his new character, he let his hair grow long enough to allow of some kind of feminine mode. And, conversely, if one suspected a woman of being a man in disguise, one could postulate a man of this type as the one to be sought for; and such a suspicion might reasonably arise if a woman who had committed a crime disappeared immediately and permanently."

"I should have thought," said I, "that the voice would have created a difficulty."

"I think you exaggerate the difficulty," he replied. "There are voices which are unmistakably masculine or feminine; but there are a good many others – more, I think, than we realize – that are not at all distinctive. Between a deep female voice, especially if the lower register is habitually used, and a light male voice, there is very little difference. On hearing such a voice proceeding from another room, it is often difficult to say whether the speaker is a man or a woman. The fact is that our ideas are based on extreme or typical forms.

"And now to resume our argument. We have considered only physical disguise; change in appearance. But there is also what we may call psychological disguise; the adoption of feminine habits and modes of behaviour and the creation of circumstances suggesting a feminine personality. These would act by suggestion and leave observers with an unshakable conviction of the personator's sex, the more powerful because unconscious. But the most convincing of all would be a love affair with a man, preferably a somewhat scandalous one which would give rise to gossip. The suggestive effect of this would be intense. It would completely forestall any possible question as to the sex of the personator.

"Incidentally, we may note that the latter would be wise to associate with women as little as possible; for women, having an intimate knowledge of the ways of their own sex, might notice some discrepancy of habit or behaviour into which a man might be betrayed by the lack of such knowledge.

"And now, having considered the 'fictitious person' method in the abstract, we may proceed to observe its application in the case of R. v. Schiller."

He paused to pay certain little attentions to his guests. Then, when our glasses and pipes were recharged and Polton had refreshed himself with a pinch of snuff, he commenced his narration.

CHAPTER EIGHTEEN

The Investigation Reviewed

"It would be a paradox," Thorndyke began, "to say that the unravelment of the complex scheme for the murder of Lotta Schiller began before the murder was committed; but it is a fact that, as each of the later developments came into view, it found me with a body of considered data to apply to the solution of the problem presented. At first, this was not an investigation ad hoc. Until Penfield proposed his case to me, I was an outsider, watching with little more than academic interest the unfolding of a train of events in which I was not personally concerned. Hence, when the question of the Presumption of Death was raised, I had not to embark on an investigation *de novo*, but only to test and verify conclusions already formed.

"For me, the starting point was the murder of Charles Montagu. The interest of that crime from a medico-legal point of view lay in the unusual method adopted by the murderer – the forcible administration of poison. But there were other elements of interest, and, thanks to Polton's enthusiasm, we were kept fully supplied with the published records of the case. We had the lurid descriptions of the murder and of the mysterious artist on whom suspicion at first lighted, and a full report of the inquest; but above all, we had Pedley's remarkable little picture of Gravel-pit Wood.

"That picture made a deep impression on me. There it is on the mantelpiece, and, if you will look at it attentively, I think you will understand its effect on me. There are three figures. One, the taller man, was recognized by Blandy as Charles Montagu; and there we see him going to his death. The shorter man must have been the murderer; and we can see him there, leading his victim to the appointed place. But, to me, the most impressive figure was that of the woman. Who was she, and why was she there? Obviously she was spying on the two men, and apparently trying to hear what they were saying. The strong suggestion was that she was in some way related to one of them; and, since she never came forward to give information, the natural inference was that she was related to, or connected with, the shorter man. For, if her relations had been with Montagu, she would surely have denounced the murderer.

"But, above all, what impressed me was the terrible position that this unfortunate woman had placed herself in; the dreadful peril in which she stood. For her life hung on a thread – the thread of her silence. If she had not actually witnessed the murder, she certainly knew who the murderer was. A word from her could have sent him to the gallows; and she alone in all the world had that fatal knowledge. It was an awful position. The man had committed his crime and vanished without leaving a trace. He must have believed himself to be absolutely safe; and yet, in fact, his life was in this woman's hands. If ever an inkling of the truth should leak out, she was doomed. The ruthless ferocity of the crime made that practically certain.

"I must confess that the thought of the dangers that encompassed that unhappy woman caused me a good deal of discomfort; which was revived from time to time when I used to see the picture hanging in Polton's room; and I was haunted by an uneasy expectation that, sooner or later, I should hear of the murder of some woman which should justify my forebodings. But the months passed, and I began to hope that the woman had had the wisdom to keep her secret and that the danger had passed.

"Then, at last, came the murder of Emma Robey; and, immediately, my suspicions were aroused. It was a bizarre, theatrical crime with many curious features; but the one that instantly attracted my attention was the method adopted by the murderer – the forcible administration

216

of poison. Not only was it the same method as that employed in the murder of Montagu; the poison used was the same poison.

"Now, when we consider the inveterate tendency of criminals to repeat their procedure, it is evident that this similarity of method suggested at least a possibility that the murderer of Emma Robey might be the same person as the murderer of Charles Montagu; and if that possibility were entertained, it carried with it the further possibility that poor Emma Robey might be the woman in the picture. There was, of course, no evidence that she was; all that could be said was that, in the only respect in which comparison was possible – the colour of the hair – they were so far alike that they might have been the same person. And at that I had to leave it for the time being. I waited hopefully for Emma Robey to be identified, assuming that, when she was, we should get into the world of realities. But she never was identified, and, after a time I decided, as also, I think, did the police, that Emma Robey was a fictitious name and that the marking on the clothing was a plant, done deliberately to confuse the issues. But who she really was remained a mystery.

"And now we come to another remarkable feature of this strange crime. I mean the absence of any real attempt to conceal its authorship."

"You are not forgetting the locked door," I reminded him, "and the elaborate suggestion of suicide?"

"No," he replied, "but I don't regard that as a serious attempt. The police did not entertain the idea of suicide for a moment, and neither did I. The whole circumstances shouted 'murder'. Nor did the murderer seem to expect that the pretence would be accepted, otherwise she would have made the discovery herself and called in the police. But she would not run this risk but took the more prudent course of absconding, and in doing so, frankly abandoned the pretence of suicide."

"But," I objected, "why the pretence at all?"

"It seems to me," he replied, "that there were two objects. First, it was a 'try-on', a gamble on the infinitesimal chance that the appearance of suicide might be accepted. What the criminal thought of that

217

chance may be judged by the fact that she did not stay to see whether it came off. She preferred definitely to incriminate herself by flight. As to the other motive, we shall come to that presently.

"To return to the crime; I repeat that, disregarding the pretence of suicide, there was no attempt to conceal the identity of the murderer. There was the corpse in Lotta Schiller's room, locked in with Lotta Schiller's key, and Lotta, herself, nowhere to be found. When once it was decided that this was a case of murder, Lotta was the obvious presumptive murderer. She alone had access to the rooms and there was no one else on whom any sort of suspicion fell. All that remained for the police to do was to arrest her and bring her to trial.

"But Lotta had disappeared; and notwithstanding the most intense and energetic search, the police failed to discover the slightest trace of her. Now, as Jervis remarked recently, it is not very easy, in these days of telephones, wireless, and a very perfect police organization, for a known person to disappear without leaving a trace; especially a rather conspicuous person like Lotta Schiller. Yet no sign of her was discovered until the finding of the handbag in Epping Forest.

"I am inclined to regard the planting of those relics in the forest as a tactical mistake. It never deceived the police, though Blandy very wisely made a search so exhaustive as to settle the question for good. Of course, the absence of a body damned the scheme. If there had been a murder, there must have been a body in the camp, and there would not have been those admirably selected clues; and the appearances could have been so easily produced by one person with two pairs of shoes. The only effect on the police was to confirm their conviction of Lotta's guilt and to spur them on to further efforts to lay hands on her.

"But, as you know, their efforts failed utterly, though the search never entirely ceased during the two years that followed; for Scotland Yard has a long memory and does not readily accept defeat. Nevertheless, in all that long pursuit, not the faintest trace of Lotta Schiller ever came to light.

"So much for the crime itself. Now let us see how these developments appeared to an experienced and deeply interested onlooker. To me, the most striking fact was the one which I have just mentioned; the virtual acceptance by the criminal of the authorship of the crime. Apart from the perfunctory suicide tableau, which the murderer obviously did not rely on, there was not the slightest effort to dissociate Lotta Schiller from the murder; indeed, it almost seemed as if the onus of the crime were being deliberately cast on her.

"This curiously defiant attitude interested me profoundly. What could it mean? This was no crime of impulse with an unpremeditated flight. It was a carefully prepared murder, the procedure of which had been arranged and considered in advance. The only explanation that suggested itself to me was that Lotta Schiller had never been in any danger at all; that before the crime was committed, a means of escape had been provided, so secure as to render any other precautions unnecessary. And here, I think, we have the principal motive for the suicide deception; to disguise the criminal's confidence in her immunity from the danger of discovery.

"But what could be the nature of this infallible means of escape? I could think of only one; and the facts fitted it so perfectly that I adopted it as a working hypothesis. I decided that here, for the first time in my experience, I had met with a criminal who had put in practice my method of the fictitious person; that Lotta Schiller was a disguised person with a fictitious personality who, having committed the murder, had simply dropped the disguise and forthwith had virtually ceased to exist.

"You will see how completely this hypothesis agreed with and accounted for all the circumstances. It was just a reproduction of the case of John Doe. Here, in the assumed character of Lotta Schiller, he lures his victim into his premises, in which everything has been prepared, commits his murder at his ease without danger of disturbance or interruption, removes all incriminating traces, and, in this case, arranges the sham suicide tableau, goes away, removes his disguise, if he has not removed it already, and, having now changed back into the personality of John Doe, watches unconcernedly the pursuit of the non-existent Lotta Schiller. If he had been perfectly wise, he would have left it at that; but he was not perfectly wise, and he elected to play the fool in Epping Forest and thereby offer to the police an unnecessary suggestion of deception.

"Having accepted this hypothesis, I asked myself the further question: assuming Lotta Schiller to be a disguised person, who and what was the real person and what was the nature of the disguise? Was she really a woman, or was she a man disguised as a woman? I decided, for several reasons, that she was more probably a man. In the first place, as I explained just now, change of sex is, as a long-term disguise, much easier and far more effective than any other kind. Then the crime looked like a man's crime. Poisoning is characteristically the woman's method; but not forcible poisoning. That requires such an amount of strength as to make it certain that the crime can be carried out. Then there was a curious little point that cropped up in the evidence at the inquest and that seemed to me very revealing. In proof of the essentially proper character of his relations with Lotta, Vanderpuye swore that he had never kissed her; that she had absolutely forbidden any intimacies of that kind.

"Now, if we assumed that Lotta was a woman, this was rather extraordinary, considering that their relations were almost those of lovers. But if we assumed that Lotta was a man, the anomaly was quite easily explained. By careful shaving, a blond beard can be rendered quite invisible. But it cannot be rendered impalpable. By the sense of touch – especially the touch of the sensitive lips – the invisible stubble would be instantly detected. Hence, in such a case, physical endearments would have to be avoided most strictly.

"The position, then, at this stage, was that I believed the murderer of Emma Robey to be some unknown man at whose identity I could not even make a guess. For he had vanished without leaving a trace; or rather, I should say, leaving only deceptive traces in the form of a well-known but non-existent woman.

"But there remained the problem of Emma Robey herself. As the time ran on and the police failed to discover any missing woman of that name, it began to dawn on me that here, probably, was another fictitious person; that the marked underclothing had been a 'plant' and that there was no such person as Emma Robey. But if there was not, then who was the murdered woman? Again, it was impossible to make even a guess; though, at this time, when I used to look occasionally at the picture in Polton's room, I would ask myself whether it might not be that the two unknown figures in that picture were Emma Robey and her murderer.

"But this was mere speculation. It could not be tested or verified and it led nowhere. As the months slipped by and no new facts came to light, it began to look as if the Jacob Street murder would have to be added to the long list of unsolved mysteries. And so the matter rested for a couple of years. And then came Mr Penfield; and with his arrival on the scene my role of the detached onlooker was exchanged for that of an authorized investigator.

"Now, before Penfield had spoken a dozen sentences, I saw that we were going to get some important new light on the problem; for we were now in a world of realities in which systematic inquiries were possible. But from Penfield himself, as he sketched out his case, I gathered several illuminating facts. Let us see what they were.

"First, we learned that Lotta Schiller was a real person. But Penfield's case dealt with two Lottas; one, the testatrix, who was certainly the real Lotta, and another, the lodger at 39 Jacob Street, who was assumed to be the same person.

"Then we learned that there was some sort of connection between Lotta and Charles Montagu. The nature of it was not clear, but there had certainly been a contact of some kind.

"We learned, further, that Montagu had apparently been blackmailed, and that the blackmail had been assumed to be connected with the murder.

"Then Penfield could give us the address where Lotta was lodging when she was last heard of; and we gathered the significant fact that those lodgings were near Gravel-pit Wood.

"Finally, Penfield gave us a description of Lotta. It was very sketchy, but, such as it was, it seemed roughly to agree with what we knew of the appearance of Lotta the lodger (as we may for convenience call her, to distinguish her from the testatrix, whom we may call, simply,

Lotta). But it agreed equally well with the woman in the picture and with Oldfield's description of Emma Robey.

"Here, then, was some valuable new material; and, as soon as I had settled definitely with Penfield, I proceeded to sort out the facts and to seek to add to them. I began by inspecting Lotta's will at Somerset House and trying to memorize her signature, and, as a matter of routine; I secured copies of the wills of Montagu and of Barbara Dalton. From the former of these I learned nothing fresh, and from Barbara's only one trivial and apparently insignificant fact; which was that she had bequeathed all her chattels to her sister Linda, with the exception of her violin, which she gave to Lotta; from which it was reasonable to infer that Lotta was able to play the violin. But that fact, though I noted it, seemed to have no possible bearing on our inquiry.

"And now I addressed myself to the really important question: Was the lodger at Jacob Street the same person as Lotta the testatrix? The most likely source of the relevant facts was Mr Thomas Pedley, with whom I accordingly communicated without delay; and, having received from him a most gracious invitation, I descended on him, supported by Jervis, at the appointed time.

"I must admit that, whatever my expectations may have been, the results of that interview were beyond my wildest hopes. Tom Pedley was a mine of information. He was a first-class observer, with an indelible memory and the valuable gift of imparting his knowledge by means of drawings. I need not go into details as most of them are known to you, but I will take the results in order.

"First, we learned that Lotta the lodger was a sham artist; an absolute sham, a complete impostor. Pedley assumed that she was posing deliberately for some reason unknown to him. This was an important fact, for, to this extent at least, she was masquerading in a false character.

"Next, we learned that, although Pedley had been on terms of fairly intimate friendship with her for many months, he knew absolutely nothing about her as to her past history or her friends or relations, excepting the rather shadowy husband. In respect of everything concerning herself, she was uncommunicative to the point of secretiveness.

"Then there were two very significant facts. One was that Tom had never seen her handwriting, and apparently no one else had; for she never wrote either to Tom or to Vanderpuye, and avoided the use of cheques by paying her rent in cash. She did not even sign her pictures. The other was her perverse refusal to have either a drawing or a photograph of her made for the locket, coupled with the fact that her own self-portrait bore no resemblance to her whatever. The great significance of these two facts was that, when the woman disappeared, all traces of her personality disappeared, too (as she believed). No portrait remained to be shown, studied, or compared with any known person, and no scrap of writing, or even the recollection of any, to be compared with letters or documents. The two facts, taken together, offered a distinct suggestion of preparation for a disappearance.

"The forced friendship with the remarkable manifestations of affection − entirely verbal and unaccompanied by any kisses or other physical endearments − was significant, especially as the woman seemed to have no other friends until Vanderpuye arrived and became the object of similar platonic affection. But I have already referred to the value of a flirtation as support for a 'change of sex' disguise.

"And now we come to the description and the incomparable notebook. That description was quite masterly, and to me an unexpected windfall. For, if I was right in my suspicion that Lotta the lodger was a man disguised as a woman, this description, with its wealth of exact detail, was substantially a description of the man himself. Thus, we learned that the woman's height was about five feet seven without her high heels, that she had ears of a certain distinctive shape (of which Tom gave us a drawing), and that her eyes were of a greenish hazel. Now, these were characteristics that no disguise could appreciably alter. It followed, therefore that the man if he existed must be about five feet seven inches in height, must have ears of that particular shape, and greenish hazel eyes. But Tom was able to supplement this description by an excellent memory drawing, the existence of which had been unknown to Lotta.

"But the real windfall was the hair. As soon as I had heard Tom's description I realized that we had got a means of definite and certain identification, since Vanderpuye's locket contained an authentic specimen which could be examined. For the condition was obviously abnormal. I suspected it to be ringed hair, since there seemed to be no other possibility; but, whatever it was, the microscope would make its nature clear. So we had got one totally unexpected item of evidence.

"It was, however, not the only one. Another point of unexpected importance emerged when Tom, in handing us his notebook, showed us the fingerprints of poor Emma Robey. They did not appear to be of any interest as the unfortunate woman was dead and buried, but I looked at them to see how Polton's improvised method had answered; and then I made a curious discovery. The fingerprints showed that Emma Robey had been a violin player."

"How did they show that?" Vanderpuye interrupted, eagerly.

"By the signs of pressure and friction on the fingertips," Thorndyke replied. "You must remember that fingerprints show other things besides the distinctive pattern; thickenings, for instance, of the epidermis due to particular ways of using the hands. Thus a professional violinist or a regular player develops thickenings of the skin – little corns, in fact – on the tips of the four fingers of the left hand which are used in stopping the strings. They do not appear on the fingers of merely occasional players, and so are indicative of the professional or serious player. The traces that they leave on the fingerprints are quite characteristic since they are raised above the general surface, and, owing to their hardness, the pattern tends to be worn flat. These, by the way, were not at all well marked; just little areas of indistinctness in the centre of each print. Still, they were quite unmistakable, and they established beyond doubt that Emma Robey had been a regular violin player.

"The significance of the discovery remained to be proved. I had inferred that Lotta Schiller had been a violin player; but the inference might have been wrong. Meanwhile, the evidence, such as it was, supported the suggestion that Lotta Schiller and Emma Robey were one and the same person.

"These were the chief facts that we learned from Tom Pedley, and you will see that it was a rich haul; for these facts were the foundation of my case. When we came away from the studio I had the skeleton of the case sketched out pretty completely in my mind. Of course, that case was purely hypothetical and it might be entirely fallacious. Its truth or its fallacy could be tested only by further investigation, and I applied myself forthwith to the task of verification.

"The first step was to examine the locket, which Vanderpuye very kindly placed at our disposal. I took it up to the laboratory at once and examined it under the microscope with a strong top light. A single glance showed that the hair was ringed hair, though, owing to its light colour, the rings were quite indiscernible to the naked eye or even through a weak lens. But with strong magnification it was perfectly clear; so we now had an infallible touchstone which could be applied confidently to any individual suspected of being Lotta the lodger.

"But we had to find that individual; and we had to seek further evidence as to whether Lotta the lodger was or was not a fictitious person. But this question was closely bound up with that of the identity of Emma Robey. For if Emma was, as I suspected, Lotta Schiller, then Lotta the lodger must be someone else. Accordingly I turned my attention to this question, and I began by ascertaining the latest date on which the real Lotta had been seen alive. Now, we knew from the affidavits that she had never been seen by any of her friends after she had left her lodgings at Linton Green. From that time she was never heard of by them until her reported disappearance in the Forest.

"The first thing, then, to be done was to find out the exact date on which Lotta disappeared from her lodgings; to which end I dispatched the invaluable Snuper to Linton Green to make inquiries of Mrs Wharton, Lotta's landlady. He began by asking if she could give him Mrs Schiller's present address, which, of course, she could not; but instead gave him those particulars which you have heard in evidence.

"This information did not appear to help us at all; for, as Lotta left her lodgings in the morning of the 13th of June 1930 and the lodger did not appear in Jacob Street until about a month later, there was nothing to show that they might not be one and the same person. So I had to look for evidence elsewhere, and I did not quite see where I was to look for it. The position was very tantalizing. I had the finger-prints of Emma Robey, and, if I could only have compared them with those of Lotta Schiller, the question would have been settled. But where was I to look for them? There is only one place in which the fingerprints of unknown persons may be found; Scotland Yard. But it seemed practically useless to look for the fingerprints of Emma Robey in that place. For whether she were or were not Lotta Schiller, she was presumably a respectable woman. Still, it was not absolutely impossible that they could be there; and, since there was no alternative, and that I might feel that I had left no possibility untested, I made a good photograph of the fingerprints in the notebook, and, armed with this, went to the Yard and sought out our old friend, Miller. He made no difficulty about taking me round to the Fingerprint Department and presenting my photograph of the prints to the search officer. And then, behold the miracle! The fingerprints of Emma Robey were actually in the files; and, of course, there were also the prison photographs and a summary of the particulars.

"At first it seemed as if the discovery did not help us much, for the name attached to the prison portraits was Louisa Saunders. We seemed merely to have got another unknown person. But the particulars were much more enlightening. It was noted that the prisoner's underclothing was marked with the initials LS, which agreed with the name that she had given, Louisa Saunders, but it agreed equally well with the name of Lotta Schiller. The most striking fact, however, was that Louisa had been arrested in the afternoon of the 13th of June 1930 – the very day on which Lotta had left her lodgings, and after her departure from them. The agreement was so complete as to be almost conclusive.

"But there was yet another agreement. From Mrs Wharton, Snuper had learned that Lotta was practically a professional violinist. But the fingerprints of Louisa Saunders were obviously those of a regular violin player. The impressions of the corns were extremely well marked; and now I understood why they had been so ill-defined in Emma Robey's prints. During the imprisonment the corns had atrophied from disuse, and become worn down.

"The facts thus disclosed left no doubt in my mind that Louisa Saunders was really Lotta Schiller; and, since Louisa was certainly Emma Robey, it followed that Emma Robey was Lotta Schiller. From this it followed that Lotta the lodger was some other person; and the question was; who could that person be? And now it was possible to suggest an answer to that question. The telegram that Mrs Wharton had received had certainly not been sent by Lotta; for it would have disclosed her address, which she had refused to give to the police. But since Carl Schiller had called at the lodgings later to settle the rent and remove Lotta's possessions, it was evident that he knew where his wife was. Apparently, he had sent the telegram to prevent Mrs Wharton from making inquiries about her missing lodger. Evidently, then, there were reasonable grounds for suspecting that Lotta the lodger was in fact Carl Schiller. But nothing more than suspicion. It had yet to be ascertained that his physical characteristics were such as to make the disguise possible; and this could not be decided until I had seen him or obtained a detailed description of him.

"At this point it became necessary to take Miller into my confidence to some extent, as I needed his help for the next stage of the inquiry. He was perfectly willing, personally, to let me have copies of the prison portraits and the particulars, but he asked for a letter which he could show to the Assistant Commissioner, whose permission was necessary, and I accordingly sent him one, with the result that, as you remember, he called on me and brought the copies with him. Of these prison portraits I made copies with the name-board masked out and put them, with a photograph of Pedley's portrait and a few dummy portraits, in a portfolio to be produced in court.

"And now I was ready for the opening of the case in the Probate Court, when I hoped to make the decisive move. But I was in a difficulty in regard to the procedure. For the correct course would have been for me to disclose the information that I possessed to Penfield, who would have passed it on to the other parties. But this was clearly impossible. Very unwillingly, I was compelled to adopt the quite irregular course of proceeding without the disclosure of material facts or discovery of documents, in the hope that I should be able to make my essential points before Lorimer objected.

"But I must admit that I was far from confident that morning when we set out for the Probate Court. For I had to settle certain questions, and to settle them quickly, and the opportunity might be lacking. And the results might not be those which I expected, in which case I should have to start the whole inquiry afresh. I have seldom been more anxious about a case than I was on that morning.

"The questions that I had to answer were: First, was Louisa Saunders actually Lotta Schiller? Second, did Carl Schiller's physical characteristics agree with Tom Pedley's description of Lotta the lodger? Third, had he ringed hair? The first question would probably be easy to dispose of, but the other two were subject to all sorts of contingencies. In the first place, Carl might not be there, although I suspected that he would; for his absence would be rather remarkable, considering his obvious interest in the case and the fact that his affidavit had to be read and that I had asked for his attendance. But even if he answered the description, there was the difficulty of obtaining a specimen of his hair. I had discussed this matter with Snuper and we had considered a number of plans, but, in the end, I had to leave it to his ingenuity and readiness to take advantage of any opportunity that should present itself.

"You know what the upshot was. When Schiller was introduced to us, I saw at a glance that he agreed perfectly with the description. He was about five feet seven inches in height, he had greenish hazel eyes, his ears exactly resembled Pedley's drawing, and the right one had a small Darwinian tubercle while the left had none; his profile, where it was not concealed by the beard, corresponded perfectly with Pedley's portrait, and, as he was talking with Jervis, I noted that his smooth, high-pitched voice would have passed quite well as a woman's voice. The agreement was complete. There was not a single discrepancy; and, for my part, I had no doubt that here was Lotta the lodger, the murderer of Lotta Schiller.

"But my belief was not to the point; nor did it amount to certainty. There remained the question of the ringed hair. That was the final test; and you will notice that it acted both ways. Lotta the lodger certainly had ringed hair. If this man had ringed hair, he was certainly the lodger. If he had not ringed hair, he was certainly not the lodger, no matter how complete was the agreement in all other respects. So that the identity of this man still remained to be proved; and I considered very anxiously whether it would be possible to get the sample of hair that was necessary for the proof or disproof. It looked an almost impossible task.

"I glanced towards Snuper, who had followed us into the court, and made the agreed signal to indicate his quarry; whereupon he got to work with his ridiculous little camera and managed to take two excellent profile portraits. Then he subsided into his seat and lay in wait for his victim; who presently seated himself close by, and then, as Lorimer made his opening speech, leaned his head against the back of the bench and closed his eyes.

"I watched Snuper anxiously and could see that he was keeping in close proximity to Schiller's head. But that was all that I could see; for Snuper has all the conjuror's skill in concealing his movements and diverting the attention of the onlookers. What he actually did was to wait until Schiller raised his head for a moment, and, in that moment to deposit a thick smear of a quick-drying adhesive on the back of the bench just where the head had been resting. It was a most audacious proceeding but apparently no one noticed it – not even Schiller himself. And it was perfectly successful, as I realized in the sequel; for, the next time that Schiller tried to move his head, it was stuck fast to the back of the bench and had to be released by Snuper's scissors. Then I saw what had happened and was on tenterhooks while Snuper scraped away the adhesive – ostensibly to clean the back of the bench – for fear the judge should intervene and impound the scrapings for examination. However, all went well, and Snuper took an early opportunity to escape; and then I knew that the sample was safe, whatever it might turn out to be.

"You know, in effect, what the result was. When we arrived at the Temple in the lunch interval, I found Snuper waiting for me, modestly triumphant at his success, and received from him his little camera and a folded envelope which enclosed some sticky material and a small tuft of hairs. I need not say that I lost no time in taking the latter up to the laboratory for examination. There I picked out a few hairs, and, laying them on a slide with a drop of bergamot oil and a cover-glass, and, placing the slide on the stage of the microscope, put my eye to the eyepiece.

"It was a dramatic moment, for the life of Carl Schiller hung on the answer to my question. And the answer was given at the first glance. The hairs were ringed hair, plain and unmistakable; and it was now certain that Lotta the lodger and Carl Schiller were one and the same person. But that person was the murderer of Emma Robey; and the final question that remained was whether Emma Robey was the same person as Lotta Schiller.

"I went back to the court confident of being able to dispose of this question before the inevitable objection. And so it turned out. When Linda Dalton identified the prison portraits, my case was complete. For her identification was so confident and positive that it left no doubt in my mind, and I now knew that abundant confirmation could be obtained. Lorimer's objection came too late to hinder me, for I could, if I had chosen, have had Carl Schiller charged then and there."

"Why didn't you?" I asked. "Why did you go on with the case in the Probate Court?"

"The rest of my proceedings," he replied, "were for the benefit of the police. They would want to be able to make out a prima facie case before they committed themselves to an arrest, and, in fact, I had promised Miller to provide him with enough evidence for the purpose. But it was as important to me as to him; for we had to make sure of a committal. It would have been a disaster if the case had failed in the magistrate's court. Besides, the latter proceedings were a sort of rehearsal; they enabled us to see exactly what evidence we could produce at the trial.

"Well, I have now retraced the course of the investigation and you can see how the mass of circumstantial evidence grew up as each successive fact came into view. There is no need to go into details of the preparation of the case, such as the composite photographs and the other exhibits which were produced in court, nor to speculate on those questions of which we shall never know the answers."

"That is all very well, sir," said Pedley, "for the learned lawyer and scientist, but simple folk like myself would like to have some sort of answers to those questions. For instance, I should very much like to know why the deuce Schiller elected to take up his abode next door to me and adopt me as his dearest friend. It could hardly have been a mere coincidence."

"No," Thorndyke agreed, "that seems incredible. But if it would comfort you to guess at his motives, I think you have something to go upon. He would have been looking about for a suitable neighbourhood where he was not known and for a likely stranger to adopt as a friend. He would have seen your name and address mentioned in the papers as that of the 'mysterious artist', and he might have noted that, as you never came forward to give information and appeared to have been unaware of the murder, you were certainly not a busy or inquisitive person. Your neighbourhood was perfectly suitable to him, and your profession ideal for the purpose of striking up an acquaintance, provided that he could pose as a fellow artist; and that the present fashion for childish and barbaric painting made quite possible, with a judicious use of the current jargon. I think he made a very good choice."

"I should have thought," Pedley objected, "that the fact of my having seen him in the wood that day would have put him off."

"But, my dear Pedley, he didn't know that you had seen him. You are forgetting. The police kept your information to themselves. It never appeared in the papers. And, after all, though you had seen him, you never recognized him. No, my friend, I don't think that there is much mystery about his having selected you; but there are some other questions that are a good deal more difficult to answer."

"You mean," I suggested, "how it happened that Lotta allowed herself to be convicted of an offence that she had not committed, for I have assumed that Schiller planted those notes on her, deliberately, and that she knew it, though, of course, she couldn't guess at his object. But why didn't she say where she had got them?"

"Probably," Thorndyke replied, "she was so terrified of him, knowing him to be a murderer, that she did not dare to put the blame on him; and it is even possible that she accepted the prison willingly as a sanctuary from him. But we shall never know the actual facts, and it is not very profitable to speculate on them."

"You speak, Jervis," said Vanderpuye, "of his object in planting those notes on her. What was his object?"

"I take it," said I, "that his object was to get her safely out of the way while he was making his preparations to personate her and be ready to make away with her when she came out, before she had time to get into touch with her friends; and I assume that he knew that she would rather go to prison under a fictitious name than make a scandal and exasperate him. What do you say, Thorndyke?"

"I think you are probably right," he replied, "but we don't know, and we never shall. Nor does it really concern us. We knew enough to defeat a really talented criminal, and that should satisfy us."

"Even though," I suggested, "it knocks the bottom out of the infallible scheme of Mr John Doe?"

"But does it?" he retorted. "I think, Jervis, you are overlooking some very material facts. In the first place, Schiller did not carry out John Doe's programme completely; and it was his departure from it that was his undoing. John Doe, having committed his crime, simply shed his disguise and disappeared, leaving no trace, and, thereafter, making no sign. If Schiller had done this, no question would ever have arisen. But he elected to stage the bogus murder in the Forest, and thereby left a loose end.

"Then you are overlooking the enormous effects of unforeseeable chance. The ringed hair was a chance in a million, and that of Polton's taking the dead woman's fingerprints and Pedley's preserving them was almost as great. Yet, if you subtract those two infinitely improbable circumstances, there is no case left. Schiller would have been perfectly safe, for I could never have got beyond the stage of suspicion.

"Further, you overlook the fact that, in spite of all these adverse effects of chance, Schiller's scheme did succeed. For two whole years he was at large and totally unsuspected. It is an actual fact that when Penfield came to me, not a single individual in the world, except myself, had any doubt that the person who disappeared in the Forest was really Lotta Schiller. Even the police, who rejected the bogus murder, did not question the identity."

"Still," I persisted, "the undeniable fact is that his scheme did fail, and that he is going to be hanged."

"Yes," Thorndyke admitted, "his scheme was defeated by the unforeseen and unforeseeable. His failure illustrates the truth of Herbert Spencer's dictum that social phenomena are too complex for prevision to be possible. But without prevision, no plan can be devised that will certainly produce the effects intended. That is where social reformers and all sorts of other planners fail. They take no account of the unknown factors. But it commonly happens that the unknown factors turn out to be the operative factors, as they did in the case of Carl Schiller."

"That is very true, sir," said Vanderpuye, "and the operative unknown factor in his case was the existence of a gentleman named John Thorndyke."

R Austin Freeman

The D'Arblay Mystery
A Dr Thorndyke Mystery

When a man is found floating beneath the skin of a green-skimmed pond one morning, Dr Thorndyke becomes embroiled in an astonishing case. This wickedly entertaining detective fiction reveals that the victim was murdered through a lethal injection and someone out there is trying a cover-up.

Dr Thorndyke Intervenes
A Dr Thorndyke Mystery

What would you do if you opened a package to find a man's head? What would you do if the headless corpse had been swapped for a case of bullion? What would you do if you knew a brutal murderer was out there, somewhere, and waiting for you? Some people would run. Dr Thorndyke intervenes.

R Austin Freeman

Felo De Se
A Dr Thorndyke Mystery

John Gillam was a gambler. John Gillam faced financial ruin and was the victim of a sinister blackmail attempt. John Gillam is now dead. In this exceptional mystery, Dr Thorndyke is brought in to untangle the secrecy surrounding the death of John Gillam, a man not known for insanity and thoughts of suicide.

Flighty Phyllis

Chronicling the adventures and misadventures of Phyllis Dudley, Richard Austin Freeman brings to life a charming character always getting into scrapes. From impersonating a man to discovering mysterious trapdoors, *Flighty Phyllis* is an entertaining glimpse at the times and trials of a wayward woman.

R Austin Freeman

Helen Vardon's Confession
A Dr Thorndyke Mystery

Through the open door of a library, Helen Vardon hears an argument that changes her life forever. Helen's father and a man called Otway argue over missing funds in a trust one night. Otway proposes a marriage between him and Helen in exchange for his co-operation and silence. What transpires is a captivating tale of blackmail, fraud and death. Dr Thorndyke is left to piece together the clues in this enticing mystery.

Mr Pottermack's Oversight

Mr Pottermack is a law-abiding, settled homebody who has nothing to hide until the appearance of the shadowy Lewison, a gambler and blackmailer with an incredible story. It appears that Pottermack is in fact a runaway prisoner, convicted of fraud, and Lewison is about to spill the beans unless he receives a large bribe in return for his silence. But Pottermack protests his innocence, and resolves to shut Lewison up once and for all. Will he do it? And if he does, will he get away with it?

1522960R0

Printed in Great Britain by
Amazon.co.uk, Ltd.,
Marston Gate.